STALL

TURNS

Books by Penelope Haines

The Lost One
Helen Had a Sister
(previously published as Princess of Sparta)
Blood Never Lies

The Claire Hardcastle Series:
Death on D'Urville
Straight and Level
Stall Turns

STALL
TURNS

A Claire Hardcastle

Mystery

PENELOPE HAINES

For information contact;

www.penelopehaines.com

Published by Ithaca Publications, Wellington, New Zealand

Stall Turns/ Penelope Haines. -- 1st ed.

ISBN 978-0-473-44971-1

For Olivia Haines,

my granddaughter

"Oh! I have slipped
the surly bonds of Earth.

And danced the skies
on laughter-silvered wings."

John Gillespie Magee, Jr

CHAPTER ONE

W E WERE LOST OF COURSE. I'D been certain of it for some minutes, but, tactful woman that I am, I'd refrained from pointing it out. Jack had stopped the car and was peering at the battered signpost marking the T-junction.

"I don't remember Pat mentioning anything about 'Retakure'," Jack said, reading the place names. "We must have gone wrong somewhere."

He pulled out his notes and studied the directions.

"He didn't mention a war memorial?" I asked. A white stele stood at the side of the road, bronze plaques screwed to its base, listing local men who had fallen in the world wars. Hundreds of these memorials were dotted around rural settlements in New Zealand, paying tribute to the price we'd paid as a nation honouring our international alliances. Pat would almost certainly have included such a landmark.

I'd listened to his directions myself as Jack wrote them down.

"'Turn left at the forestry block and drive for about 10 kilometres. You'll be tracking alongside the river, so you can't go wrong. When you get to the fork, turn right. You'll see the Fitchett's place on your left. About five kilometres on, you'll reach the crossroads. Turn right again and then take the second on the right. The old woolshed will be on your left. The farmhouse is two kilometres further on. You'll probably recognise it once you get there. You can't miss it.'"

Famous last words!

The route Pat described had followed vague and strictly locally sourced criteria which had foiled the skill of the GPS navigation system in Jack's car.

Pat hadn't mentioned the roads would turn to gravel soon after we left the highway, making it hard to distinguish between farm tracks and promulgated roads. We'd already wasted time driving up one track, only to come up against a closed gate saying 'Private Property'. Nor had Pat thought to tell us there were several more turnings and crossroads than those he'd specified.

Consequently, on that fine spring morning, Jack and I were well and truly lost in the hilly countryside south-west of Te Kuiti.

"You don't remember this from when you last visited?" I asked.

Jack shook his head. "Nah. I was about ten then. I suppose I'll remember the farmhouse when we get there, but nothing else seems familiar. We'll have to turn around and see if we can pick the route up further back. I don't recall Pat saying we'd have to cross the river. He'd have mentioned a bridge, I'm sure of it. And this is a no-exit," he said, pointing to the sign.

"Why don't we find the nearest farm and ask directions?" I suggested. "They're bound to know where Pat's run is if it's anywhere near here."

Yes, I know real men don't ask for directions, but I was relying on Jack's common sense to get us past male stereotyping clichés.

His "Hmm," didn't sound convinced, but he turned across the bridge towards Retakure.

A short distance further, just beyond a bend, we came to a wide gateway framed by a high, square archway spanning the entrance. On each side the bordering fence line was neatly planted with low shrubs. The track that ran beneath the arch and led away up the valley was wide, well gravelled and tidy. Clearly a substantial and prosperous property, it was a marked contrast to other farms we'd passed where weathered barns and sagging fences displayed utilitarian values with no aspiration to being aesthetically pleasing.

"There must be someone about," I said as Jack turned into the drive. Sure enough, in a few hundred metres, we'd reached a sizeable woolshed with a red ute parked beside it.

"Stay here," said Jack. "I'll go and see who I can find."

I watched as he tried the woolshed door which seemed to be locked. He gave me a wave as he made his way through the sheep yards around the side of the building towards the rear.

It was too nice a day to stay in the car, so I climbed out and looked around. Well-fenced and tidy paddocks ran into the distance. Beyond them, cleared land gave way to bush-covered hills which framed the valley. It was a beautiful spot. I leaned back against the bonnet and listened. The only thing filling the silence was the gentle sound of bees buzzing in the clover-filled pastures.

Jack had parked near a small stream, its banks fringed, not with the usual flax, but with bulrushes. I've always admired the austere architecture of these oddly shaped plants, so I made my way through the long, spring grass to have a closer look at them.

Getting to them was more of a mission than I'd anticipated. Not only was the grass unpleasantly damp, drenching the bottom of my jeans, but I hadn't appreciated the stems of the bulrushes were well protected at their base by a mixture of pig fern and blackberry tangled among their roots. I picked my way over the uneven ground until I reached the nearest one, only to discover it was all an illusion. The kebab-shaped heads were clearly well past their use-by date and must have been hanging there since last summer. Those that remained were shabby, their rich velvet coating rubbed away in uneven patches. What I had assumed were entire flowers were ghostly shapes held together by the spiders' webs which covered them.

"Well, that's depressing," I muttered to myself.

I had to bend to untangle the mess of fern, biddy-bids and blackberry clinging to my legs. I glanced back at the woolshed; Jack hadn't reappeared. I didn't want to go back the same way –

it was too messy to tempt me again. I saw a clearer route to my right that would take me between a couple of clumps of reeds and looked free of any nasty creepers.

Unfortunately, I wasn't savvy enough to see the whole area, cunningly disguised by the tall grass, was actually swamp. I hadn't taken two steps before I sank ankle deep into the morass. I floundered across to the reeds and, by balancing on their roots, hauled myself out of the smelly, wet mud.

I was furious. Yes, it was entirely my own fault and stupidity, but that didn't make me feel any better. My shoes were soaked, my jeans were foul, and I stank: a rich mix of rotting vegetation, sour mud and stagnant water. Worse, I could imagine Jack's hilarity when I made it back to the car. At least, I thought, his laughter would die once the stench I now carried with me like a toxic plague infested his vehicle.

I took a deep breath before launching myself from my safe-haven and across more swamp to the next cluster of stalks. I stumbled and tripped on snags concealed in the quagmire and grabbed gratefully onto the rough blades of the reeds to pull me to safety.

My right foot had been gripped so firmly by the mud I had to bend and pull it out by hand so as not to lose my shoe. There was a nasty sucking noise as it emerged. My shoes were ruined. I couldn't imagine any wash cycle that could clean them up and render them fit for purpose again.

I looked around to plan the next stage of my trip back to the car. The ground ahead looked solid, but I'd been proved wrong already. I checked behind, to see whether I could improve on my track and saw, probably due to extricating my shoe from its grip, my passage through the morass had caused other matter to rise to the surface. I squinted at the thin, white branches that emerged from the mud.

They were probably what I'd trodden on. I was lucky they hadn't caused me to fall face first into the swamp. I'd half turned away to concentrate on the rest of my escape before my brain clicked into focus and screamed for my attention.

I turned to face the branch. *Shit.* It wasn't a collection of twigs

I'd seen but the very identifiable, if skeletal, shape of a human forearm. If I'd just seen the ribcage, I suppose I'd have assumed it was the remains of a long-dead sheep or cattle beast. The structure and shape of the arm and fingers was unmistakeable. And I'd just tripped and trodden over it! I felt a surge of nausea. Too late I realised the debris hanging off those twigs wasn't rotten vegetation, but probably rags of skin.

"What're you doing?" called Jack, back at the car, observing me. "You look a little worse for wear."

"Come over here," I shouted.

"Are you stuck? Do you need a hand?" Jack's amusement was palpable. "I'm not going to get myself all dirty for you. If you were silly enough to go in there, you can get yourself out."

"Just come here." I gritted my teeth against the sickness in my stomach. I couldn't bring myself to explain I thought I'd found a body. Let Jack work it out for himself.

He must have registered my distress, because he stopped teasing and picked his way across to help.

"Are you OK?" he asked when he reached me.

I nodded. "Look at that." I pointed towards the bones, although I didn't look at them again. I wanted Jack to tell me I was being dumb, that there was nothing to worry about.

"What?" He looked where I was indicating. "What's the probl . . . .? Oh, holy crap. What have you found?"

"They came up when I stirred the mud up wading through it. I trod on them. It's a person, isn't it?" My voice wobbled.

He put his arms round me and hugged me to him. I was shaking with reaction.

"You coping?" he asked at last, once I'd settled a little. I nodded. It wouldn't help if I went to pieces.

"Go and sit in the car," he ordered. "I'll just have a closer look. Then we need to phone the police."

Normally I'd have reacted to this automatic assumption of authority. For once, I was grateful to be with an alpha male. Jack was a member of the police force himself, serving as Detective Senior Sergeant Body.

I extracted myself from the swamp as best I could and plodded back to the car. I didn't want to watch whatever examination he intended to carry out.

There was still no one about so I took the opportunity to change into a spare pair of jeans and take my shoes off. I wiped my feet on the damp grass and bundled the soiled clothing into the boot. I couldn't do much more about cleaning myself or my clothes, but at least I'd improved my smell quotient.

Jack was still investigating the swamp and its contents. I looked away, swept by a purely selfish wave of frustration. Jack and I were supposed to be on a much-overdue holiday, the first we'd shared since we got together. We'd met when he was investigating a murder and so far, either his work or mine had intervened each time we planned to take a break.

The only reason we'd managed to organise this holiday was because I'd recently been a victim in a kidnapping case. As I was needed as a witness at the trial and there was some gang involvement, the police had suggested it would be better for my health if I were out of the reach of persuasion or retaliation until after the court case.

If I was forced to go into hiding, then as far as I was concerned, Jack was going with me. It took some negotiating, or as Jack put it, 'his people spoke to my people' but eventually his boss and mine agreed and we'd been granted four weeks leave.

My employer, Roger, looked a little sick when he made the concession and I'd been hit with a wave of guilt at abandoning him. I knew perfectly well that in any small business, like Paraparaumu Aviation, each staff member and their contribution was important, and in my absence my colleagues, Greig and Nick, were going to have to pick up the slack.

Less high-mindedly, I knew they'd also be picking up all my flying hours and wondered whether I'd have any students left to call my own when I came back from leave.

Maria, our office manager had sensed my conflict. "Work-life balance," she'd reminded me. "Don't worry about us, Claire, we'll be fine. You need to get somewhere you can be safe for the next few weeks. Enjoy the break. It's time you got away."

I'd agreed, but even so, every time an aircraft passed overhead my head snapped up automatically to follow its path across the sky. Some addictions are hard to break.

We had spent the first three weeks of our holiday in a bach at Taupo which had been lent to Jack by a police colleague. The spring weather had been chilly, but we'd enjoyed ourselves and soaking in the hot pools at DeBretts Spa Resort had been a romantic way to end the evenings.

Five days ago we'd driven to Kihikihi to meet Jack's family. I'd been dreading the visit. Who isn't nervous about meeting their partner's family? But they were lovely, warm, welcoming people who had made me feel at home. Doug, Jack's lawyer dad, was a quiet man, and it didn't take more than a short conversation to establish the range and scope of his intellect. I'd been wary of him before I'd realised he'd got a wonderful acidic sense of humour. Jack's mum Beth was a quintessential New Zealand housewife. She baked, sewed and nurtured her large family. I watched Doug roll his eyes a couple of times when she was over-enthusiastic with her caring, but it was obvious he adored her and that she held the family together. I enjoyed their company and their large extended family.

We were only up this god-forsaken valley because Jack's Uncle Pat had invited us both to join the Labour Day weekend muster, held every spring on the hills at the back of his farm. It sounded like an opportunity to see a real slice of Kiwiana, so I'd agreed enthusiastically enough when the plan was proposed. It was to be the last family-related activity before Jack and I headed back home to Paraparaumu.

Now, with the discovery of a corpse, we were likely to be detained and delayed, and if I knew Jack at all, he wouldn't be able to resist the challenge of investigating exactly why a skeleton was residing in the swamp. I hoped with all my heart that the bones were centuries old and didn't relate to any recent crime scene.

CHAPTER
TWO

WE WEREN'T DETAINED FOR AS LONG AS I'd feared. Once the police arrived they dealt with me and Jack with crisp efficiency and allowed us to go on our way.

"They didn't want you to stay and help?" I asked. I'd wondered whether Jack might feel proprietorial about *his* skeleton.

He gave a wry chuckle. "Quite the reverse. I don't think they have a lot of time for their colleagues from the big smoke. I was quietly encouraged to enjoy my holiday and leave them to their investigation on their own patch. If I have anything else to add, I'm welcome to call them."

I suppressed a smile. Apparently, the world of policing was as competitive as small aircraft aviation, where instructors jockeyed fiercely for flying hours.

One positive outcome from the drama of the morning was that Jack had taken advantage of a constable's local knowledge to get more reliable information about how to get to his uncle's farm.

"We took the wrong turning," he explained. "Pat's place is in the next valley over and his run borders the bush and scrub behind the hills we've been looking at. No distance at all as the crow flies but about forty minutes by car."

Armed with accurate directions, we had no further problems finding the farmhouse.

"Now I remember!" exclaimed Jack as he parked the car and looked at the old wooden farmhouse.

I rolled my eyes. "It would have saved us a lot of hassle if you'd managed to remember a couple of hours ago," I grumbled.

Jack grinned. "Then we'd have missed out on an adventure."

Pat and Joanne came out to greet us. Pat was tall, thin and rangy and in his sixties. Joanne was some ten years younger, slender and sporty looking.

"Sorry we're late," Jack apologised. "We got lost. It's a long story. I'll tell you all about it later."

"No worries," said Pat. "We didn't wait on lunch. Come on in. We'll show you to your room so you can settle in and freshen up, then come through to the kitchen and we'll find something to eat."

I enjoyed the casual acceptance of circumstance that seemed the norm in Jack's family. His parents had shown a similar tolerance for the vagaries of their large family's arrangements. It made them particularly restful to be around. I could only contrast it with memories of my late mother's hospitality. I'd loved her dearly, but she'd have been deeply rattled if her guests had arrived three hours' late. In my mother's world, routine and order had reigned supreme.

"We'd just about given you up for the afternoon," Pat told us, when we joined him and Joanne in the kitchen. Joanne busied herself cutting bread into thick slices.

"Help yourself to ham, mustard and anything else you want," she said, indicating the supply on the kitchen bench. We made impromptu sandwiches and washed them down with tea while Pat explained we would be going riding that afternoon.

Because of the distances covered, there would be no time the next day to ride up the length of the gorge, then turn around and muster the flock back down.

"We'll ride up as soon as you two have refreshed yourselves. It will only take a couple of hours or so," Pat told me. "We leave the horses in the overnight paddock so we get an early start tomorrow morning. That way both riders and horses are fresh."

I glanced at Jack, trying not to let my uneasiness show. I'd been to pony club when I was a teenager, but I wasn't sure trotting round a paddock in Waikanae equipped me for back country bush-bashing. As always, Jack looked relaxed and comfortable. Not a lot rattled my man.

Five minutes later, dressed in my oldest, softest jeans, I felt I was as ready as I possibly could be.

Pat drove us down to the yards and introduced us to our horses. Toby turned out to be a solidly built, friendly looking creature. I politely said I thought he 'had a kind eye' when Pat brought him over to me.

We were joined by Pat's oldest son, Matt, a couple of years older than Jack, and Ian, the next-door neighbour, who was coming to help with the muster.

I wondered just how fresh I would feel at five o'clock the next morning after a two-hour ride today. But I said nothing. This was a man's world and I wasn't going to embarrass Jack or myself if I could help it.

Jack had known Matt since they were children. Matt, had introduced him to country life when they were growing up. Apparently, he had always been kindness itself, even if teasing was part of his repertoire.

"He taught me the rules," said Jack. "Never grumble, never complain and you'll earn respect. If you whinge, you're likely to be the butt of some friendly country humour. Even worse, if you make a pain of yourself, the humour is likely to turn acid and you might never be invited out again."

Jack had laughed as he shared Matt's dictates, but I'd taken them to heart, determined to blend in. As it was, the cobalt-blue Kathmandu rain jacket I'd tied to the front of my saddle irrevocably marked me as a townie. I didn't want to make any social gaffes.

I made a mental note to make no mention of my trepidation to Jack, or to Matt. My fingers fumbled around the saddlery I was putting on Toby. It had, after all, been a very long time since I had done this stuff. But I completed it myself, and if I took a little longer than the others, well, they were still putting other horses on leading reins.

"Most of the guys coming can't afford the time to ride the horses into the hills, so we'll be leading the spare horses for them," Pat explained. "We've also got a couple of visitors who'll be coming out tomorrow. They're staying at Retakure Lodge, just over the ridge from us. They sent a couple of guests out with us last year as well, so I suppose we're now part of the entertainment provided for visitors."

"Well I hope the ones this year are better than last year's bunch," grumbled Ian. "The last two spent the whole day jabbering at each other. God knows what they were saying, but it didn't sound friendly."

"Yeah," grinned Pat. "They're a feisty lot, the Chinese. There wasn't much peaceful zen about them."

I scrambled up on to Toby and had a lead rope thrust into my hand. I tried to look as if I knew what I was doing as we moved out along the road. The occasional car passed us, heading up the gorge to the remote freedom camping site at its head for the Labour Weekend break.

Soon the sealed road gave way to gravel, traffic became scarcer and we relaxed, allowing ourselves to spread across the road. I wasn't particularly surprised to find I was the only female in the party. To my relief, Toby proved to be a quiet horse and we went at walking pace. I smiled at Jack as Toby plodded alongside him.

The gorge road was defined by the steep hills on either side. Much of the time the road ran 30 metres above river level, and at one point it was carved right into the edge of the cliff.

A rubble of small rocks lay in the middle of the road. I looked around. "Looks like there's been a rockfall," I said.

Pat looked up at the steep cliffs towering over us and grunted.

"Yeah, It's a bloody unstable piece of road. I'm always glad when we've ridden past it. We've had a wet spring and a lot of water has fallen up there. The run-off penetrates cracks in the rock and weakens it, so it doesn't take a lot to bring a slip down. The council must hate it. Every year or so it costs them big bucks to fix the damage. Frankly, the only reason they keep at it is that Joe Bryce has been a councillor for more years than you've been alive. He lives further up, at the head of the valley, and makes sure the road's kept open."

I looked at the steep slope and quickened Toby's stride. Jack grinned as he kept pace with me.

Every now and then the gorge would widen into river flats, well above and protected from the water. Sheep and goats grazed these areas and tumbled remains of stone walls were evidence of previous, failed, farming attempts.

"They were built after the Great War or in the Depression," remarked Pat when I commented on them. "The government gave returning soldiers land grants and handed out farms in areas like these. The soil's poor and it's as remote as you can find, but folk were desperate."

He gestured around. "No one knew, but these hills are seriously deficient in trace elements, particularly cobalt. The first thing most of them did was burn off the native bush and sow grass seed. The first year or so they got a bumper crop, but after that the soil failed. They didn't understand you had to top-dress it to get a crop of grass. Poor sods." He shook his head in regret.

"After the soldiers quit, there was a move towards felling the remaining timber. This place is so remote transporting stock or timber in and out is difficult, so after a while that industry failed as well."

He pointed to the unusual sight of a well-maintained drive, with a neat letter box, that left the road and wound into the hills above.

"Now that we've got yuppies or whatever you call them nowadays, who are 'reclaiming' the land, I suppose the cycle will start all over again. They don't intend to farm here, just have somewhere with paddocks and a pony for the kids. Trouble is, mortgage rates have started to rise again, and they're all squealing because they can't sell the land - no one in their right mind wants to buy up here."

"What goes around comes around," commented Ian.

Shortly after there was an excited tooting behind us and a

Land Rover with Joanne at the wheel overtook us.

"That's our afternoon tea," said Matt.

The 'overnight paddock' was a roughly fenced area that ran over a rocky ledge some way above the river. Joanne was already there. We unsaddled the horses and left them to roam free. The saddlery was piled on the ground and covered by tarpaulins Joanne had brought up. Spare saddlery for tomorrow's additional riders had also been brought in and the trough checked for enough rain water for the animals.

Afternoon tea was served on the flat deck of the Land Rover – hot thermoses of tea and Anzac biscuits. I sat on a rock, allowing the late afternoon sun to soak into me, and smiled up at Jack. "I may be saddle-sore tomorrow, but I'm enjoying this more than I can say."

Pat overheard and smiled. "It's neat, isn't it? It's why we live here. I can't imagine living anywhere else. It's not perfect, but it's the best place in the world."

I caught his enthusiasm and smiled. Perhaps he thought he was being too emotional because he looked slightly abashed.

"Silly, isn't it? I still feel that way after all these years," he mumbled.

"No," I murmured. "I don't think it's silly at all. I think you're very lucky to live here." Work, dead bodies and other mysteries all seemed a million miles away from this place. The peace and tranquillity made me realise how rattled I'd been this morning.

Matt overheard me. "I'll be interested to hear you say how lucky you are at four-thirty tomorrow morning!"

"Well, that's nothing for a pilot," I retorted.

"Good on you girl," laughed Pat.

Ian snorted his approval beside him. "We'll see if you're that staunch tomorrow."

I smiled to myself. I felt among family.

Later that evening, back at the farmhouse, Jack broke the news about our discovery that morning.

"We stopped at a place the next valley over. Big imposing property with huge gates."

"You mean the hunting lodge," said Pat.

"Hunting lodge?" I asked. "We never got to see the farmhouse or whatever was further up the road. It seemed very affluent."

"Retakure Lodge. It's impressive and very exclusive," explained Pat. "Celebrities and the very rich fly in by helicopter for a few days' hunting or fishing there. It's the place I was talking about when I said we had visitors coming out with us tomorrow."

"Isn't it a bit far away from everywhere?" asked Jack. "I thought tourists would want more than just a farm at the back of beyond."

Pat laughed. "It's a nice secluded holiday spot where they do whatever rich people do, without any publicity or media attention. We don't know much about what goes on up there. Most of their staff are imported. A posh chef, foreign housemaids, foreign hosts. It's owned by an Asian outfit we assume are Chinese. The only locals employed work on the farming side of the operation, or as hunting guides."

Jack went on to elaborate on what had happened and that we were late because we'd been held up by the police.

"So why would human remains be hidden in their swamp? Has anyone gone missing from there?" he asked.

Pat shrugged. "Not that I've heard. You'll have to ask Phil tomorrow. He's their farm manager. He's coming out with his dogs to help us with the muster and bring the guests. They're his charge to manage, not mine, thank the lord. I don't think Phil's too pleased about it, but I guess it comes with his job."

"Hopefully the bones will turn out to be ancient. Some early settler, like those returned soldiers you told us about," I said firmly.

"Maybe," said Pat. "It wouldn't be a good look for the lodge if one of their guests drowned in that swamp."

Later that evening there was a short report on TV.

"Earlier today a woman stumbled upon a body hidden on a property in the King Country. The body is yet to be identified and will remain overnight where it was found, west of Te Kuiti on the grounds of Retakure Lodge. A scene guard has been stationed at the site. A police spokesperson said they were notified just after 1 o'clock. Formal identification is yet to take place, and police are seeking forensic information to help them establish the identity of the body."

CHAPTER THREE

AT FOUR THIRTY THE NEXT MORNING, there was a knock on our door. The guest bedroom was small, and I struggled up into my clothes, trying not to fall over Jack who was doing the same thing. We went down to the kitchen where Joanne had prepared an early morning breakfast of eggs, bacon, toast and lots of tea.

"Eat up girl," urged Pat. "There's no weight on you and you're going to need some energy today. I don't imagine sitting inside a plane keeps you very fit."

I smiled. "Well, we do a fair amount of walking around the airfield, and we get to push aircraft around, but I agree, it doesn't match up to what you've got in mind."

It was pitch black outside when we went out to the ancient Land Rover. It was at least an hour before sunrise and bitterly cold.

Shamelessly, I pushed my way through to a seat in the cabin of the Land Rover, leaving the places on the flat deck to the men and their dogs. I squeezed myself between various supplies and the gear stick, then had to squash up even tighter when Ian leaned over and stashed a couple of guns into the well of the vehicle. I accepted guns were part of country life, but after my recent experience as a kidnap victim, I was wary of them. I twisted my knees to keep out of their way.

The Land Rover seat was decrepit, with bits of lining and springs extruding from the seat and back. I hoped there weren't too many bumps between the farm and the overnight paddock, although I had a nasty feeling there would be. It was amazing what you didn't notice on horseback but could feel in a car.

We rendezvoused at Ian's place. He had his own vehicle loaded up, and as we waited, two other utility vehicles drove up. The men climbed out of the utes, and Matt nodded a good morning as Jack and I were introduced to Phil, the hunting lodge's farm manager and his two guests. Another Asian man called Wu was introduced as a staff member from the lodge. He appeared to be there as minder for the visitors.

Phil introduced the visitors as 'Lee and Ray Chan from China'.

They were quietly spoken men.

"Lee, Ray." I smiled as I shook hands with them. "You're brothers?" I hardly needed to have asked; the family resemblance was very strong. They were surprisingly tall and fine boned.

"Yes, we're staying at the lodge and they offered us the opportunity to see what New Zealand farming was all about."

Their English appeared flawless.

"So, you two have come out to experience a slice of the real New Zealand?" Pat asked.

"It's not something we see in Shanghai." The older man, Lee, smiled politely.

Pat cracked a laugh. "I don't suppose it is."

Dogs ran all around the place and as each new set arrived there were a few minutes of power play between the packs. Some snarls were heard, which were quickly broken up by the men who simply kicked the offending animal. There was no time on a busy day to worry about a bit of territorial display from a dog.

It was still dark as the vehicles moved up the gorge, and all I could see in the headlights was the dusty gravel road and the tall, pale grass at its edge. Twice I saw the bright eyes of a possum reflected, before they disappeared. By the time we arrived at the paddock, the first traces of light were appearing in the sky. It was just enough for me to identify my horse, catch him, and get a saddle and bridle on him.

"Good boy, Toby, nice horse," I crooned, trying to make him stop jiggling as I did up the buckles. All the horses were excited, picking up their mood from the dogs and men. I had to climb on the stone I'd sat on the day before and throw myself onto Toby's back, as he wouldn't stand still. Then I had to reach down and tighten the girth while he shifted and fidgeted below me. By the time I'd settled into the saddle, I was warm from my exertions, despite the bitter morning chill.

I was proud I'd accomplished it all myself and wasn't obviously slow compared to the others although, they were doing a lot of other tasks as well. They loaded themselves up with guns, Swanndri jackets and their lunches before getting their dogs into working order. The brothers saddled up their own horses. Phil came over to check on them, but they seemed surprisingly competent for city-dwelling Chinese.

As we moved off, the light had changed to a pale daylight. It was still too early to make out much detail, but the light now limned the far-off ranges and painted the ridge lines with pale gold. High on the hills, wisps of mists clung to the cliffs. Dew-drops hung on the lichen that dangled from the tree branches. There was just enough light to make them sparkle like diamonds. Around us was the first chatter of bird-song as the dawn chorus kicked in. It was going to be a perfect day.

I followed Pat and Phil who were riding in front with Lee and Ray. Jack was some way behind me talking to Matt. A kilometre or two up the road, we turned off onto a track that took us down to the water. Everyone dismounted and led their horses down the steep trail. I followed, aware of Toby's big feet right behind mine, as I slipped and scrambled my own way downwards through the steep bush track. He was so sure on his feet, I thought I'd have been safer if I'd stayed on his back.

The river bank itself was a mass of rocks and boulders. We picked our way carefully over them to the edge of the river where everyone climbed onto their horses again. I made use of a convenient rock as a mounting block, which caused some amusement.

"Come upstream of me," ordered Pat, "and stay close." I pulled up beside him and we entered the water. It was clear and quickly deepened as the horses plodded further into the river. By midway the water was up to the soles of my shoes. I wondered how Toby was finding it, having icy-cold water all the way up his legs and belly. I was very aware of the strength of the current around us. I could feel its power pushing against Toby's side as he angled his way across. But the horses were strong, and Toby forged along beside Pat's horse, finally climbing out on the bank on the far side. The dogs had to swim for it and in the fast-flowing current were pushed down-stream, but they dog-paddled gallantly and made it to shore safely.

Toby stood there dripping for a minute before he shook himself like a dog. I held on grimly while he shuddered and shook beneath me. Pat laughed at my expression as I gripped the front of the saddle.

"You hang on there, girlie," he said.

I was taken aback. I'd never been called 'girlie' before! Pat undoubtedly didn't mean to be patronising, however archaic his language, so I contented myself by rolling my eyes and ended up grinning.

Once the group had all crossed safely and reformed, we tracked across the stony beach to the grassy sward that lay below the cliff above us. Here the men dropped their bags.

"We'll stop back here when we break for morning tea," explained Pat, "but before that we'll get the sheep off the hills above."

A brief discussion between Pat, Ian and Phil established that Ian, Matt and Jack would move further upriver and climb the cliff that bordered the river there. Pat, Phil, the two brothers, their minder, and I would work our way down stream for a bit, before we, too, climbed the bluff. I was conscious that Pat had appointed himself my guide and guardian for the day, for which I was grateful, although I was determined to keep my end up. I smiled across at Jack who'd been left to make his own way.

He grinned back, and it struck me how relaxed he was. He

had the happy ability to get on with almost everyone, and his innate physical competence made him useful in most situations. I envied him his poise and confidence.

"Once we're high above the river, both groups work the sheep in a pincer movement to bring them off the higher hills behind," Pat explained. "When we've formed them into a mob, we can start them flowing on the track that goes downstream by the river."

I followed him along the bank, sticking to the grassy areas wherever possible. There was a faint track here. I assumed it was made by sheep, but at least it followed the easiest contours and made passage effortless for horse and rider. In a short while we came to a shallow creek and Pat turned inland to follow the waterway up into the hills.

I was aware of Phil, on his own horse, and the two guests following silently behind me.

We splashed in and out of the shallow creek bed until we arrived at the foot of a bush-covered cliff. Here the track disappeared completely. I stared at the featureless hillside and narrow stream and assumed we'd carry on further up the waterway.

"We climb here," announced Pat.

"Where?" I asked.

Pat pointed.

"Up there? But there's nothing there," I said.

"Don't worry," he replied, correctly interpreting my expression. "You'll be perfectly safe. Just lean forward, stand in your stirrups and hold on to Toby's mane. You'll be fine. He's done it before. He's very sensible."

I wasn't about to betray my terror if I could avoid it, so I nodded with what I hoped looked like confidence and watched Pat duck under the curtain of creeper and branches that hid the bank behind it. Beneath the canopy, I now saw a narrow sheep track zig zagging up into the darkness above. It seemed barely wide enough to accommodate a horse. I had no alternative but to grit my teeth and follow Pat. The other men were behind me and I couldn't block the way.

The track quickly became so steep I was forced to follow

Pat's advice and stand, leaning right forward in my stirrups, clinging to a portion of Toby's mane up by his ears. I could feel the strength and power working in his hindquarters as he pushed and scrambled his way up, but it wasn't easy work for him. The ground was some type of crumbly rock that fractured into rubble as we climbed, and I felt Toby's feet slipping on its unstable surface. One hand clutched his mane, the other slid on the reins I was holding, and I realised they were wet with nervous sweat.

Ahead I could see Pat's horse clambering in a series of surges as he levered himself up the steep track. Pat himself, a tall man, was bent low over his horse's back to avoid the supple-jack and bush lawyer that threatened to grab him at every stride.

I bent my head low and prayed Toby did indeed know what he was doing. Although it was fully daylight out in the open, it was horribly dark and gloomy down under the canopy. I avoided looking back behind me down the hill, and focused every fibre of my being on reaching the top of the hill.

Suddenly I turned another zig, or was it a zag? There was light ahead, then I was in a grassed clearing high on a ridge above the river. Pig fern and fox gloves grew in wild profusion and bordered the open space, blocking a closer look at the river. Pat had stopped a little ahead of me and stood listening.

He slid off his horse and I copied him. "You OK?" He gave me a searching look. "That's the worst of the climbing. Everything else is pretty plain sailing now we're up here."

I was happy to hear it but determined to remain staunch.

"I'm fine," I managed in a casual tone. "What an amazing view."

"Yeah" said Pat shortly. "Can you hold my horse for me? I can hear someone in trouble down the hill." He handed his reins to me and strode back down the track we'd just climbed.

Left with nothing to do, I enjoyed the sun, looked at the view and watched the horses cropping the grass at my feet. Occasionally one or other would shift and I would have to rearrange their reins in my hands, but otherwise, I simply enjoyed the dreamy peace. That place was an archetypal New Zealand tourist's dream. Beautiful, surrounded by bush and bird song and a million kilometres from civilisation.

A few moments later, Pat climbed back into view, his dogs running ahead of him. "One of the visitors got caught in bush lawyer vine," he explained. "I had to cut him free. He was blocking Phil and the other guys."

Behind him, the men and dogs emerged from the bush. Lee seemed pale and shaken but said nothing.

Pat looked thoughtfully at me and the horses I was holding but was casual in his remark. "Watch where you're standing. The edge of the cliff is only a couple of feet into that pig fern, and if one of the horses goes over, there won't be any saving them. It's a long drop to the bottom."

Pat's laconic comment jerked me from dreams and back to reality. There was no indication to the casual eye that the swathe of pig fern hid anything like the edge of a cliff. Now I was aware it was close, I was pleased enough to shove Pat's own reins back into his hands. I pulled Toby away from the dangerous edge before mounting up and following Pat onto the clear hill paddocks ahead of us. I was shaken by the danger I'd unwittingly put myself and the horses into. Beautiful this place might be, but for visitors like me who wandered around unwarily, the dangers were both hidden and deadly.

With their teams of dogs safely assembled, Pat and Phil were in business. They sent them high up the hills at the back of the plateau and I watched in admiration as, with a shrill whistle or an arm movement, they ordered the dogs to climb above the sheep and bring them down. The dogs must have been incredibly fit to run up and down that impossibly steep bit of land. I certainly wouldn't want to be running over it myself.

The minder, Wu, had followed Phil, leaving the brothers to trail behind with me.

Lee smiled at me. "This is a very interesting experience."

He was picking a long strand of vine out of his horse's mane. I noticed there were additional leaves and twigs clinging by their thorns to his jacket and saddle blanket.

"It is," I agreed. "It's a privilege to see this." I checked him over. "Are you OK after getting caught on that cliff?"

He nodded. "Yes. Wu was close behind me, which edged my horse into a loop of creeper that got tangled around him. It was a little frightening because the hill was very steep, and I was afraid the horse would panic, but Pat came down and cut him out."

"It was more than frightening," said Ray. "It was deliberate. Wu's supposed to be looking out for us, not trying to kill us."

His voice was harsh with anger. I stared at him.

"You think Wu was trying to attack Lee?"

"I think there's a lot of odd stuff going on, and Lee was definitely shoved into that creeper deliberately."

Lee shook his head at his brother. "There's no reason to say so. It was just an accident."

Ray looked as if he'd argue the point, but Lee rode his horse forward and placed himself behind our leaders.

I hadn't known them long enough to know if I should take Ray's accusation seriously. Lee had dismissed the claim, and perhaps Ray was a drama-queen, inclined to making dramatic statements. All the same, there'd been enough certainty in his voice to be unsettling. I looked ahead to where Wu rode with the other men and resolved to stay well clear of him.

Quietly we followed the men as they worked their way up the ridge, then across the next flat. Toby hesitated at one point and I kicked him on. Phil grinned.

"Don't go too far that way, girlie, it's all swamp," he advised.

I peered at the land and realised that had Toby not stopped, I would have cheerfully ridden into the rough marsh grasses that hid the mire without even noticing. It was too reminiscent of what I'd done the day before, and I shivered. For a moment, pleasure drained from the day.

Pat smiled at me. "At least your horse has more sense than you have. Trust him, he knows what he's doing." I nodded, put the moment behind me, and smiled back, determined not to spoil a perfect day.

In the distance, I could hear whistles and shouts coming from Ian and Matt's party. I hoped Jack was having as much fun as I was.

Gradually, at first in twos or threes, but then in larger numbers, the sheep started to move down from the hills above us towards the middle of the plateau, where it seemed there must be a broader way that led down to the river far below.

Pat set a slow, steady pace as we followed them. Both he and Phil had their eyes fixed on their dogs and sat relaxed and completely at ease in the saddle.

For a man in his early sixties, Pat looked very fit. Phil was younger but had a tough, wiry presence that made it clear he could last all day in the saddle. I was already aware of tension in my thighs that would certainly present as sore muscles later, even though it was still barely breakfast time. I'd put up with the discomfort. It would be worth it for a magic experience like this.

As they drew nearer to the spot where the sheep were ducking over the edge of the cliff, Ian and Matt joined us. It was immediately obvious that Pat and Phil's quiet, easy control over their dogs wasn't a skill shared by Ian. His dogs were managed mainly by him shouting at them.

"Bloody wally," I heard several times. "Go out, left… stupid bloody dogs," he swore in disgust as his animals ran around in circles.

I smothered a smile. If there's a noise-to-effectiveness ratio, it was getting over worked by Ian. I saw Matt raise his eyebrows at Phil and his father and saw the same thought shared, with some amusement, between them. Still, Ian and his dogs seemed very happy in their chaotic way.

Jack rode up beside me. "Enjoying it?"

I nodded with enthusiasm. "I feel like an extra in a *Country Calendar* programme," I said. "Incidentally, I won't be able to walk tomorrow."

"Me neither." Jack shook his head ruefully.

When we reached the edge of the plateau we found a broad track leading to the river flats below. The group paused at the top to look back at the hills. Ian got out his binoculars. "I think we missed one up there behind all that scree," he muttered.

I gazed across but couldn't see anything.

"It'll be that old ewe that got away last time," said Pat "She's as wily as."

Ian continued scanning the hills with the binoculars. "I've been trying to get a sight of the bull," he said.

I gave a start that Ian noticed. For fuck's sake, no one so far had mentioned bulls.

"There's at least one feral cattle beast up here, possibly two," he explained. "I've had my eye on them for the last year or so, but they're cunning and hide deep in the fern if they see anyone coming." He shrugged his shoulders. "Nothing yet, but if I see him, I'll try and get us some pot roast."

He grinned at me. "I'll get a bit of beef for you and Jack to take back to that city place of yours, eh?"

I smiled, hoping devoutly that Ian would be unsuccessful. He swung around and scanned across to the far side of the river.

"There's a car about early over there," he observed. "I didn't expect anyone to be stirring on a Labour Weekend morning until a lot later."

"You never know who's around," agreed Pat.

He pointed back up the way we'd come to the hills above us. "You guys were talking about the hunting lodge place? It backs on to my land along the ridge line up there."

"Up there?" asked Ray in surprise. "I didn't realise it was so close. I've lost my sense of direction."

"That's easy to do in this sort of country," said Pat. "The two valleys run parallel, with that ridge separating them. It's quite close as the crow flies, but much longer by road."

I studied where Pat was pointing. "Can you get through to the lodge by going up there?"

Phil shrugged. "The bush is all secondary regrowth. There are tracks all through these hills, if you know where to look. A lot of logging took place until fifty years ago, and tracks were put in to get the timber out. When I was a kid growing up in this valley we used to ride our ponies along them and later our motor bikes. You could get through once. Nowadays they're so overgrown and degraded, I doubt you'd manage it."

I thought of the climb we'd taken up from the river and agreed no stranger was likely to stumble on such a route by chance.

CHAPTER FOUR

W E FOLLOWED THE SHEEP TO THE bottom of the cliff where the packs the men had piled up earlier still lay.

"Tea time," called Matt

We all dismounted. Pat took my horse and tied him beside his own to a low-hanging branch.

The thermos of hot tea was passed around with some of Joanne's biscuits. I sat on a boulder and thought I had acquitted myself adequately so far.

"How are you enjoying it?" asked Jack, sitting down beside me.

"I love it!" I said, "but I do feel like a bit of a townie in this environment."

Matt heard and smiled at me. "I've always loved the muster. It makes no economic sense to run anything over this back-country land nowadays, and with the Department of Conservation getting more aggressive about keeping stock from native forest, days like these are numbered. It's a special experience though, while we can still do it. I wanted to bring my girlfriend, but she's a nurse and had to work today. I'm glad you could make it."

"So am I."

The biscuit tin had reached me, and I passed it to Ray.

"I hear there was a bit of excitement over at your place," Pat remarked to Phil.

Phil nodded. "The police. Yeah. Swarming all over us yesterday afternoon. They found a body in the swamp by the woolshed."

I heard Ray give a slight gasp.

"It was Claire and Jack who found it," said Pat. "They got lost on the way to our place, ended up at the lodge, and Claire stumbled over the remains. I don't suppose you've any idea who it was or what happened?"

Wu, who was sitting beside Phil, turned his head sharply towards Jack and me. I hadn't heard him speak yet, but I picked that he at least understood English.

Phil shook his head in reply. He wasn't, I'd noticed, a very talkative man.

"You've got to ask yourself how long the body's been there," Pat continued. "You said there was still some flesh on it, didn't you, Jack?"

Jack shrugged. "I only gave it a cursory examination, and it was still in the swamp, so I couldn't see much. I didn't want to disturb the site. It looked like the remains of flesh to me. It'll be up to forensics to determine how long it's been there, I don't know how quickly a corpse would decompose in that environment."

"It doesn't take that long," said Phil. "Not that I know about human remains, of course, but I've seen a cattle carcass disintegrate. We had an animal caught in a boggy area right out the back of our place. We didn't find the poor beast until it was too late to save it. It had wedged in a narrow spot where we couldn't get to it. Anyway, it rotted quite quickly. Within a year, all you could see were bones."

We sat for a while in silence while we contemplated that thought. I found I could cope with yesterday's discovery more easily if I thought the body had been peacefully lying there for years. It was much more disturbing if the death was recent.

"You don't think it was one of those bog-men?" I asked. "You know, like the ones they dig up in Europe. They've been dead for centuries, but their bodies have been preserved by the swamp."

"They were found in peat bogs," objected Pat. "The swamp around here probably wouldn't have the same chemical effect. It's more likely a recent death."

"You haven't had anyone disappear from the lodge then, in the last year?" Matt joked as he turned to Phil.

Phil gave a cautious glance at his two guests who were sitting quietly. "I don't know much about what goes on up at the lodge. They've always got visitors coming and going, and many of them don't speak English. I run the farm, so I don't have anything to do with the guests, unless they take an interest in agriculture, or there's something interesting happening, like this muster. They're usually only want to get into the bush so they can go hunting. The rest of them get carted out to the golf courses in the chopper for a round or two, or go down to Taupo for the fishing. I can't see why one of them would have been out on the farm, let alone wandering into the swamp."

"That's assuming the dead person put themselves into the swamp," said Jack. "If they were murdered and dumped there, it would be a different story."

"Is that what you think happened?" Pat asked Jack.

Jack shrugged. "How long is a piece of string? I'm on holiday and don't know any more than you. We'll just have to wait and hear what they report on the news."

Lee had been listening to the conversation.

"Excuse me," he interjected, "you said a body had been found yesterday. You mean a human body?"

Pat nodded. "That's what it sounds like. Didn't the people up at the lodge tell you about it? I'm surprised the police didn't say something."

"No," Lee said, "we were told nothing." He glanced at his brother.

"This interests us very much," said Ray. "Is anything known about this dead person?"

Phil shook his head. "The police haven't said anything to us. I suppose, as Jack says, we'll have to wait until they have some forensic results before they can tell us anything."

"Are you sure it couldn't be a bog-man?" asked Matt. "It would be fascinating to find one here in New Zealand."

"And maybe not," said Pat with a snort. "The police will release details as soon as they know something. Although I am surprised the lodge themselves didn't say anything to you two, seeing as you're staying there," he said to Lee and Ray.

"They probably didn't want to alarm their guests," said Jack easily.

Ray and Lee looked as if they wanted to continue the conversation, but there was a mumble of dissent from the other men and no one else commented. Phil and Wu, employed by the lodge, presumably had to be cautious about what they said. But I thought the other men were embarrassed by the coincidence which had turned a local, titillating event, into something more sensational to be picked over by transient foreigners.

We mounted up again and moved downstream along the river. The dogs still worked above us on the hills, sending sheep down to join the mob ahead, but for us riders it was easy going. We were following a properly formed, flattened and benched track even though it was now overgrown. The pace was leisurely and relaxed, with plenty of time for banter and chat.

We passed a ruined cottage, covered in creeper, with tall foxgloves and docks growing around its base.

"That was old May's cottage," said Pat "It's been empty for years. People come and go up here. I dare say the present breed will do the same."

Talk turned to the new subdivisions that were working their way up the gorge. The men were pragmatic. Days such as this might soon be a thing of the past, but, as Pat remarked, human habitation came and went depending on economic conditions.

"This was big business in those days," he remarked, pointing out old workings from logging operations. "Everything is gone now of course, but back then there were a lot of men up here, taking timber out before it became uneconomic."

Lee and Ray had been silent since we remounted. It occurred to me they had been disturbed by the knowledge police were investigating the grounds of the lodge. Like Jack, I thought the lodge had kept quiet about the body to avoid any unease amongst their guests. It was unfortunate, in that case, that Lee and Ray had heard about it from us.

The track had widened, and riders were now able to proceed two or three abreast. Wu moved up to ride beside Phil.

Ray manoeuvred his horse beside me.

"Was it you who found the body?" he asked.

"I wandered into the swamp by mistake, and I was trying to get out when I disturbed the mud. By the time I'd reached solid ground, some of the skeleton had floated to the surface. I only saw it from a distance."

"Then how did you know it was a body?"

I turned to find Lee had ridden up on my other side.

"Because an arm had risen to the surface and the shape of the fingers was quite distinctive," I said. I didn't want to talk too much about it, partly because it was a police investigation now, but more particularly because I didn't want to remember how sick I'd felt when I realised I'd stood on the thing. It felt like the worst sort of desecration, even if it had been an accident.

"And your boyfriend? He studied it as well?" Lee persisted.

I glanced over to where Jack was riding beside Matt. "You'll have to ask him what he saw," I said discouragingly. "He's a detective, so he might have seen more than I did when he went to have a look."

"He's a policeman?" asked Ray. I intercepted a glance between the brothers.

"Yes. But he's not working on that case," I replied. "We're on holiday. It was just stupid chance that I found the body."

I couldn't mistake Ray's excitement, a lively curiosity which I realised was mirrored in Lee. I was beginning to regret the subject had ever been raised at all. Ray and Lee seemed a little too curious for it to be healthy. I clamped my legs against Toby and asked him to move forward, away from their questions.

From behind me I heard a rapid exchange in Chinese. I ignored it and quickened my pace until I was beside Jack and Matt.

The hills rose steeply up from the river on our right. The

lower levels were covered with an impenetrable mixture of pig fern and creeper. I spared a moment to hope Ian's feral bull wasn't concealed in the thick scrub. It was unnerving to think it could be watching us. There was a clear demarcation between this lower growth and the rough grasslands above, a bizarre, natural Plimsoll line I assumed was the result of river activity. I imagined the river could easily fill the gorge from side to side after a few day's rain.

Above us, the dogs were still working through the clearer areas, picking out recalcitrant sheep trying to hide, and driving them down to join the mob in front of us.

We rode in companionable silence for a few minutes. I was happy just to be beside Jack. Occasionally my thigh would lightly bump against his and he'd give me his warm smile.

The widening track allowed Ray and Lee to join us and ride abreast.

I moved aside to let them in, at the same time making sure not to let them come between Jack and me.

"Enjoying yourselves?" Matt leant forward from the far side of Jack to ask.

Lee nodded. "Very enjoyable." The banal reply gave the impression his mind wasn't focused on what he was saying. I saw him glance to where Pat, Phil and Wu were riding. Phil and Pat were chatting although I couldn't hear what they were saying. I gazed ahead, wondering whether joining them would be preferable to remaining with the brothers who were beginning to creep me out.

"We need to ask you about the body you found," Lee said a few minutes later. I felt a surge of irritation. Not only did I think it was in poor taste to metaphorically pick over the bones of the person whose remains we'd found, but Lee was sabotaging my peace and comfort. I gave him an unfriendly look.

But Jack was as relaxed as ever. "What do you need to know?"

I wondered whether he'd read my mood and had stepped in to deflect it.

"Claire said you are a policeman?" asked Ray

"I'm currently on holiday," Jack said, "but yes, I'm a

detective."

"Then there is something we need to tell you," said Ray.

Jack raised his eyebrows but said nothing.

"We are very interested in the body you and Claire found."

I took a deep breath in to protest, then shut my mouth. "Let it rest," I thought.

Ray glanced at me. "This is not just random nosiness," he assured me. "It involves me and my brother."

I sighed and concentrated on the spot between Toby's ears.

"A year ago, our father came to New Zealand on holiday," said Lee. "He stayed at the lodge. We have evidence he came out on this same muster last year. Then he disappeared. He has never been seen since. We can't help wondering whether this body you found is his."

"I'm very sorry to hear that," said Jack. I could tell he'd switched into his professionally courteous 'dealing with the public' mode. "When you say he disappeared, what do you mean? How did he disappear?"

Ray and Lee seemed relieved to talk.

"We don't know," said Lee. "He came for a holiday and some hunting. My father doesn't speak English, but the lodge caters to Asian business men, so it was a natural choice for him, particularly as he didn't come for pleasure alone. It was also a business meeting. He was here to discuss plans for a merger with another Chinese company.

"He reached here safely, because he called our mother when he arrived. He also emailed us to say he was riding out on a muster and being a shepherd for the day. The idea amused him." Lee shook his head. "That was the last time we heard from him. It was also the last time *anyone* heard from him. He never arrived back in Xian."

"You mean he never got on the plane?" I asked, my attention jerked from the track in front of us. No wonder the poor men were frantic for information.

"The airline had no record of him having boarded the aircraft in Auckland," said Ray. "At first we assumed he'd missed the flight. We tried to call, but his mobile phone was on answerphone.

When we still hadn't heard from him two days later, we became seriously worried. My father was a busy man. He wouldn't, he couldn't, disappear from his responsibilities for two days without an explanation. Even more worrying, his social media accounts have been deleted. For the first few days after he went missing, we were able to check them in case there were new postings. Now they've all gone."

Lee picked up the story. "We made enquiries with the airline, the police, with the embassy and the New Zealand Government. They all agreed to help, but no one could find any trace of him since he booked out of the lodge on his last day here. He'd settled his account and that was the last transaction on his credit card. The owner of the lodge reported they'd helicoptered him to Taupo to catch the plane on to Auckland, but there was no record of him boarding that flight either. Nor did he appear on any CCTV film at the airport. Since then, nothing. Our mother is, of course, frantic with grief and worry. Our father's business is in limbo, and its stock market value has dived. Until we know what has happened to him, we can't make plans or decisions, and we have no certainty about the future. If he's dead, then his estate must be wound up, but without proof, no one can do anything. His company has stalled. His competitors have taken over his place in the market. If he's alive and maybe lost his memory . . . ."

"Amnesia," supplied Ray.

"Amnesia," repeated Lee. "He may not want to be alive when he sees what has become of his business. We do our best, but we have limited authority to act on his behalf. Our father was relatively young, with no reason to plan for his death. We have no power of attorney to help us. Also, dealing with events in another country and in another language, makes everything harder to manage."

I heard the frustration in his voice and, it shamed me. Lee and Ray must have found the talk about a discovered body highly significant and I'd dismissed them as being vulgarly curious about my macabre discovery! Would it would be better, or even more awful for them, if the body turned out to be their missing father. They'd want closure of course, but on the other hand, confirmation of their worst fears would be gut-wrenching.

"What line of business was he in?" asked Jack.

"Manufacturing. He started with a small stall at our local market, but years ago, when we were very young children, he began an export business into Australia and New Zealand selling cheap, fashionable, Western clothing. Even as imports, these goods were cheaper than any other brand at the time. He had a team of women making the clothes. Initially, they worked from their homes, or set up their sewing machines on the pavement outside their apartments. The marketing model proved to be successful, so he shifted his workers into a factory in Shanghai. Eventually he channelled a large portion of the business through Alibaba.com, which of course gave him access to a wider market. As Alibaba expanded, so his own business grew and prospered. He became a wealthy man. Within China, he was well respected."

Ray smiled as he took up the story. "He moved our mother into a larger apartment. He even became wealthy enough to afford to holiday at a luxury lodge in New Zealand. Educating me and my brother had always been important to him. For the first time there were no issues about what it cost. He wanted us to have the best. There was a high expectation of academic effort and excellence so we would come back and join him in the firm."

We rode in silence for a while, absorbing what the brothers had told us.

"It's an obvious question," Jack said eventually, "but do you know why he might have wanted to hide? Or indeed of anyone who might have wanted to kill him, or cause him to disappear?"

I made a move to interrupt, but he shook his head at me. "Yes, I know it's reasonable to assume the body we found in the swamp could be their father, but we don't know that yet. It might be coincidence and there's another reason for his disappearance."

The brothers both shook their heads. "We've been over this so often," said Ray. "There's nothing we can think of. He loved our mother. He loved us and his family. His business was successful. I can't think of anything which would have made him abandon us."

"Nothing," echoed Lee.

"What about his politics?" asked Jack. "Could he have offended people in power back in China?"

"That's a bit extreme, isn't it?" I asked. "Are you suggesting some cloak-and-dagger international conspiracy?"

"I'm just searching for possibilities," said Jack calmly. "If the man's missing, there must be some reason. There've been other cases where wealthy Chinese have disappeared, and it's been assumed by Western police and observers there has been a political connection."

"My father firmly supported President Xi Jinping. I believe he even once did him some personal service, helping dispose of assets, a few years ago. He didn't discuss the details with us," said Lee, "but he would be regarded as a friend by our president – certainly not part of an anti-Xi coalition. There'd be no reason to kidnap him."

"If he'd been kidnapped for profit, there'd have been a ransom note," reasoned Jack. "I'm afraid your best hope of a quick solution is for that body to be identified as his. Failing that, it's a cold case, and without fresh evidence, there may be nothing the police can do for you."

"Can you help us?" asked Ray. "I realise it's discourteous to ask you. Claire said you're on holiday, but we are desperate. We've been here five days and there are no leads at all."

"I can put a call out to my friends in Wellington," said Jack, "and see who's working on the missing person case. But frankly, there's not much to go on unless the body in the swamp does indeed belong to your father. In that case – and if there's signs of foul play – it will be handled by homicide and you'll need to speak to them. Your father's name would be Chan? The same as yours?"

There was a sudden silence. I looked up to see the brothers exchanging glances.

"No," said Ray. "Our father's name is not Chan. Nor is ours. When we made the booking for the lodge, we didn't want anyone to associate us with him in case there was some scandal we had to uncover. We called ourselves Chan to conceal our name."

"Our family name is Zhang," said Lee. "Ray and I use anglicised names because it was easier at school and to travel. But our real name is Zhang."

"I'm not sure our deceit worked," said Ray. "We think someone went through our papers last night when we were at dinner. We also think someone accessed Lee's computer. We'd put our passports and other documentation away in the safe in our suite and Lee had booby-trapped the papers."

"I saw it in a James Bond film," said Lee, looking embarrassed. "007 put a hair on the safe so he could tell if it had been touched. I thought it was a good idea, so I draped a hair over our documents. When we got back to our room after dinner last night, I checked, and the hair had disappeared. It's not proof, of course, but I'm certain our stuff had been tampered with."

"What about the computer?" asked Jack.

"I'd used it earlier in the day to Google one of the people at the lodge," said Lee. "I've got a good memory for faces and I thought I recognised him as someone my father and I met once in Shanghai. My research was inconclusive, but I'm still certain it's the same man, only with a different name. There was some back story to him, but I can't remember the details. I think there was a scandal of some sort."

"So, what makes you think someone accessed the computer?"

Lee shrugged. "I can't be certain. I hadn't logged off when we went down to dinner. I just had a feeling the mouse had been moved. If someone looked at my search history, they'd know who I'd been researching. It may be coincidence, but I have an uneasy feeling about it."

"Then again, they didn't tell us about the discovery of a body," said Ray. "Maybe it's made them nervous for some reason. I think Wu is suspicious of us and why we are here."

"Is that why he came out with you today?" Jack was asking.

Ray shrugged. "They told us it was normal practice for the lodge to supply an assistant for their guests on trips such as these. Maybe it is." He hesitated for a second and turned to speak to me. "When Lee got caught in the creeper on the hillside, I'm certain

Wu deliberately drove him into the vines. I think he wanted to cause an accident."

I looked at him, the urgency of his accusation earlier very clear in my mind. Originally, I'd misjudged the brothers' interest in the remains as gratuitous curiosity, yet they'd had real cause to want more information. Ray had been very certain Wu tried to cause an accident that could have seriously injured Lee. Maybe I shouldn't dismiss this claim either as overly dramatic nonsense.

Lee said something sharply in Chinese which shut Ray up. "We don't know that," he said. "I apologise for my brother. The strain of worrying about our father is telling on us both. It is easy for us to imagine devils in every doorway. The hill was steep and treacherous, and it was probably an accident. Pat sorted it out very easily."

Maybe Pat did sort it out, I thought, *but the brothers both looked shaken when they'd reached the top of the climb. What would have happened if Pat hadn't been there to intervene?*

CHAPTER FIVE

A COUPLE OF HOURS LATER WE STOPPED for lunch. My legs were so wobbly after the hours in the saddle, I could barely stand when I slid to the ground.

By now the track had widened to the width of a road, and the sheep moving ahead of us were several hundred in number.

Ian was still scanning the surrounding country intent on searching for his bull, while I continued to hope, with equal fervour, that there was no possibility of him finding it. I held a strong conviction that I didn't want to be in close proximity to a feral bull, alive or dead.

After a while Ian said "That's odd. You know that car we saw earlier? That same fellow has come down-stream again. Looks like he's tracking us. Maybe he's taking photos of us."

I looked up and saw Ian had swung round and was now focusing his glasses on the opposite side of the river.

Pat snorted, "You'd better powder your nose and put some lippy on then, Ian. Only way they'll take photos of you is if you get some make-up on."

I smiled to myself. I was lying in the warm grass beside Jack. Close behind me I could hear Toby munching on the long grass. Above us in the bush, the cicadas were rasping. It was unbelievably nice to do absolutely nothing at all.

I wondered whether I'd ever flown over this particular valley and what it had looked like from the air. It was quite possible I'd done so. I'd once taken a wedding party on a charter between New Plymouth and Hamilton. This valley must be close to the line I'd taken that day.

I felt the early spring sun warm my face and body. I heaved a sigh of satisfaction and allowed my mind to drift.

"I tell you what," announced Ian, "that bastard's watching us as well. I can see the glint on the lens."

"You did say you felt like an extra in a *Country Calendar* clip," Jack said to me. He was propped up on one arm watching Ian with amusement.

"Bloody odd sort of a car to be up the gorge in," Ian continued. "A bit fancy, I'd have thought, to be driving around on gravel roads. I can't see what it is from here, but it's a bit low to the ground for all the bumps."

"Can you see its registration number?" asked Pat quietly.

"Nah, the guy's standing right in front of it. Ah well, tourists," said Ian, lowering his binoculars.

"Can I borrow those for a second?" asked Jack.

Ian handed them to him and Jack focused on the car across the river. It was a long way away. I stared across to where Ian had indicated, but without glasses I could only get a very vague impression of a vehicle. Ian must have good eyesight if he could make out more.

"Can you see anything?" Lee asked. "Why would someone be interested in what we are doing?" I glanced across at him and Ray. There was an urgency in the way Lee spoke that seemed disproportionate.

I considered what the brothers had told us: Their father was missing; they thought the safe in their room had been tampered with and their papers and computer examined, although they hadn't indicated anything had been taken. Then there was the business with Wu and Lee on the hillside.

Ray at least had seemed concerned and jumpy when they'd discussed it. The trouble was, I couldn't see why anyone would want to hurt or intimidate them. Even if their connection to the missing man was discovered, there had already been an investigation into his disappearance that had found nothing. Unless, of course the body I'd stumbled over really was their father. In which case, I still couldn't see why there would need to be any threat to the brothers.

The men were continuing to study the car across the river.

"I expect it's fascinating to a townie," Matt replied. "A muster must be almost as exotic to an Aucklander as it does to you guys from Shanghai. Not everyone in New Zealand is a farmer."

After a few moments' scrutiny, Jack handed the binoculars back.

"I guess you're right," he said. "He's just a tourist who's watching a muster."

"It's most likely someone from the lodge checking we're OK," said Phil phlegmatically. "There's a footbridge across the river about a kilometre further on. If our guests are tired or uncomfortable, it's the only opportunity for them to leave the muster."

He looked over at Ray and Lee. "Once we're past that point, you're committed for the rest of the day. Are you still certain you want to carry on?"

Both men nodded. "Yeah, we're fine," said Ray.

"Did you know they were coming out to check?" Pat asked. He sounded puzzled.

Phil shook his head. "Nah. But it wouldn't surprise me if that's who it is. If you remember, we had a bit of trouble last year. They may have decided to control things better this time and check everything is OK."

Pat shrugged.

We mounted up again and followed the track downstream. I kept a look out, but the car had disappeared as we turned a bend in the river. Probably Matt was right, and the vehicle contained nothing but a weekend driver enjoying the sight of rural New Zealand at work. I realised I was responding irrationally to tension I imagined emanating from the brothers and made a conscious effort to simply enjoy myself in the moment.

While we'd been stopped, the sheep had continued ambling down the track. It seemed once they were set in the right direction, they took care of the rest themselves. Occasionally the dogs would rush around to chivvy a slow animal or cut one off that made a break for the hills, but otherwise it was an orderly mob they followed.

A thought had occurred to me, and I nudged Toby up beside Jack.

"You realise it was their father on the muster last year? He emailed them and told his family he was going on it, remember? And Pat said the visitors were quarrelling all day. Maybe that's why their father disappeared. Maybe it was an argument that turned deadly."

Jack nodded. "It could be that's relevant to his disappearance, but it's purely speculative. We've nothing to go on. We don't even know whether that body relates to him or not. We'll have to wait until the police get the forensic report."

Ten minutes later we came to the bridge. It was, as Phil had said, a footbridge suspended from metal cables that spanned the river. It was narrow and swayed, and there was no way a horse would have crossed it, but a man could.

As we reached the spot where the cables were anchored into the ground, a slender Asian man stepped on-to the span from the far end. He waved as he walked across towards us.

There was a muffled grunt from Phil. "Told you so," he muttered to Pat and kicked his horse forward to the end of the bridge where he swung his leg over and jumped to the ground.

He stood waiting while the man made his way across and joined him. Phil shook his hand. I was amused at the contrast between them. The man crossing the bridge was tall, well-built and elegant, casually enough dressed in jeans, open-necked shirt and a leather jacket, but every article of clothing shrieked quality.

The jacket looked supple, with the soft sheen of high-class leather. The jeans were well cut, and I could see enough of the exquisitely pressed, brilliant white shirt to tell it was of a heavy, expensive looking fabric.

Phil, like the rest of us on the muster, was dressed in

comfortable old trousers of some antique provenance, a scruffy T-shirt and a loosely hanging bush jacket. If you passed him on the street you'd assume he was a tramp. My own fashion choices for the day didn't stack up much better.

We watched as Phil greeted the newcomer, then turned and introduced him. "This is Charles," he announced. "I don't know whether you've met before, but Charles Wong is the manager and owner of Retakure Lodge. Charles, this is Pat Crombie who owns the land that borders yours along the ridge line up there. He's the one to thank for his hospitality today."

I studied Charles. Close up, he had the high-cheek-bones and stern look seen on ancient terracotta warrior figures. It wouldn't surprise me to find some long-distant ancestor had been the model for those statues.

If he was the owner of the lodge, then had he been involved in the disappearance of Ray and Lee's father?

Pat leaned from his saddle to shake Charles's hand. "G'day," he said amiably. "You've come to see how your guests are getting on?"

Charles nodded as Lee and Ray rode forward to greet him. "Yes, I've come to check how these two are going and if they're happy to continue." He smiled at them. "You're not too saddle-sore, or tired? If you are, I can give you a lift home."

Ray shook his head. "No thank you. We're just fine." His brother nodded in agreement.

"I wouldn't want to miss this experience," added Lee.

"That's excellent," Charles said. "We're very lucky we have good neighbours who are kind enough to allow our guests to ride out with them. I must thank you, Mr Crombie, for permitting this."

Pat shook his head. "You really owe it all to Phil over there," he said. "He twisted my arm last year, saying I should let your guests come out on the muster. Having let him persuade me once, I couldn't very well say no to him this time. Phil can be very convincing when he wants to be."

"That's very true," said Charles. "But it's good for me to meet my neighbour at last, as well, and be able to thank you in person for your generosity in giving my guests such an opportunity. Perhaps, in repayment, you and your guests would care to come to the lodge tomorrow for dinner? Come early and spend the afternoon enjoying our facilities before the meal. It's the least I can do to repay you."

What a stroke of luck! Aside from any other consideration, it was likely the only time in my life I'd get to see the inside of a luxury hunting lodge. My finances and future expectations of income didn't run to that sort of hedonism. Plus, it could be an opportunity for Jack and me to snoop around a bit for evidence about the missing Mr Zhang the elder.

"Well, yeah, thanks." Pat appeared startled by the invitation. "I'm sure we'd all be keen to visit the lodge. I hear you had a bit of trouble up there yesterday?"

Charles's face darkened. "Ah yes, indeed. Such a sad discovery to make. That poor man. How he ended up in the swamp is a mystery. The tragedy must have occurred many years ago before we bought the property. None of our employees have disappeared, and we take very good care of our guests. I hope this doesn't put you off visiting us?"

Pat shook his head. "Not at all. Unfortunately, Matt and I'll be busy with the shearing until late afternoon tomorrow, but I'm certain my wife and the others here would be happy to come around earlier. We've all wondered what sort of a place you're running up there. Matt and I could join you all later, if that's OK?"

"Of course. You will be welcome whatever time you choose to arrive. Join us for the meal when you're ready, and your wife and guests are most welcome to come early afternoon. Shall we say two?"

"Yeah, that's great," said Pat. "Yeah. The wife *will* be pleased. We'll see you tomorrow then."

I glanced at Jack to see what he thought about this offer, but he was his usual imperturbable self and I couldn't read his expression. Ray and Lee were smiling, so I assumed they approved. They waved goodbye to Charles and made their way to the back of our group.

Charles paused to exchange some words with Wu. They spoke too softly for me to make out individual words, not that it would have helped as I wouldn't have understood the language anyway.

Charles glanced at the brothers a couple of time as Wu spoke, and his reply was a quick fire of sharply pronounced words.

Pat had been right, I reflected. The Chinese were a feisty-sounding lot. If I hadn't known better, I'd have assumed Charles was ripping in-to Wu for some reason. As it was, I supposed the aggressive pace and tone of the conversation was normal for them. Wu was probably being instructed to keep a close eye on his clients and ensure they had a good time.

The conversation finished, Charles turned to the rest of us.

"Until tomorrow then."

"Until tomorrow," echoed Pat.

Charles marched away across the bridge. Although his steps made the construction sway, he made no attempt to steady himself by grasping the rail. Instead he seemed to have an enviable, cat-like ability to keep his balance.

"What do you make of him?" I asked Jack.

"Very polished," he replied, "although I *do* wonder why he was certain the remains you found were male."

"Oh! You're right, he did, didn't he? Perhaps he was just generalising? Using 'he' as if it's a gender neutral term?"

Jack shrugged. "Maybe."

We waited until Charles drove off, before we turned our horses downstream and continued on our way.

CHAPTER SIX

W E'D BEEN FOLLOWING THE TRACK FOR about half an hour before Ian leaned over towards Matt who was on the far side of Jack.

"Fancy a bit of fun, mate?"

Matt's eyes lit up. "Sure thing. What's the deal?"

We were in a wider part of the gorge. To our right, set back some hundred metres from the river itself, was a moderate slope which led upwards towards the ridge. The hill curved around towards us, and ahead the gorge narrowed dramatically as the ridge descended steeply to the river bed below. It was the narrowest the gorge had been since we forded the river earlier in the day. The opposite bank also sported a steep cliff, so the current ran deep and fast between the two banks.

I could follow the line of the road high above on the other side and realised we were opposite the place Pat had mentioned which suffered road closures regularly due to slips. There was no danger to us, situated as we were on this side of the valley, but it was clear how easily a slip could occur. The scree-covered cliff was bare of any vegetation and looked distinctly unstable and prone to erosion.

Our own track climbed as we approached this point on our

side of the gorge, and I could see the narrowest part was below the point.

"The bull often hangs about in the pig fern up on that ridge," said Ian. "What say we take a tiki-tour there and see if we can find him?"

Personally, I couldn't think of anything I'd have wanted to do less, but Matt was keen. "Do you want to come as well, mate?" he asked Jack.

"How do you get down again?" asked Jack, eyeing up the steep fall into the river.

"Easy," laughed Ian. "Don't be put off by that cliff. Once we reach the top of the ridge line, you'll see there's an easy route down on the far side. You won't even have to get off your horse."

"OK," Jack nodded, then looked doubtfully at me. "Do you want to come?" he asked.

I got the impression Ian and Matt were surprised the question was even asked.

"Hell, no," I said with deep feeling. "Nothing would convince me to join a hunt for a bull."

Ian gave a chuckle. "Leave it, man," he advised Jack. "There's not too many sheilas would join us."

Matt snorted, which he converted into a cough when he realised I was watching him. "I'll go and tell Dad," he said. "Chances are he and Phil want to join us."

"You'll be OK?" Jack asked.

"I'll be fine as long as I don't tangle with a feral bull," I assured him. Jack's the most grown up-person I know. He's kind, thoughtful, competent and a real mensch, but I couldn't miss the boyish grin spreading across his face at the prospect of adventure. Boys will be boys, I guess.

"You go and play with the big kids," I laughed at him.

He rolled his eyes, and he and Ian rode forward to join the others. Matt had been right – Pat and Phil wanted to be part of the action as well.

"No need to hurry, but when you're ready, carry on along the track for about two hundred metres or so around the bend you can see up ahead. Not too far beyond that, the road drops down to the river and a flat, wide-open area. We'll meet you there when we come down from the hill. You'll be able to see us anyway," advised Pat.

Matt gave me a wicked grin. "We'll call out to you if we find the bull."

I watched as their horses climbed the slope. Remaining with me were Ray, Lee and Wu.

"You didn't want to go with the others?" I asked the brothers.

Ray shook his head. "I think we are safer staying on the track," he said. "It's sufficiently exciting for us to herd the sheep. Chasing wild bulls isn't part of our programme."

"Fair enough."

Jack and the men climbed higher until we lost sight of them in the scrub above us on the slope. Our own horses ambled forward along the track, climbing as we headed for the point.

I indicated the other side of the gorge. "That's where we saw the rocks on the road yesterday when we rode the horses up the gorge. I recognise where we are now."

"I'm not surprised rocks fall down that cliff," said Lee, surveying the bleak expanse of scree. "It needs a retaining wall."

"It's probably not worth the money," I said. "This is a pretty remote country road. I doubt the local council wants to spend any more cash on it than they have to."

We reached the point and stopped to look down into the gorge some twenty metres below. The cliffs on either side of the river crowded nearer and blocked out the direct sunlight so the river ran fast and dark. Nasty-looking rocks jutted above the surface of the flowing water, and the river swirled around them, the white of the rapids the only lighter shade in the dismal monochrome.

It was a beautiful and rather eerie spot, like Coleridge's 'deep, romantic chasm'. I felt in my pocket for my mobile phone and pulled it out to take a photo. Toby shifted beneath me. It didn't matter how still I tried to stay to keep in focus, on Toby's back I couldn't steady myself sufficiently to get a clear shot.

"Crap," I said, as I dismounted. Secure on my own feet, I snapped away happily and when I checked the results of my photographs I was happy that I'd captured the moody, dramatic nature of the place.

There was a holler from somewhere on the hills above us. The men were out of sight and I hadn't made out the words.

"They say the bull is coming this way," said Lee.

"They did? I bet it's not true," I said scornfully. "That's just Matt trying to wind me up."

The call came again, more urgently and this time I recognised the voice as Pat's.

"Shit." I scrambled on to Toby's back with the speed of a stunt rider. As I'd spent all day searching for handy rocks to help me mount, I allowed myself a pat on the back for my new-found athleticism.

Ray looked both ways down the track. "He didn't say which way it's coming," he complained.

I waited nervously. "Perhaps we should move," I suggested. "Pat said the track opens up further on." Encountering an enraged bull on this narrow portion of the trail was unattractive.

As I spoke, there was a long low grumble of sound, and the ground began to shake. We'd barely had time to register it was an earthquake, not a rampaging bull, when Ray gave a startled cry as the cliff on the far side of the gorge slipped and fell outwards, curving out over the river.

We froze, awed and fascinated by the display. Then, above and behind the first slip, two more slabs of cliff fell forward, like so many slices of carved meat. They hung for a moment, high on the cliff opposite, before crashing with a wild tumble of rocks and gravel into the river.

Abruptly I was spun in a fine demonstration of centrifugal force as Toby barged forward, shoving his way past Lee, who'd been standing beside me, and bolted from the group along the track.

I barely maintained my place in the saddle. My right foot had lost its stirrup, making my seat precarious and I clung by my thighs with a strength born of desperation as I tried to regain both my balance and some control over the horse. We were running downhill, a factor increasingly threatening my tenuous safety in the saddle as we careered down the track.

The ground was still shaking, and Toby's pace was uneven as he tripped and stumbled along in his wild rush. The world had turned insane. I'd lost control and had no idea how to get it back.

CHAPTER SEVEN

IT MUST HAVE BEEN THE BEST part of a kilometre before I managed to get a proper grip on the reins, before Toby's pace moderated to a slow canter and he finally came to a stop. His sides heaved, and there was a heavy sweat on his neck.

I wasn't in much better condition. Throughout the muster, Toby had been such a placid animal that his action had taken me completely by surprise. While he heaved and puffed below me, I trembled with shock on his back. At least the earth had ceased its wild rolling, although every few minutes I thought I felt aftershocks, but equally that might have been the wild, uneven beating of my heart.

We'd travelled downstream from where we'd been standing. Ahead, startled sheep raised their heads to consider whether our sudden appearance in their midst represented a threat. They seemed placidly unconcerned about the earthquake that still sent rumbles through the ground, and were content to continue ambling along the track, stopping for a few mouthfuls of grass every now and then.

Eventually our breathing patterns steadied. I patted Toby's neck in a futile gesture of reassurance, as much to convince myself I was safe as to give him comfort, and looked around.

We'd come to a halt in an open area where the pig-fern covered hills on our left descended, at some distance from the river, into a wide, level bowl, slightly raised above the water, forming an expansive and protected area of grassy land. It was beautiful and isolated and a perfect spot for a picnic. Some fragment of memory surfaced through the turmoil in my brain and I realised this must be where Pat had told us to rendezvous with the group chasing the bull.

Once our panting had subsided, Toby and I were surrounded by limpid silence. I heard no birdsong, the rumbling sound of the earthquake had faded away and the sheep were quiet. Even the noise of the river was muted.

I looked up to the hills which Jack should by now have been descending, but could catch no sight of the party. Of course, there was fern, and the scrub above it was thick. The men could well be half-way down the hill already but hidden from view. I waited a few minutes, hoping they'd turn up. More particularly I was hoping that Pat, who seemed a competent sort of man, would arrive to take control of the situation. It was, after all, his farm, his muster, and so far, he'd shown admirable leadership traits. Failing Pat, Jack would have done nicely. He had a way of making me feel safe, whatever situation we found ourselves in.

Alone, if I was honest, I felt out of my depth. This wasn't territory I was familiar with and the earthquake, followed by the wild ride on Toby, had rattled me in more than one sense of the word.

Eventually I pulled on the reins, asking Toby to turn and retrace the course of our wild charge. I expected some resistance, but he seemed happy enough to comply with my request. We were still half way through the turn, standing at right angles to the track, when I looked up, hearing the loud clatter of hooves on gravel, to see a rider-less horse charging towards us.

We didn't have time to move and for a moment I thought it would plough straight into us. Instead, the bolting animal, realising he'd reached the safety of another horse's company, came to a plunging stop barely a metre in front of us. I let him calm down for a moment or two while he greeted Toby. I recognised him as Lee's horse.

At some point the animal must have trodden on its reins, as they were broken. I eased Toby alongside, reached over and gathered the two ends up. Tied in a knot, they would be short but still serviceable. As it was, I grabbed the longer of the two as a lead rein and pulled the animal behind us as I steered Toby up the track. Perhaps Toby's bolting had triggered a similar flight instinct in this animal and Lee had been less successful at staying on. I hoped he hadn't been hurt in the fall.

I hadn't realised just how far Toby had carted me. The track led uphill around a couple of bends until I began to see, on the far side of the gorge, the damage we'd witnessed during the course of the earthquake. I kept an eye out for Lee in case he'd fallen on the track, but there was no sign of him. We had to round one more bend in the road until I'd be able to see where I'd left my companions.

I reached the corner, looked up and ahead to the point, and stopped, staring at the spot where we'd been standing. The hillside had collapsed. Of the track and the cliff that had towered above it, there was no sign. All that was left was a long slope of rocks and gravel that smothered every detail of where we'd been. The rubble carried on downwards. I edged to the side of the trail to see the river which I knew was several metres below me. The weeds and scrub at the side of the track were dense and it took a few moments before I found a spot where I could stop the horses and look over the edge.

"Oh, shit," I said out loud. I could barely take in what I was seeing. Fortunately, the horses stood placidly enough, as I tried to absorb the scale of the destruction below me.

The collapsed cliff on my side of the river had merged with the fallen debris on the opposite side and now blocked the entire gorge, shutting off the flow downstream. There was still water in the river bed, but most of that was the remains of what had previously been a substantial body of water. Only a very small amount of moisture seemed to be seeping through from the impromptu dam.

I had thought the muted sound of the river had been the result of my own shock and lack of focus. Instead, the river was dead.

I was guessing that upriver from the dam a substantial lake must be forming behind the blockage. I wondered how long the dam could hold and what would happen further down when it eventually collapsed under the pressure of water. I was fairly high above the old river level, so assumed I would be safe enough for the present.

More urgent was the question of what had happened to the three men. I saw no sign of them and urged Toby onwards. A knot of terror was growing in my belly. Surely I couldn't be the only person still alive?

Trust your horse, Pat had said. *He knows what he's doing.* His words circled in my head. If Toby hadn't taken us away from the danger zone, I could well be lying badly injured or even dead in that pile of rock and rubble.

I was two hundred metres away when I saw the first sign of movement. The horse on the lead rein trotted along obediently beside me as I hurried Toby along. At first my eyes couldn't work out the shape I was seeing. Then I realised it was another horse, but not one standing tall and proud on four legs. This poor animal must have been crushed in the fall. One of its hind legs was broken, the torn flesh and shattered bone poking through. Something was wrong with its shoulder as well, so it stood crooked and bent.

Toby nickered gently, and the horse turned its head. It was covered in an ugly muck of sweat and dirt and its eyes rolled wildly. I sensed its desperation. The pain must be driving it crazy and yet it was incapable of movement. I felt sick. The only possible course of action was to euthanise it immediately, but I had no gun. And even if I could have mustered the moral fortitude to cut its throat, which was far from certain, I had no knife. I stared at it helplessly and felt useless, impotent, tears of pity well in my eyes. I hate to see an animal in pain.

I dragged my attention away from the injured animal and scanned ahead. A mere fifty metres or so ahead the track disappeared completely beneath the rock fall. Close by, large boulders lay strewn about with smaller rocks dotting the space between them. It was no ground for riding a horse over.

I dismounted and tied the horses by their reins to a scrubby bush. I hoped I was doing the right thing. If I lost the horses, it was going to be a long trek out of the valley. Even more concerning was that the only route out lay downstream, with the nightmare scenario of that dam breaching behind me.

I gave a slight whimper and realised I was panicking. I took a deep breath and gave myself a mental shake down. This was no time for inventing problems that might never arise. The first imperative was to find the rest of our group.

"Hello! Is there anyone there?" I realised I sounded like an actor in a cheap horror film, a silly, fleeting thought that helped steady my nerves. I called again, then stood listening. Silence. I fancied I could hear noises from the rubble in front of me shifting as it settled.

I pulled out my mobile phone – one bar of reception. I gave a small cheer, but even as I celebrated, the line flickered and disappeared. There was no signal and no easy way to reach the outside world. Who knew where the earthquake's epicentre had been, or how bad the damage was everywhere else? At the best of times mobile contact wouldn't be easy in this steep-sided gorge and the earthquake could well have hit much further afield than here.

I shoved the phone back into my pocket and shouted again. This time I heard a reply. It was faint, but I thought it came from the hills above me.

"It's Claire. I'm on the track below the slip!"

His reply was too faint to make out the words, but at least I knew someone else was alive in this place. I hadn't recognised the voice. It wasn't Jack's. I'd know his voice anywhere. It was Matt's, I thought, or maybe Phil's. The knowledge I wasn't alone stiffened my spine and gave me a burst of confidence. I walked to the edge of the rockfall.

I knew Lee's horse had survived, and I thought, although I couldn't be certain, one horse looking much like another to the uninitiated, the injured animal had been ridden by Wu. That left the three men and Ray's mount unaccounted for.

I stared at the fallen mass of boulders and gravel that covered the path, trying to sort out where I should begin searching for them. They could be in the rubble ahead, or it was possible they'd been swept downwards, carried off the track as the land fell away and into the gorge below.

The task was hopeless. Even if I'd had the help of heavy excavating equipment and a search and rescue team, I wouldn't have known where to begin looking. I estimated at least fifteen minutes had elapsed already since the earthquake. If there was any hope of finding the men alive, timing was critical. The scale and magnitude of the destruction was daunting, and I stared at the wreckage in despair until a grain of common sense reasserted itself.

Discipline and systems, I reminded myself. Panicking about the big picture won't help. Focus on essentials, or as pilots would say, *Aviate, Navigate and Communicate*. These essential tools are drummed into every trainee pilot. Flying the aircraft safely is the critical consideration in a crisis. Second comes sorting out direction and destination and third, letting others know what is going on. Deviation from these principles has caused many an unnecessary plane crash.

In the current situation, the prime consideration had to be finding the men and the easiest way to do that was with a systematic grid search of the scree before me, starting with the most likely areas in which to find them.

Taking a deep, steadying breath, I focused on the slope, drew mental grid lines from boulder to boulder to guide me, shut out the voices that told me it was futile and settled down to a slow square by square search over my impromptu grid.

I narrowed my focus to the area ahead of me. I scanned every rock and the jumbled gravel and scree that lay between them in the hope of seeing something that would lead me to a survivor. I could see nothing.

I'd been avoiding going too close to the edge of the bank. It had been an unnerving experience looking over when the landscape had still been intact. Now, the slippery, unstable slope of rubble with the wall of debris blocking the river higher up was frankly terrifying.

I gingerly picked my way across through the strewn debris and looked down at the mess below. As I'd expected, it was a wasteland of utter desolation and destruction. It wasn't just the rock fall that was distressing, it was the clear damage to trees and plants that lay wrenched and ripped along the fringes of the rubble.

My eyes narrowed on a small movement out on the slope. Had it just been gravel settling? I concentrated on the area, trying to make sense of the shapes and colours of the new landscape.

I saw the flicker of movement again, but this time my vision had adjusted to interpret what it saw. It wasn't a jumble of boulders. It was a man. A dirty man, so covered in dust and dirt from the avalanche that he'd initially been indistinguishable from the rest of the debris. A man clawing at the slope below me. A man with a purpose.

"Hey," I called out. "Are you OK?"

There was no response. I wondered if he'd even heard me and thought the answer was probably no. I was rattled enough, and Toby had taken me to a place of relative safety. Whoever was below me had endured the whole experience and was probably in deep shock. At least they were alive, up and moving.

I sat on the edge, swung myself round to face the wall of the bank and climbed backwards down the steep, unstable, slope. I scrabbled for hand-holds and somewhere safe to put my feet. Often, I simply fell into an uncontrolled slippery-slide that scared the seven devils out of me until I regained control. In the end I made it down with little more damage than a few superficial scratches and grazes to my hands and a couple of broken nails.

I came to a spot I thought abreast of where I'd seen the man, stopped, and checked his position. He was some distance away across the slope, but I was closer to him, which was good.

I called again, but still got no reply. I was going to have to follow him out across the rubble. I thought, I'd better do it then, while I still had momentum. If I'd stopped to think about the dangers of venturing onto the scree, I'd never have nerved myself to do it.

I bent and did up a loose shoe lace, then stood, gritted my teeth and followed him out onto the slope. At least his track was quite clearly marked.

I hadn't gone very far before I realised if I put my feet into his footsteps printed in the soft rubble, it would make a simpler and firmer track for me. I concentrated fiercely on placing my feet. There was no point looking up. I'd know when I caught up with him and that was all that concerned me. It was impossible to tell who it was. Dust had covered his face and form leaving no identifying features.

I scrambled and floundered on the unstable ground until I reached him. He was kneeling, his back to me, hammering at something on the ground with a large stone. I called, but still received no response. I weighed up the options. If his hearing had been impaired I didn't want to frighten him by coming up behind and touching him on the shoulder. I gazed up the hill. Circling around in front of him seemed the best choice, but to do that I would have to leave the footprints I'd been following and climb the slope.

It was a small thing, but it took a real act of concentration to lift my feet from his track and clamber up the slope on a line above his own to bring me to a place where he could see me before I startled him. I managed it with a lot of swearing and sweating following an arc that took me above him, then descended to his level. Eventually I stood a few metres in front of him. I wanted to attract his attention without giving him a scare.

My first real look at the man told me two things. It was Wu, and he was busy hammering at something buried in the ground.

I stepped forward and he finally became aware of my presence.

"Hi, Wu," I said.

He gave a startled shriek when he saw me and toppled back off his heels so that his bum landed on the slope.

"What are you doing?" I asked, peering at the area he'd been attacking with the rock. Even before the words had left my mouth I saw a flutter of material in the earth by my feet.

"Oh shit." I fell to my knees. "Is that someone in there? What are you doing? Are you trying to kill them?"

I plunged my hand into the loose rubble and started digging.

I followed the line of material down and found an arm. I was digging frantically now, pushing the earth out of the cavity I was uncovering as fast as I could. The arm gave way to a torso. Wu was on the other side of the body.

"Dig," I yelled at him. "For fuck's sake, dig."

It wasn't just earth that had to be shifted. There were stones here as well, some of them large. Had Wu been trying to move one with his hammering? Wu's side seemed to have more rocks than mine, so I redoubled my efforts with the rubble. In fairness, Wu was digging as well. I looked at him properly for the first time and saw he was only using one arm. The other hung useless on his left side and I realised it was probably broken. There was no time for sympathy or reprieve. Whoever was under this pile of earth took priority over any other consideration.

I tried to work my way up to the face and clear a passage for breathing. *God help me*, I thought, *I hope he'll still be able to breathe.* A couple of rocks lay beside the head, but at least the soil here was lighter and I was able to brush much of it away. I found the nose, cleared his eye sockets and discovered it was Lee.

Wu reached across with his hand and picked away at the earth covering the nose. I nodded.

First clear the nose and mouth, I thought.

I opened Lee's mouth and hooked out a wad of clay and pebbles from between his teeth. I had no way of knowing if he'd got stuff stuck further down his windpipe. Wu was back on his haunches now, watching me. He still said nothing, and it occurred to me that he might not speak English.

I'd never done it before, but I'd been shown how to do CPR and mouth-to-mouth resuscitation.

I gestured to Wu to keep on digging Lee from the earth, while I took a deep breath, leaned forward and started breathing for Lee. I knew I'd never have the courage to attempt this if I let my imagination get carried away, so I put aside the strong probability that I was kissing a corpse.

For what it's worth, it was much harder to do CPR on a real

person than it had been in the first aid course I'd attended. I huffed and puffed, trying to keep up the rhythm I'd been shown. *Push down on the chest hard and fast. Seal your lips over the mouth and breathe. Repeat.*

My knees hurt where they pressed on the stones, my head was getting dizzy with trying to breathe properly and my lungs felt exhausted.

I could feel tears of frustration gathering. I hated to think this was going to be in vain. It was then that I felt the face beneath mine give a slight shudder as I shared another breath with him. I sat back and watched as Lee gave a cough, then another much larger. His eyes snapped open and I saw him look at me in incomprehension before he turned his head away and gave a series of retching, body shaking coughs. I searched my pockets for an unused tissue and used it to wipe his nose and face as best I could.

The coughing seemed to have worn him out, because he closed his eyes again and lay quietly. I thought for a panicked moment that he'd stopped breathing, but then the steady rise and fall of his now uncovered chest reassured me.

I turned my attention to helping Wu clear the rest of Lee's body and it soon became clear that Lee wasn't going to climb out of this mess of rubble unaided and ride off down the valley with us. His right leg lay twisted at a horrible angle and there was no way of telling whether he'd got internal injuries. He'd opened his eyes again, but he wasn't moving and I was forced to consider that he might have sustained spinal injuries.

I'd never felt so helpless. There was no way I knew of making contact with an ambulance service to get the rescue helicopter up here to lift Lee out. I sat back, pulled my knees up to my chest and shut my eyes. The only hope of help now was whoever had called back to me from the top of the hill. Assuming they were well and able, perhaps they could ride down the valley and eventually find some way of organising help.

As if I'd summoned it, I heard the beat of rotor blades coming nearer. Above us, following a route up the river valley, flew a dark-coloured chopper. I scrambled to my feet – an ungainly procedure on this slope – and waved my arms. I believe I shouted for help. I even dragged my jacket off and waved it to make me more visible.

I hoped he'd seen us and would circle to see what we needed. I held my breath waiting for the response. Instead, the helicopter proceeded up the valley, over the level of the dam and after a few minutes the sound of the blades faded into the distance.

He hadn't seen us. I had to assume that, because I couldn't believe any pilot would ignore an emergency and simply fly off.

I turned to look at Wu who'd also been following its path. He met my gaze.

He pointed in the direction the helicopter had disappeared and said something. I shook my head in frustration.

"I don't understand."

He glared at me. I could tell our mutual ignorance annoyed him, but there was nothing I could do about it. I shrugged and kept looking up the gorge in case the chopper came back.

"He says it's his boss's helicopter."

I spun to look at Wu, who looked as startled as I was.

"You speak. . . ?" Wu shook his head. My eyes travelled down to where Lee lay on the ground between us. His eyes were open, and he was looking at me.

"It belongs to the boss at the lodge." He shut his eyes again.

I knelt by his side. "Lee, how are you?"

He gave a groan. "I hurt."

"I'm not surprised." I hesitated. "Can you feel your legs?"

"It hurts."

I nodded. "Your right leg looks broken. It must really feel crap, but at least if you can feel it then you probably haven't had your spine crushed or anything."

He moaned again and I winced. Even if I had been a trained nurse and had known what to do, we had no painkillers, or leg splints, or any equipment to get him off this hill. Even worse, our best hope of assistance had just flown further up the valley.

I'm a pilot. I like taking control and solving problems. It's no part of my philosophy to indulge myself with 'poor little me' thought processes, but I just didn't have a clue what to do next.

There was a rattle of falling stones from above and I looked up to see a lithe figure making his way down the slope towards us. For once I didn't let inhibition hold me back as I pushed past Wu and flung myself at Jack. He steadied me as I fell against him, and he hugged me very tightly indeed. I shut my eyes as I clung to him.

"Thank God, you're alive!" I said in relief when my emotions had settled enough to allow me to step back and release him.

I heard him chuckle as he let me go.

"Yes, we're alive. Matt was with me when the quake struck, and when we realised how bad it was, we went back down to look for you all. We found Ray on his own. He'd been standing just clear of the rock-fall. You can imagine how we felt when we saw the mess that had tumbled into the river."

"Toby looked after me," I said shakily. "He didn't hang about waiting for the rock-fall. He took off, with me on him."

"Sensible horse," said Jack. He looked across at Wu. "Are you OK?"

I suppose "'OK'" is universal.

Wu nodded in response.

"I don't think he speaks English," I said, "and I think he's broken his arm."

Jack looked at him critically. "It's more likely his collar bone, or maybe his shoulder. Either way, it must hurt like hell, poor bastard."

Jack turned his attention to Lee and winced as he took in the crooked line of his leg.

"Your brother will be pleased to know you're alive," he said.

Lee opened his eyes again and gave a slight nod. "Ray is OK?"

"He's fine," said Jack. "Our next problem is to get you out of here and up on the track. I don't fancy our chances if that pile of rubble gives way."

As he spoke, I looked up and saw Matt and Ray start down the slope towards us. They trod carefully as they made their way over the unstable surface.

Matt waved to us when they were half-way across and I gave him a big grin of relief.

There was a sudden crack of gun shot from the hill above us. I started and looked at Jack.

"The injured horse," he said tersely. "Pat and Phil are up there."

"Oh. Poor thing." There wasn't anything else to be said. I was glad the animal was out of pain.

A few moments later, Pat made his own way down and joined us. After a short conference, the men cut poles from a fallen manuka tree, sorted out splints for Lee's leg and rigged up a stretcher with their jackets. It was rough and ready, but an effective solution. There was no dithering where the men were concerned!

It was painfully difficult to get Lee up the slope, but between them, with a lot of heaving and puffing, they managed it. It must have been agony for Lee who groaned each time the stretcher moved, but at least it got him clear of the risk posed by the loose rubble. I couldn't help but be impressed by this evidence of male strength and competence, and I was content to let them take control of the situation while I brought up the rear.

I helped Wu make the climb. At least he had two sound legs and one good arm, but he was in a lot of pain. Every now and again I would have to pull on his sound arm, adding my strength to his, to give him traction up the slippery slope.

We collapsed once we were safely back on the track where Phil was waiting for us. He rummaged in his backpack, produced a thermos, and passed cups of tea around. I sat on a rock, grateful to be alive and safe, sipped my tea and smiled at Jack. I was careful not to gaze in the direction of the carcass of the dead horse.

A few minutes later we heard the helicopter return. This time it flew right over us and hovered. I thought the pilot waved.

"He wants us to follow him," said Pat, interpreting the pilot's gesture more accurately. "He'll probably put down on the flat land around the corner. Come on, guys."

They carried Lee down to where Toby and I had stopped our gallop. Pat and I followed, leading the horses. Pat offered Wu a ride, but he just shook his head and marched along in silence, his body hunched over, clutching his arm in support.

As we approached the chopper, a man came to meet us.

"Charles?" said Phil to his boss in surprise. "I thought you were on the other side of the river."

"The road's blocked further up," said Charles. "It's not as big as the slip opposite us here, but it's going to be a long time before any motor traffic gets along the gorge road. Thankfully I was stranded in a spot that got reception, so I phoned and got Brett to come and pick me up. I've had to abandon my car." He shrugged. "Brett saw what had happened to your party on his way up the gorge, so we've come to lend a hand. First of all, are our guests OK?"

"Two of your guys are injured and need medical attention, and frankly, I was racking my brain wondering what we were going to do for them. Your appearance is a godsend," said Pat. "We don't have mobile phone coverage this side of the gorge and it was going to be a long ride down-river to reach help for them."

Being Pat, he was carefully casual, but there was no misinterpreting the tension in his voice. "We were trying to work out how we were going to get out of here."

Toby decided he wanted to eat a particular blade of grass and dragged me to the side of the track so he could reach it. As I was leading three horses, this resulted in a muddle of reins and animals which took some time to untangle.

"It would be helpful if you could take Claire with you as well," I heard Pat say. "Is that OK with you, Claire?"

I looked up to see the men lifting Lee into the chopper.

"Sorry, I missed that. Do you want me to leave?"

"Would you mind?" asked Pat. "I'd like to get Charles's guests safely out of here and Wu and Lee need to get to hospital. I thought it would be good if you could go with them as support. The rest of us can finish up getting the sheep down to the barn and we've got enough hands to lead the spare horses."

"No, that's fine," I said. I understood. Pat was ruthlessly clearing out the unfit and less able. I didn't blame him. The day had turned out a lot more exciting than any of us had envisaged.

"We'll take Claire back to the lodge when Wu and Lee have been seen to," said Charles. "We'll look after her until you guys make it home, or we can run her back to your place. Whatever you choose."

"It will probably take some time to get the guys through A & E, especially if the quake has caused a lot of damage elsewhere in the region," said Jack. "If we're back in reasonable time, I'll drive over and pick Claire up."

I gave Jack a small smile. "See you later then."

"Yeah, we'll play it by ear, if that's alright," agreed Pat.

Charles nodded. "Keep in touch." He gave a wave as he turned away.

"Look after yourselves," I said. It wouldn't do to turn all girlie in front of the guys and say I didn't want to be parted from Jack. I patted Toby in farewell, blew a casual kiss to Jack which sparked a ribald comment from Ian, climbed up into the helicopter and took the seat beside Charles.

CHAPTER EIGHT

IT FELT LIKE FOREVER, BUT IT was more like five hours, to get Wu and Lee seen and treated at the A & E Department at Te Kuiti Hospital. There were several casualties from earthquake-related accidents and these, added to the usual daily crop of injured folk, meant the staff were over-worked and the queues were long.

While we waited, Ray, Charles and I watched the news on the waiting room TV. The earthquake epicentre was to the south of Lake Taupo, but the damage was widespread. The only fortunate aspect of the quake was that it had occurred outside the main metropolitan areas. Even so, there were reports of serious damage to buildings in both Auckland and Hamilton, and peripheral damage throughout the Bay of Plenty. Bizarrely, Wellington, our earthquake capital, had got off relatively lightly, which was a relief.

We shared stale sandwiches and tepid coffee in the cafeteria, and Ray formally introduced me to Charles. I nodded politely and shook his hand. I had the wry thought that this, my one chance of being on first-name terms with an owner of a luxury lodge, was being wasted in a hospital cafeteria.

I phoned my sister Kate to check on her and my nieces. She

assured me the earthquake had barely been felt on the Kapiti Coast and they were fine. I was a little surprised how casual and off-hand she was. Usually Kate manages to turn my misadventures into a three- ring circus and blame them all on my incompetence. Today she sounded preoccupied and was quick to end the call.

I considered phoning my boss Roger, but decided against it. He hadn't been happy about me taking leave in the first place. If I contacted him, he was liable to summon me back to work.

I tried calling Jack, but there was no answer.

It was evening by the time we left the hospital and flew to the lodge. We were a subdued group. Charles and pilot Brett, exchanged a few words, otherwise we sat quietly, absorbed in our own thoughts. It would be safe to say mine focused on Jack, and whether he and the others had made it through to the farm safely.

Wu returned with us. Jack's diagnosis had been correct – a broken collar bone. It wasn't serious, and he'd been given pain relief, but I imagined he was still uncomfortable.

Lee's leg was a more complicated matter. Te Kuiti Hospital was going to transfer him by air to the much larger hospital in Hamilton where he'd be admitted. They told Ray there was a high probability the leg would need to be operated on, with a gloomy prognosis of several weeks in hospital, in traction.

Ray stared silently out of the window. He'd been with Lee throughout the medical examination and his frustration was palpable. There'd been no confirmation the remains I'd found related to their missing father, and now his brother was confined to a hospital bed for an unknown period. I couldn't begin to imagine how this glitch would affect their plans.

I checked my phone to see what time it was and whether Jack and the others had finished bringing the sheep in yet. It had been a long and eventful day. I subdued a yawn and wondered how I was going to get back to Pat's farm.

Earlier I'd been looking forward to the opportunity of doing some sleuthing around the lodge, but now I simply wanted to get home, have a hot shower and enjoy a quiet evening with Jack.

It was dusk when we landed, and the lights were on inside the lodge, shining a warm welcome out into the twilight. Charles steered us through the enormous entrance doors into a large hall from which a flight of stairs ascended to the upper floor. He stopped to speak in what I assumed was Mandarin with the woman who'd opened the door for us. I imagine he was explaining the events of the day, as she exclaimed several times as he spoke.

While they talked, I studied the numerous photographs on the walls. I thought I recognised Bill Clinton shaking hands with Charles. More notable people appeared with him in other similarly posed shots – world leaders, sporting heroes and a couple of past New Zealand prime-ministers. As a visual guest-book it made for an impressive display, particularly as they all had dates recorded on the frames. I found it remarkable so many great and famous people had visited here while I – and, I assumed, the average New Zealander – hadn't even known of Retakure Lodge's existence. Which, when I thought about it, was the sort of discretion their business was based on.

"Mary will look after you, Claire." Charles' voice broke my concentration. "I've asked her to settle you in and get you some refreshments. If you will excuse me now, I must attend to a few matters."

"Thank you, that's fine," I said and watched as Charles headed for a door on our right.

"Hi," I said to Mary as she came over and shook my hand. She was short, with black hair, bobbed and cut in a formidably straight line above her brows. I envied her fair skin and beautiful complexion. She wasn't fat, but every part of her person was rounded. I thought her antecedents might have been from some Mongolian tribe. She was a completely different ethnic type to the slender-boned Charles.

I turned back to the photographs again.

"They're a pretty impressive record," I said. "I like the way they're all dated. It gives you a real sense of history."

"Please follow me?" Mary gestured towards one of the other doors, but I lingered, my attention focused on one particular photograph.

Charles stood in the centre, flanked by a small group of men and two women, in front of the lodge entrance. I recognised one of the women as Mary, but it was the other woman the eye was drawn to. Something in her pose and bearing conveyed immense grace and dignity – qualities only enhanced by her considerable beauty and slender figure. Surely some ancestor of hers had graced the palace of a Chinese emperor. She was turned slightly, her head inclined to the man standing beside her.

It was the date on the frame that had caught my attention – October the previous year.

"Are you enjoying our gallery?" Mary asked.

"They're fascinating," I said. "It's fun spotting the famous people in each of them. The lodge has had an impressive guest list."

Mary nodded. "It's known as a safe place for celebrities to come. There are no paparazzi here to harass them."

"It's obviously been a very successful venture for whoever built the place," I observed.

She nodded but said nothing.

"I don't recognise anyone here." I indicated the photo I'd been studying. "Well, apart from you and Charles, of course. I was wondering who the famous person was in the group and whether I should know who they are."

Mary glanced at the photo. "They are all successful Chinese business people," she said dismissively. "Unless you were Chinese and also in business, it would be very unlikely you'd ever have heard of them."

I maintained an encouraging silence and after a moment she continued.

"The most successful man in the group is Li Qiang." She pointed to the one in the middle at the back. "He's a multi-millionaire who made his fortune in electronics. Nowadays he's an investor."

I nodded, and Mary indicated the next man.

"Wang Lei's fortune came from mining. The next one is Xi Yong who is in construction, then Li Jie who is well known for computer manufacturing. In the front row, Zhang Lei is a clothing manufacturer and exporter. You'll recognise Charles and me, of course. Beside Charles is Wenjun, another guest who you will meet soon, and beside him is Lui Wei whose company manufactures consumer goods, such as refrigerators and air conditioners." She smiled slightly. "As I say, in China these are our elite business leaders. In New Zealand, you will never have heard of them."

"Who is the woman?" I asked. Had Mary had ignored her because she was unimportant?

"Li Na. She used to work here, but she left." Her tone was dismissive. I wondered whether this was a case of simple jealousy.

"She's extraordinarily beautiful," I said.

Mary gave a slight shrug. "She knew it."

I waited for her to continue but she turned her head away, and I accepted the conversation had ended.

"Thank you for explaining. You're right, of course. They're not people I've heard of." I moved on to the next photograph. "Now Tom Cruise I *do* know."

But I *had* recognised one of the names Mary had mentioned.

I allowed her to show me into a large and luxuriously furnished living area which opened on the opposite side of the hallway. She settled me on a couch.

"Can I get you a drink?" she asked, indicating the fancy looking bar in the corner.

"Yes, a Sauvignon Blanc, please."

The wine arrived on a silver tray and she gave a formal bow as she delivered it to me.

"I must leave you for a short while. Please refill your glass from the bar when you are ready. We serve evening cocktails and snacks in here for the guests in about half an hour, so you won't be alone for long. If there is anything else you need in the meantime, please pull the bell in the corner." She pointed to an elaborately brocaded cord discreetly placed in the corner of the room.

She bowed deeply again before leaving me to my own devices.

Ray had excused himself in the hallway and gone to have

a shower, and Charles and Wu had disappeared off together elsewhere in the building.

A fire was already burning in the enormous open fireplace, spreading a welcome warmth throughout the room. Rugs full of jewel-rich colours were spread across the polished, heated floor, and the ceiling, I noticed, leaning back in my seat, was a mirror. I gazed up at my reflection for a while. It made for depressing viewing. Horse-riding, digging through rock falls and the general wear and tear of the day had done nothing for my appearance. At the very least I needed a brush through my hair. To fit into these surroundings I needed to be dressed like Marie Antoinette.

I sat sipping a pleasant Hawke's Bay Sauvignon Blanc, gazed at the ceiling and looked about me. Pat had said this was a luxury hunting lodge for wealthy Asians and he wasn't kidding. The emphasis was on opulence. I'd assumed the walls of a hunting lodge would bristle with mounted stag and boar heads, or alternatively, displays of guns and fishing rods. There was nothing like that here. I felt as if I was in a palace. The décor was a confusing mix of baroque European and imperial Oriental. Lacquer-ware jostled beside gilt. The effect was overwhelming. I wanted to share this luxury with Jack and see what he made of it.

This time he answered the phone.

"Hi. How did things go at the hospital? Where are you?"

"I'm back at the hunting lodge," I said. "Lee's being transferred to Hamilton Hospital for surgery and will probably be there for some time. Wu came back with us. You were right about the collar-bone. They gave him pain-killers and stuck his arm in a sling, but there wasn't much else they could do for him. It took us hours to get through A & E. The place was crowded."

I heard the smile in his voice. "Most emergency services are permanently over-worked. We've only just got back ourselves. We had to cross a couple more slips as we came down river. Fortunately, they were small ones, but they slowed us down while we picked our way over them. The poor dogs will be stuffed after today. They had to keep the sheep together and get them past the obstacles."

"I'm glad you're back safely," I said. "I was a bit worried that blockage in the river would give and you'd all get swept away in the flood."

"We were all thinking that." Jack's voice was grim. "No one admitted it until we were a long way downstream and the track had climbed to high ground above the river for the rest of the ride. Then we all looked at each other and sighed with relief. But that brings me to the bad news. The road out of here is blocked with another slip about a kilometre south of us, so I can't get out to come and pick you up. Pat's been on to the council, but they won't have it cleared until tomorrow morning."

"Oh bugger," I said. "I've been looking forward to getting home and cleaning up. I feel a right grub sitting here in my dirty riding stuff. I suppose I'll have to see if Charles will put me up for the night. He's not here at the moment. In fact, I'm on my own, sitting in a place that looks like a palace."

"Really? Is it pretty flash?"

"It's not what I thought a hunting lodge would be. The guests don't come here to rough it, that's for sure."

"I look forward to seeing it tomorrow, assuming Charles's invitation still stands. I'm sorry about tonight though. Let me know if there are any problems, but I can't see Charles chucking you out."

"Let's hope he doesn't," I grumbled.

When Jack hung up I sat back and considered my options. I assumed Charles would be hospitable, but that still left me with dirty clothes and no toothbrush, hairbrush or pyjamas. I'd be a blot on the landscape in this palatial environment. Even sitting on the sofa seemed risky, given the grubby state of my clothes.

The seats and couches were large and comfortable, and any part not upholstered in expensive-looking brocade was lacquered. Enormous paintings, surrounded by massive, gilded frames lined any wall not occupied by bookshelves crammed with books.

I couldn't help it. I've always been a book lover, and those books were calling to me. I put my wine aside on the ornately decorated table and walked across to investigate.

Unsurprisingly, the volumes were in Chinese and therefore incomprehensible, although the unfamiliar script was aesthetically pleasing. I browsed through several shelves before giving a choke of laughter. Clearly identifiable by the artwork on the cover, not to mention the hero's name printed in English, was a Chinese edition of Harry Potter. After that I began to recognise other novels by their covers and amused myself picking out Dan Brown and James Patterson.

"Are you looking for something to read?" Mary had returned.

"I like books," I explained. "I always check out people's bookshelves. It's an automatic habit, even if I can't read Chinese."

She set the tray she was carrying down on the table. "Most of the collection is in Mandarin. The English section is over there." She indicated shelves at the far end of the room.

"Ah, I hadn't got that far in my exploration," I replied.

"I thought you might like something to eat with your wine while you wait," she said, placing a plate of small biscuits on the table. I understand you've had a busy day."

"Thank you," I said with real gratitude as I sat down and helped myself. "This is great."

She smiled. "My pleasure."

"Is the lodge busy at the moment?" I asked.

"No, this is our quiet season. Most of our guests come for deer hunting, so they mainly arrive between February and July. Trout fishing season has already started, but the majority of our guests won't arrive until next month, when the weather warms up and those who like golf will come in summer. So we're in-between activities at the moment. One party went home yesterday, and we've only a couple of guests here at present."

"Do you mean Ray and Lee? I met them today when we were up the gorge mustering."

"The poor man who was taken to hospital? Of course. I'd forgotten you must have been with him. I hope he recovers soon."

"So do I," I said. "It was an awful thing to happen. He's lucky to be alive. We had to dig him out."

A thought struck me. "Did you have any damage here from the earthquake?"

She shook her head. "The place shook very badly and some glasses fell off the shelves in the bar, but otherwise we were lucky. Fortunately, the lodge is sturdily built."

"It's a beautiful place," I agreed. "It's like a palace inside. It would be nice to see outside in the day time. It was too dark to see much when we arrived. Earlier today, Charles invited us here tomorrow, but I don't know whether that still stands after everything else that happened today. Which reminds me – I've been told the road is blocked and I won't be able to be picked up. Is there any way I can stay here tonight?"

"Oh, no! How unfortunate for you. I'll have to ask Charles. I'm sure we can find you a bed for the night. I'll go and see what I can arrange."

"Thank you. I don't like having to ask."

Mary gave me a smile as she left.

I wondered how many staff the lodge employed. So far I'd only met Mary and of course Wu. I assumed Mary's role was housekeeper, in which case there was probably a chef in the kitchen. I hoped Mary didn't have to do everything, even if it was a quiet time.

The tepid coffee and stale sandwiches I'd bought earlier at the hospital had been both unpleasant and unsatisfying, and Mary's biscuits were very welcome. I nibbled one as I thought about what she had said.

Lee and Ray's father had been at the lodge this time last year, a season when they hosted few resident guests. Surely, in that case, the sudden disappearance of one of them would have been cause for concern at the least? And if the body in the bog did turn out to be the missing man, then what had happened to him? Supposedly he had checked out, paid his account and been flown to Taupo. He should have been miles away from here. How had he returned? Perhaps the missing man and the unidentified corpse both being associated with the lodge was just coincidence, and the two weren't related at all.

I considered how the person in the swamp might have died.

I suppose there was a possibility they'd unwisely ventured in there by accident. After all, I'd walked into it myself. But although the experience had been smelly and unpleasant, there'd been little likelihood of it being fatal. The bog wasn't quicksand and wasn't going to suck anyone down into it. Maybe the shock of being caught in the mud had brought on a heart attack? We wouldn't know until forensics had completed their examination of the body and the site.

My thoughts were interrupted when Charles entered the room.

"Mary tells me the farm is cut off by slips and you can't get home tonight? Of course you can stay. We are nearly empty, and half the rooms have been shut up. Mary is preparing a room for you now, and if there are still problems with the road in the morning, I'll get Brett to fly you over in the helicopter."

"Thank you very much. I feel a bit embarrassed, as if I'm gate-crashing in this lovely place."

"Not at all. In fact, I should thank you instead. Wu told me how competent you were today in saving our guest's life. I feel I owe you a great debt. To have a guest die in such a terrible way when they were enjoying our hospitality would have been a calamity. Terrible for our reputation, but even more terrible on a personal level. We think of our guests as friends and pride ourselves that they can relax here and really be at home when they visit us. It's distressing enough the poor man has been so badly injured and his travel plans thrown into chaos."

"Whose plans have been thrown into chaos?" Another man had come in.

He was short. So short, in fact, that I was conscious my eyes, previously focused on Charles's face, searched the room for an appreciable moment before I dropped my gaze half a metre to find the new speaker. He was much shorter than me, and I found myself looking down at him.

Although he'd spoken to Charles, his eyes were on me. I felt myself flush with embarrassment, hoping my struggle to locate him hadn't been too obvious.

Charles had turned to include the newcomer in our conversation.

"One of our guests had an accident during the earthquake. He's been admitted to hospital in Hamilton. I was thanking Claire here for the help she gave him. She probably saved his life today."

"It was nothing," I murmured.

"Claire, may I introduce you to Ding Wenjun?" Charles said.

"Hi," I said.

The man nodded politely but made no effort to shake my hand or otherwise greet me. Instead, after a brief pause, he headed for the bar and poured himself a whisky.

"Same for you?" he asked Charles.

I wondered whether I was being snubbed, but if so Charles didn't seem to have noticed.

"Yes, thanks. Claire is staying the night," he explained. "The road's blocked and won't open until tomorrow. If it isn't open then, I'll get Brett to fly her back."

The conversation slipped easily into discussion of the earthquake, Charles's stranded car and what Wenjun's experience of the shake had been. They spoke English, and I was content to sit back on the sofa, listen and relax.

In a short time Mary returned.

"Would you like me to show you to your room?" she asked. "I imagine you'll want a chance to freshen up after your day. You've got plenty of time before dinner."

I nodded goodbye to the men and followed her up the stairs.

The room she showed me into was luxurious but less ornate than the lounge downstairs.

"En-suite." Mary opened a door on the long side of the room. "I've left clean spare clothes for you to change into if you would like to." She looked at our reflection side by side in the bathroom mirror and smiled. "I hope you don't mind, but these were left by a previous guest so they're nothing special, but we are very casual here. She was much the same size as you, I think. If you leave your dirty clothes in the bathroom when you've finished, they'll be laundered, ready for you tomorrow morning."

"Thank you. I can hardly wait to change out of this gear. I feel so dirty I was embarrassed sitting on the sofa downstairs."

"It's not a problem," Mary smiled. "There's a full range of toiletries for you to use. Let me know if there is anything else you need. Dress for dinner during this season is relaxed. I've left you a skirt and top that should fit."

She smiled again and left me.

I made full use of the luxurious products and was pleased to find the toiletries included a toothbrush kit and a small folding hair brush.

The skirt and top turned out to be more glamorous than Mary's words had implied. The long, layered black skirt was an Annah Stretton and the soft cashmere top from Karen Walker. I held them out dubiously. Mary had thought they would fit. To my delight, she was right.

I wouldn't have bought the garments myself if I'd been choosing them in a shop, as I'd have considered them too old for me, but when I checked in the mirror I had to admit the effect was quietly sophisticated and understated. I felt a renewed burst of self-confidence as I abandoned my dirty clothes on the bathroom floor and made my way downstairs to join the other guests.

CHAPTER NINE

MARY NODDED WITH APPROVAL WHEN I entered the room. I smiled my thanks for her help. She had described the required dress as 'casual', but it was obvious everyone had made an effort to smarten up for dinner, and I was relieved to be dressed appropriately.

Charles and Wenjun had been joined by Ray, the pilot Brett and Wu. A trolley with canapes was now in the middle of the room and the men had gathered around it, helping themselves to minute spring rolls, puffs and chicken satay sticks.

I accepted a plate from Ray and helped myself to the wonderful food.

"Save some room," Ray warned. "The chef is talented, and you don't want to blunt your appetite for dinner."

"I'll try," I said, "but I'm starving."

"Dinner won't be long," Charles, overhearing my remark, assured me. "Mind you, the chef's in a bit of a temper, which doesn't bode well. Apparently, he'd prepared some delicate desserts which were ruined when the earthquake shook them to bits. When I spoke to him he was threatening to return to China until I reminded him they had earthquakes there as well. So now he's sulking."

"Even sulking, he won't allow himself to serve an inadequate meal. He's a maestro." I found Wenjun had come to stand beside me.

"I look forward to his food then," I smiled. To my surprise he smiled back, an unexpectedly charming smile. I put him in his fifties or sixties, although he could have been older. Whereas the other men had interpreted 'casual' as buttoned shirt and trousers, Wenjun was dapper in suit and tie. The odd note of formality suited him and seemed part of his personality.

I speculated what brought such a man to a remote lodge in the New Zealand countryside. I couldn't imagine Wenjun tramping the hills in search of deer, or wrestling trout out of a stream. Perhaps he played golf.

"It is our custom during our low season for the senior staff to eat with our guests," explained Charles as he escorted me to the dining room. "When we're at full capacity of course, the two are separate, but while our numbers are low, we think it brings a friendly informality to our meals and allows us to share our family with our clients."

I nodded. I hadn't been sure where Mary, Wu and Brett fitted into the hierarchy, but I was all for informality. I'd been afraid I'd wandered into a scene from *Downton Abbey* but it seemed common sense operated here.

The dinner was excellent as the men had said it would be. Course after course of small, exquisite portions of food arrived, served by a young waiter.

He introduced himself as Stephen, and I was aware of his quick admiring glance as he helped me sit down. However, he was totally professional as he explained each course and how it matched the wine.

The courses ranged from tiny squares of salmon topped with caviar, deconstructed French onion soup, sashimi, New Zealand venison and two desserts. I felt the bruises and cares of the day begin to drift away on a happy tide of food and alcohol.

Consequently, I felt a stab of annoyance when Ray said casually,

"When we were out with the muster this morning, we heard

a body had been found on this property. Has it been identified yet?"

There was a second of silence, and I thought I heard tension in his voice when Charles replied.

"No, we only heard about it when the police arrived yesterday. We assume the death occurred before the lodge was established here, as we know nothing about it. We were hoping not to distress our guests, so we didn't make it open knowledge." He gave a wry smile.

"Of course, it was inevitable there would be talk. Perhaps we should have pre-warned you. If you were upset by the news, I apologise."

"It wasn't a matter that need concern the guests," added Wenjun in a tone of finality.

"Maybe," said Ray, "but it was disturbing hearing about it in such a manner. Are you aware that Claire discovered the body?"

Everyone turned to stare at me, and I immediately felt I'd committed a breach of good manners. I had to fight the urge to apologise, and instead gave a slight shrug and said nothing.

"Then you can tell us about it!" exclaimed Mary. "What did you see? Was it a man or a woman?"

I shook my head. "I accidentally stumbled over some bones in the swamp, that's all. When I realised they were human remains I got out of there as quickly as I could. I didn't stop to examine them."

"Claire's partner is a detective," Ray added.

I glared across the table at him. If he wasn't careful, he was going to destroy the tone of the entire evening and ruin my one night of luxury.

"He's an off-duty detective," I said firmly. "We're on holiday, so he's not involved at all in what was just a chance discovery. Your local police will have it in hand."

"This dessert is very fine." Wenjun obviously wanted the subject changed as much as I did.

There was a soft murmur of agreement from around the table. The conversation moved to the earthquake and what arrangements Ray would have to make for his brother's care and eventual travel to China.

I was glad to have the spotlight off me. I couldn't contribute any useful knowledge and speculating about the body raised uncomfortable memories about how I'd stumbled over it.

When the meal finished, we returned to the lounge. I paused in the hallway to study the photographs I'd seen earlier. I had been right. It *was* Bill Clinton shaking hands with Charles. I looked closer and thought I recognised Wenjun among a group of men in the background. A discreet plaque on the frame informed it was October 2003.

I found it even more remarkable, when I looked closely, that Wenjun was in the background of each shot. When we'd been introduced, I'd assumed he was another guest, and Charles hadn't said anything to alter that impression. He must be cracking up points at a great rate of knots on whatever loyalty programme the lodge offered.

A card table had been set up in the lounge, on which a neat square of tiles had been built.

"We have a regular evening game," explained Wenjun. "Do you know how to play mah-jong?

"No," I said, shaking my head. "My mother used to belong to a group that met each week and played it, but I never learned."

"Would you care to join us then and learn?"

"Be careful with this lot," warned Charles. "These guys are very good players, and they play for high stakes. It's like stepping into a pool with sharks."

"All Chinese like a gamble," expostulated Wenjun. "It's our tradition. Anyway, *you* win your fair share of hands yourself."

Charles chuckled and took his place at the table. "Ah, but I'm the boss. I can chuck you all out if you don't let me win enough."

I laughed. "I think it would be a very good idea if I let the experts play and stayed right out of it. I'm very happy to sit and watch you for a while, if I you don't mind. Then I think I'll turn in early. It's been quite a day."

"I'll join you in a second, if I may," said Ray. "I'll just phone the hospital and check Lee's OK before we start playing."

"How is he?" I asked when Ray returned from his call.

"Asleep. They sedated him pretty heavily for the flight up to Hamilton. He's only just been admitted. I just have to hope that they can operate tomorrow and get him fixed up."

"If you get a chance later, please pass on my best wishes," I said.

Wu, Wenjun, Ray and Charles settled into their game. I watched as they stirred the tiles and drew out the pieces. The game was fast moving as they picked up and discarded tiles. I watched them long enough to gather that, like many card games, the purpose was to collect a specific run of tiles. The first to complete a hand and say 'mah-jong' won the pile of tokens.

Initially they spoke English so I could follow the comments, but as they grew more absorbed in the run of tiles, they slipped into Chinese. The competition seemed amiable enough. I heard occasional moans of frustration when one or other lost a hand. These were punctuated with excited shouts of 'mah-jong' indicating another win.

I sat for a time, too tired to make the effort to get up and go upstairs. Mary and Brett had left after the meal, so I had no one to talk to. The men's voices rose and fell on the roll of the dice. I felt my eyes getting heavy.

I woke to a shout and peered blearily around. The game had apparently become passionate, and Ray was shouting at Wenjun, who was returning the abuse with equal vigour. I remembered earlier in the day thinking the Chinese were a feisty people.

They were speaking Chinese so I had no idea what they were on about. I thought it was a suitable time for me to leave.

"Goodnight all," I said as I stood up.

Charles noticed and absent-mindedly waved a hand in my direction without taking his eyes off the two arguing men.

I turned in the doorway for a last look just as Charles jumped to his feet with an enraged roar and slammed his fist down on the table so hard the neat tiled walls went flying.

Whatever he said effectively shut the other two up. I kept on walking. Discretion was definitely the better part of valour I reminded myself as I shut the door behind me.

In my absence, the bedroom had been tidied, the sheets turned down and my dirty washing removed. A black nightie was folded ready on my pillow, and I was free to fall into the enormous bed, shut my eyes and sleep the night away.

Naturally, sod's law had it that two hours later I woke from a nightmare in which a giant wave threatened to engulf Jack while I, who should have been helping him bury something, was carted away on a strange animal to a land that turned into a swamp with nasty things swirling below the surface.

I awoke, sweat-drenched, my heart pounding with fear and an utter inability to go back to sleep.

It was useless reminding myself I was safe, Jack was safe, and the nightmare was merely nervous reaction to an overexciting couple of days. I tried lying still with my eyes shut; I rolled to my right side, then to my left. I missed Jack, I missed my cat Nelson. I wanted something to cuddle, and the big bed was cold and empty.

There was a digital clock on the bedside table. I watched the minutes roll over. 12.00, 12.30. By 1.30, I'd had enough. I was wide awake, alert and with no possibility of sleeping for the next few hours.

In my own home I'd have turned on the light, made myself a cup of tea and gone back to bed with a book, which I'd read until I was ready for sleep again. Unfortunately, I'd forgotten to browse the English-language book-shelves for something to read before coming to bed, and I didn't want to disturb anyone by switching on lights that might wake them up.

I tried to stick it out, but as the digital numbers rolled towards 2.00 I gave up again, swung my legs out of bed and tiptoed towards the door.

To my relief sides of the hallway were lined with subdued night lights that led me to the top of the staircase. Individual lights were set on the right side of each step and the line continued around the perimeter of the hall below me.

Easy-peasy. I followed the lights down, entered the lounge and looked to where Mary had told me English editions were kept. There was just enough illumination for me to be able to read the titles.

I found a fine range of leather-bound classics, but I wanted something more contemporary and less cerebral. Chick-lit would be great, although I doubted the lodge would run to it. To my surprise, I eventually discovered a Sophie Kinsella paperback I hadn't read. Guests must leave their books behind when they check out, and they end up in the library.

Pleased with my success, I headed back to bed. I crossed the room to the door and had just turned the handle when I thought I heard a noise in the hall outside. I froze, consumed with the embarrassing thought of encountering one of the guys while I was in my scanty nightdress and having to apologise for disturbing them.

I listened for a second or so but heard nothing. Maybe I'd been imagining things. As the handle was already depressed, it was easy to pull the door back towards me. Fortunately, the hinges well-oiled so they didn't squeak, as I cautiously opened the door and looked outside.

There was no one in the big hall, but I could see light beneath the door where Charles had gone earlier in the evening. Apparently someone else was up, but at least it didn't seem I'd been responsible for waking them. I imagined they'd be as embarrassed as I would to be caught in their sleep wear, so I crept across the hall, making sure I kept silent.

I'd made it to the stairs and was starting to climb when the door opened. I was on the darker side of the staircase, away from the night light, but I'd be easily enough visible to anyone who had their night vision. Fortunately, whoever opened the door, was coming from light into dark. Equally fortunately, they'd turned to continue their conversation with someone else inside the room. I was close enough to hear the man with his back to me.

"I'm telling you, you'd better think of something. I lied for you once because you told me it was important. I won't do it again. What's with this body they found in the swamp? Whose is it?"

The reply from inside the room was too faint to hear.

"You'd better be right, mate. But if it's nothing to do with you, how come it's hidden on Lodge land? And why was it so badly stashed away that bloody woman fell over it?"

That settled it. The man with his back to me was Brett. I wasn't sure who he was speaking to, but of one thing I was certain – it wasn't in my interests to be found eavesdropping on such a conversation. In spite of the risk, I carried on up the stairs, hoping my luck would hold.

The noise of my own heartbeat drowned out the rest of the conversation as I climbed.

I'd just reached the safety of my bedroom door when I heard Brett say, "Fuck off."

In a sudden rush to reach safety I turned the handle and slid inside. It was silly, I know, but it felt like I'd reached sanctuary. For an appreciable time I stood with my back jammed against the door while I waited for my heartbeat to slow.

Eventually my panic subsided and I felt able to walk across the room and climb into bed. Sophie Kinsella notwithstanding, there was no way I was going to be able to sleep again tonight.

CHAPTER
TEN

I TRIED TO MAKE SOME SENSE of what I'd heard. Brett had confessed to previously lying about something – but what? He'd been sufficiently rattled to raise the spectre of murder in relation to the body I'd found. Yet it had also sounded as if the other person had denied it.

I tried to put things into context. Did Brett's words involve Lee and Ray's father? Had Brett lied about flying him to Taupo Airport? If so, why? It would be a stupidly easy detail to check. Airports keep a log of traffic in and out so they can charge landing fees. It would have been easy enough for police to establish whether Brett had landed there that day.

What else would make Brett concerned that a murder had occurred?

My mind whirred uselessly in circles. Flights of imagination, fantasies I was creating out of nothing – that was all they were. I needed to hear what police forensics had found. Most of all, I needed Jack, that most excellent representative of the police profession, to provide me with some sanity and steadiness.

I hoped the council were quick off the mark in the morning clearing the blockage in the road to Pat's place. The sooner I was out of there, the better I would feel. This lodge was lovely, but there were too many unanswered questions buzzing around.

I was aware some of my discomfort was based on the foreign ownership of the lodge and the complications of the language barrier. I hadn't been able to ask Wu to explain his actions, so I was deeply suspicious of them. Even Charles and Wenjun, fluent though their English was, were still indefinably different. I wasn't sure their values aligned with mine.

In the end, I did sleep again and woke at seven feeling heavy and exhausted. Every pain I'd been too busy to feel yesterday had blossomed overnight into full misery. My hands were sore from the scrapes they'd suffered digging out Lee. My thighs ached from all the riding, and there were numerous other niggles and bruises that clamoured for attention.

I rolled out of the most luxurious bed I'd ever slept in feeling like a walking corpse and tried to work out what I was going to wear. The skirt and top from last night were clearly inappropriate. My brain was processing thought with great difficulty, but it finally occurred to me to check outside my door and there on the floor in a neatly folded pile, were my freshly laundered jeans, top and polar-fleece.

I stretched protesting muscles as I bent to pick them up. As I straightened, a small glow of red light high on the wall to my left caught my attention. I stared at it realising everything I'd done last night had been caught on security camera.

I retreated to my room. It was too late to worry about any possible repercussions. I'd been nervous last night, but some of that had probably just been night-time fears. If anyone asked, I'd heard one side of a private conversation, that's all. Maybe I wouldn't even have found it significant if I'd been able to put Brett's remarks in their full context.

The small shock of adrenalin that had shot through me when I recognised the camera had been enough to jolt me out of my lethargy. I was up, dressed and going home that morning.

I made my way downstairs and was guided to the dining room by the smell of coffee.

"Good morning." Ray looked up from buttering his slice of toast. "Did you sleep OK?"

"Not bad. Have you heard any news about Lee?"

"No, it's too early. I don't expect any until the doctors get on duty, and I can't imagine that happens before about nine at the earliest. I'll phone then. I don't want to wake Lee if he's sleeping."

Ray saw me hesitate. "Guests help themselves. Choose anything you want," he said indicating a row of dishes on the side-board. "Stephen's just gone to get us a fresh pot of coffee."

I investigated what was on offer. The food was an eclectic mix of Asian and Western cuisine. I helped myself to scrambled eggs and toast and joined Ray at the table.

"I'm considering moving out today," he told me. "It's a long way from here to Hamilton, and if Lee's going to be stuck up there for weeks, I should move closer to be with him. Charles has offered me the use of the helicopter for today, but that's going to be an expensive option over the long term."

"I suppose that would be best," I said. I knew how expensive chartering a helicopter was, and even though Ray and Lee appeared to be well-heeled, the costs would add up quickly. The little Hughes 300 we kept at Paraparaumu Aviation was pricey enough to hire. The lodge's flash Eurocopter would cost a fortune to keep running, and guests would be charged accordingly.

"I'm torn," confessed Ray. "Part of me wants to be with my brother, but I also want to be here at the lodge to find out what the police discover about that body. I can't help feeling those are the remains of my father. Even if they're not, I want to be here to force a thorough investigation into what happened to him. We've had a year of trying to solve his disappearance long-distance, and it's been most unsatisfactory. Lee and I thought it wisest to keep a low profile when we arrived, but now I think I need to confess my interest and push for the case to be reopened."

"Your interest in what?" Charles asked. "Good morning, Claire. I trust you slept well?"

I watched as he helped himself to food. He seemed casual and relaxed and showed no sign that Brett had been accusing him of murder only a few hours earlier. If, of course, that person *had* been Charles. I so wished I'd been able to identify that speaker.

I'd assumed it was Charles, but there was nothing to say it hadn't been Wu, Wenjun or anyone else.

"Yeah, I slept well, thanks," I said. "I borrowed a book from the library. I hope you don't mind?"

"Not at all. If it's in English it's probably been left here by a guest. You are welcome to take it with you." He turned to Ray. "You were talking about an interest?"

"Yes, my interest in the body Claire found." Ray looked directly at Charles. "Lee and I didn't just visit your lodge for the beautiful surroundings and experiences it offers. We are on a pilgrimage. Our father disappeared a year ago after he'd been a guest here. We've come to pay our respects to the last place we know he visited and to see if we can find what happened to him."

"You are talking about Zhang Lei?"

Ray nodded.

"My dear friend, I wish you had told us this earlier. How terrible this must be for you and your brother. I am so sorry, but I cannot help you. We know nothing about his disappearance." Charles shook his head. "Zhang Lei checked out from here on his final morning and our pilot flew him to Taupo Airport where he was picking up a flight to Auckland. We know nothing more than that. A few days later the police came and got us to sign statements. They asked questions about what state of mind your father was in when he left here, whether we'd observed anything odd or unusual in his behaviour, but we'd noticed nothing. He was just a guest, one of several business colleagues, who was enjoying our hospitality."

Charles sounded sincere, but I'd been watching him, and I'd swear he hadn't been surprised by Ray's admission. He had already known who Ray and Lee were. While it gave substance to Ray's earlier suspicion that their passports had been examined and possessions rifled, the big question was 'Why?' If the lodge wasn't involved in Zhang Wu's disappearance, they'd have had no more than a passing interest in a visit by his sons.

Charles's phone rang, which effectively stopped any conversation. I listened to his call with half an ear while I tried to sort out possible explanations for what was going on at the lodge.

Charles put his phone away. "That was Pat," he explained, "phoning to say their road is expected to be cleared by midday and is the invitation still on for dinner here tonight. I've said of course it is, and people are welcome here any time after two o'clock."

I groaned inaudibly. It didn't make sense for Jack to drive over and pick me up, take me back for a change of clothes and then return at two. That meant another day in these clothes which, although now clean, had been handpicked as comfortable for riding a horse all day and weren't really my best look.

"Would you like to get back there before this afternoon?" Charles gestured vaguely in my direction. "So you can get some fresh clothes, perhaps? The helicopter is flying Ray to Hamilton, so it could drop you off at Pat's place. It's on the way."

I sighed with relief. "Thank you. Yes, I'd love to change, even though Mary looked after me so well last night." I gave him a smile. "I'm also looking forward to another trip in your helicopter. I was too tired and stressed yesterday to really appreciate it."

"Then it's done," he said. "You're leaving at 9.30, aren't you Ray?"

Ray nodded. "Yup."

"I'll get my stuff," I said. "How's Wu this morning? Is he OK?"

"It's his day off," said Charles. "I imagine he'll take things easy. It will give him a bit of time to recuperate. Unfortunately, as they told us at the hospital yesterday, there's not a lot anyone can do for a broken collar bone. It's not as if you can put it in plaster."

"Give him my regards if you see him," I said.

'Getting my stuff' consisted of grabbing my jacket from the bedroom. I took the opportunity of calling Jack and bringing him up to date with the arrangements.

"So you won't have to drive down to pick me up," I concluded. "I'll get flown into Pat's place in a fraction of the time."

"I'll be waiting." Jack's voice sounded as mellow as always.

"You'll have to tell me how you enjoyed being an overnight guest at the lodge."

"There's a lot I need to tell you," I said. "I'll see you soon."

My hand hovered over the Sophie Kinsella novel for a moment before I decided to take Charles's offer at face value and keep it. If my holiday with Jack returned to our original plans, then having relaxing reading matter with me would be useful. I shoved it into the deep pockets of my jacket, did a quick look round and headed downstairs.

Brett was waiting in the hall. I jumped when I saw him, last night's overheard conversation still on the surface of my mind.

"Hi, Brett," I said, trying to disguise my slight nervousness. "I believe I'm getting another ride in the chopper with you."

"Yeah, Charles just said. That's fine. Pat's place is just over the hill. Dropping you off won't delay things much for Ray. He should be here in a second. Do you want to go out to the helicopter?"

"I wouldn't mind having a proper look at it in daylight," I replied. "She's a rather beautiful specimen, isn't she?"

I'd touched on the one thing all pilots have in common – a willingness to discuss any aviation related topic. It was obvious Brett was immensely proud of the Eurocopter.

"It's a magic machine to fly," he said with enthusiasm. "Really responsive to handle and yet not twitchy, if you know what I mean."

"Well, I'm a fixed-wing pilot," I said, "but my boss has let me have a play in our Hughes a few times, so I sort of know what you're talking about."

Brett focused on me properly for the first time. "You have a pilot's licence then?"

It was my turn to pause. There'd been a patronising note to his question, as in, 'you amateur, do you only have a private pilot licence?' My job is such a part of my identity that it is always a slight shock when someone doesn't automatically recognise I'm a professional pilot – although, in fairness, there was no reason why Brett should know.

"I'm a commercial pilot," I explained, "and a flying instructor.

I fly out of Paraparaumu."

A reassessment worked its way across Brett's face. I saw the frown soften and his mouth curve into a smile. Now we were colleagues – bonded by the magical world of aviation.

"Do you work for that old chap down in Paraparaumu? Bad-tempered sort of a bloke? Runs his own business. I can't remember his name."

"Roger? Yes, although he's not really bad-tempered."

"He gave me one hell of a bollocking one day when I put the chopper down in the wrong spot. All I wanted was to pick up a client from Paraparaumu."

I had to grin. "Yep, that sounds like him. But his bark is worse than his bite. He's a good guy to work for."

Now that we'd bonded, Brett was a changed man. He walked me outside and enthusiastically showed me around the helicopter. Even a mere fixed-wing pilot could see that it was a thing of beauty and by the time he'd finished discussing its collective and its fenestron, I was as convinced as I could be that this was a wonderful machine.

"We'd better go back and find Ray," he said, looking at his watch. "He's probably waiting for me in the hall."

Ten minutes later Ray finally turned up by which time I was running out of patience.

"Sorry," he said. "I was on the phone to the hospital and it took ages to get through to Lee's ward. He's awake, and I said I'd be there to see him this morning."

"No worries," said Brett, while I gave a cursory smile.

We walked out to the helipad. The ground was wet – it must have rained during the night but I hadn't heard it. The heavy, grey sky promised more rain to come soon although the visibility was fine at the moment. I was just about to climb in when we heard a shout from Charles who came running across the lawn.

"Hold up, you lot. The police have just been on the line. They want to talk to Ray."

"To me?"

"They phoned to ask a few questions and I told them you were here, Ray, and that you were Zhang's son. They want to interview you. They'll be here in five minutes."

I groaned under my breath. Every minute we delayed was a minute longer before I could change into better clothes and see Jack. Actually, those two imperatives were interchangeable. I was hard – pressed to say which was the more important.

I'd realised for some time that I loved Jack. Unfortunately, a few weeks ago I'd had a vulnerable moment when I'd declared myself and told him so. That had been a mistake. So far, he'd failed to return the sentiment. I didn't know whether he, all evidence to the contrary, really didn't care for me, or whether some dumb, male stupidity blinded him to the importance of saying the words. Whichever it was, it rankled.

"OK," Ray said. "I guess I'd better wait for them." He gave a sigh. "I hope they don't take long, I wanted to see Lee before he went into theatre."

Charles nodded, then looked at Brett and me.

"Why don't you take Claire home now," he suggested. "It's only ten minutes away. By the time you get back, the police will have finished with Ray and you can go straight to the hospital with him."

"OK." Brett turned to me. "Get yourself onboard."

I climbed into the helicopter, found the seat belt and buckled myself in. I watched Brett exchange a few words with Charles before he joined me. I couldn't help noticing he looked rather pale.

"Thanks for dropping me home. At least I get to ride in the chopper again."

Brett gave a sort of grunt. I left him alone while he flicked switches and powered the machine up. I listened to the whine of the rotors as they wound themselves to full speed and then, smoothly and easily we lifted from the pad.

We turned and flew over the lodge. Seen from the air, it was a spectacular estate. The main building was surrounded by large areas of lawn and backed by the dramatic dark of the bush-covered hills. It was a beautiful site. On the edge of the northern side of the lawns a stream tumbled attractively over large grey boulders. Another substantial building was tucked away behind a copse of trees, hidden from the guest house.

"It's a really lovely place, isn't it? Have you worked here long?" I asked.

"Just over a year." Brett's earlier enthusiasm and conviviality had evidently disappeared. I shrugged. I'd be home soon enough, so it didn't matter.

We followed the line of the estate road down the valley and in seconds we passed over the wool-shed and the swamp. I looked down at the police activity below us. Tape had been put up surrounding the area I'd floundered in, and numerous cars were parked at the shed. I wondered how the police were getting on with their investigation.

Brett's words burst over my thought. "They probably think the fucking corpse you found is Ray's father. It'll be why they are so keen to speak to him now they know he's at the lodge. I suppose he'll have to identify it."

I swallowed my nausea. "Poor Ray," I said. "What a bitch of a job." I was trying to suppress the memory that I'd stomped right over the remains. No culture on the planet would regard that as acceptable behaviour and I had a nasty feeling that Chinese were particularly hot on respect for their ancestors. Brett and I shared a silent moment.

I waited until he had set the course for Pat's place before I asked my question.

"Did you know Ray's father? I think you told police you flew him to Taupo?"

The Eurocopter, previously described as 'un-twitchy', gave an ungainly lurch. Brett scrambled for the control his nerves had cost us.

I let him recover and glanced at him. His face was an unattractive grey, and I could guarantee his hands were sweating.

Moments passed in silence. We flew across a ridge then turned to follow the riverbed. I realised yesterday we'd been riding along this valley. The blockage was behind us so I couldn't see the dam, but the river looked dead. Small pools and a thin trickle were all that remained of the powerful flow we'd forded the day before.

The silence from Brett was deafening.

"I couldn't sleep last night, so I got up and went looking for a book in the library. On the way back, in the dark, I overheard a conversation. I heard you say you'd lied."

I let a silence build between us and I could sense his tension in the change in his breathing and the slight jerk in his manoeuvres as he steered. I didn't know whether I'd been wise to mention what I'd heard, but this was likely to be my only chance to question him.

I tried to keep my voice calm and impersonal.

"What did you lie about, Brett? Ray's father?"

I had to hand it to him. The landing in the paddock beside the woolshed was spot on. I doubt if Roger, a hard taskmaster, could have faulted the approach or the execution.

"Out you get." Brett's voice was unemotional.

I looked at him, refusing to budge until I got my answer.

He just stared right back at me.

"Whatever you thought you heard, you were mistaken, OK? Now get out of my chopper. Stay away from me, stay away from the Zhang brothers and most of all, stay away from the lodge or you'll be up to your neck in shit before you know it."

I'm not easily intimidated, but Brett's bleak little speech cut right through me.

I grabbed my jacket, climbed out and marched across the paddock to where Jack was waiting for me.

I waved a tentative hand as Brett took off again but received no acknowledgement. Apparently the bond we shared as pilots had disintegrated.

CHAPTER ELEVEN

"I PHONED PETE LAST NIGHT AND asked him to find out what he could about Zhang's disappearance" Jack said.

"He called this morning and confirmed Lee and Ray's story. Their father disappeared after being dropped off at Taupo airport. The helicopter's arrival with two people on board was logged by air traffic control, but the trail ends there. Zhang didn't board his flight to Auckland and the helicopter left after ten minutes on the ground. There are no more details. Alastair Taylor was in charge of the investigation. It's still open."

Jack followed me up to the bedroom.

It was wonderful to climb into fresh clothes. None of the clothes I'd brought with me were up to the level of sophistication of those I'd worn to dinner the night before, but at least my shirt and black trousers looked passably dressy and would have to do. I pulled my hair into a high messy bun to complete the look.

I briefly told him about what I'd overheard in the night.

"So where do you think it all stands now?"

I sat on the bed beside him.

"I don't know. There's definitely something not right at that lodge. Brett, he's the chopper pilot, seemed very edgy when we flew over the police cordon. Then there was that odd conversation

I heard. I just wish I knew who Brett was talking to and what it meant. He's very twitchy and unsettled. He'd been friendly but went right off me when I asked him about it. I was lucky he didn't push me out of the chopper. Charles, on the other hand, seems cool and calm. Nothing's rattling him. I'm quite certain Ray's right that someone has gone through their things. Charles tried to hide it, but he already knew who Ray was and that he was looking for his dad."

"Are you sure you want to go back there this afternoon? We can make our excuses if you like. We're still on holiday, you know."

I gave Jack a grin. "No, I want to go back. You know me, I'm a nosy-parker. In particular, I want to talk to Ray and find out how he got on with the police this morning. I also think it would be a good idea for you to be there and pick up the vibe. I may be too imaginative, seeing things that aren't there."

"Fair enough."

"There's also a photo of Zhang and a group of other guests, hanging in the hallway. You should look at it."

I lay back on the bed and looked up at the ceiling while I thought.

"Pete said air traffic control logged a chopper with two people on board flying into Taupo. But there's nothing to say that Brett's passenger actually was Zhang, is there? There's only Brett's word for that. He'd have signed a passenger manifesto, of course, but again, it's only his word. Maybe that's what he lied about. Was there any security camera footage of the passenger?"

"Not that Pete mentioned."

"Suppose Brett took someone else to Taupo – or didn't even have a passenger at all? That could mean Zhang never left here. Maybe that body in the swamp *is* his."

"And the motive for all of this?" Jack sounded amused.

"I'm working on it," I replied. "Yesterday you asked Ray and Lee whether their father might have had something to do with politics. What made you ask that?"

He gave a slight shrug. "Politics seemed an obvious consideration. There was an international case a few months back when a Chinese businessman was kidnapped from a Hong Kong hotel. A few days later it was confirmed he was in mainland China. The assumption was he'd been arrested for some illegal political activity and whisked away by Chinese police. Hong Kong is part of China, but its laws are different and it's supposed to be independent so it caused an international outcry. There've been other similar cases, so I wondered what Ray and Lee knew about their father's politics."

"They seemed fairly certain he was on the right side of party lines," I said.

"They did," Jack said lightly.

"So again, no motive." I was stumped.

Pat, Ian and Matt were still at work in the woolshed.

"Pat wants to get all the sheep shorn before the rain comes down," said Joanne.

"Fat chance," I said. "It looks as if it's going to pour down any minute now."

"The yards themselves are under cover, so they can carry on even if it does rain. It's just a nuisance when they have to put them back out on the hills. The rain only needs to hold off for another couple of hours or so," she said, giving the lowering sky a hopeful look.

We piled into one of the farm's utes. Our advance party to the lodge consisted of Jack, Joanne and me. Joanne was excited and asked me endless questions.

"I'm jealous," she admitted. "I'd have loved to spend the night there. Is it really as flash as they say?"

"It's very impressive. I'd have felt better about it if I hadn't looked like a scruffy refugee. If Mary hadn't found me something decent to wear to dinner I'd have been really stuffed."

"Ah, you'd look beautiful dressed in a sack," she said. "You don't have to worry." I rolled my eyes, but I appreciated the compliment. However competent, polished and sophisticated we are, there's nothing like feeling inadequately dressed to bring out our neuroses.

We'd packed our swim-suits in preparation for enjoying the

spa pool Charles had promised us.

"It's all very well for you townies," said Joanne, "but we don't have the luxury of a spa pool at our place."

"Well, I don't have one at mine either," I replied.

Joanne, who was driving, carried on telling us the story of a movie filmed some years ago on the Whanganui River and the American actress who insisted a spa be installed in some remote little hamlet so she could enjoy her creature comforts.

"Thankfully New Zealanders don't behave like that," she declared with scorn. "I heard she was a temperamental woman. A fine set of airs and graces demanding all sorts of things. Just like a child! Mind you, she was a very good actress."

Jack was silent and I listened with half an ear. I was more concerned about the reception we would get at the lodge.

There was plenty of evidence along the roadside of yesterday's earthquake in the form of small slips and falls. We reached the largest one, responsible for blocking the road last night, and found the road-clearing crew having smoko.

Joanne pulled over and opened the window.

"Hi, Kevin," she called.

Kevin came over. "G'day, Joanne. You guys were OK in the shake yesterday?"

"We were, yes. I bet your lot have been busy cleaning up after it, though."

Kevin chuckled. "It'll take days to clear everything up in the area. We've opened the road here, then we're moving up to McCartney's Line to clear another slip there."

Jack leaned across to ask, "Do you know what they're going to do about clearing the river?"

"That's a curly one," replied Kevin, looking doubtful. "I dunno. Our boss and some council people have gone up there today to look at it and work out what's best. They did a fly-over first thing this morning. They reckon 80 million tonnes of material came down in that slip."

"Jeez, that's enormous," said Joanne.

"It is. That lake behind it is 50 metres deep or more already, and rising. There's no water leaking from it, so each day it's only going to get deeper. Civil defence guys are going around the neighbourhood warning potentially affected residents. The main thing is to make sure they stay out of the riverbed. The dam might fail at any time, and there's one hell of a lot of water behind the landslide."

"So what happens next?" asked Jack.

Kevin shrugged. "No doubt head office will develop a management plan. They'll have to get in specialised engineers to assess the risk. It'll be a money-go-round, paid for out of rate-payers' pockets, no doubt. Frankly, everyone would be happier if it rained like hell, flooded, and nature took its own course in clearing it."

"They'll have to figure out something," said Joanne. "Too many people depend on that river. It could be a disaster if it stays dried up."

"True enough," said Kevin, "but there are real dangers in trying to clear it. The ground's as unstable as anything. I don't think the boss would be too happy to put our people in there. It would be very risky.

Jack nodded. "Good luck."

Kevin and his crew waved as we moved on.

I looked down into the empty river bed as we crossed the bridge that connected Pat and Joanne's valley with the road to the lodge.

"Is it going to be a real problem for you?" I asked. "I mean, without the river."

"Not for us so much," Joanne replied, "we've got big water tanks. Further downstream though are a couple of farms that use irrigation, and they'll be affected. Then there are all the small businesses that rely on the river for their work, like kayaking and adventure tourism."

"Perhaps they'll have to bomb the blockage," I said.

We reached the entrance to the lodge and were stopped at the gate by a policewoman who enquired of our business and took our names.

She looked up when Jack gave his.

"Were you here yesterday?"

"I was. How's it going?"

"I couldn't say. Do you want to speak to Detective Inspector Alastair Taylor?"

"Is he here? That's good news. Yeah, I'll have a word with him."

"You don't mind?" Jack asked Joanne. "I know Alastair, and it would be good to get a heads-up on what they've discovered."

Joanne shook her head. "I don't mind at all. See if you can find out some juicy details for us."

We waited in the ute. Rain had started to fall as a light drizzle.

I watched as some minutes later Jack shook the hand of an extremely tall, thin man who clapped him on the back as he left. Both men were grinning.

"Any news?" I asked, as Jack climbed back into the car.

Joanne started the engine and we continued up the valley.

"Not really. Alastair said it's too early to tell very much. Forensics are having a field day. It's a cold case and the body is badly decomposed, so analysis could take a while. They've established it's a homicide though. There's a bullet hole in the back of the skull, so whoever you found there didn't walk into that swamp voluntarily."

"Ugh," said Joanne.

"Yeah, well, they've taken all the evidence they need, and will be out of here in the next couple of hours."

I gave a shudder, before something the policewoman said registered. "Did she say that Alastair Taylor is an inspector now? He wasn't when he interviewed me a few months ago."

"Yes. He was promoted soon after that. I was teasing him about it just now. He's a good bloke is Alastair. If they've brought him in for this case, it must be a tricky one."

"I wonder how the interview with Ray went this morning."

"Alastair didn't discuss it. If Ray's still at the lodge, you can ask him this afternoon."

Charles met us as we pulled up outside and I introduced him to Joanne and Jack.

"Welcome, welcome," he said, shaking their hands. "It's lovely to meet you."

He smiled at Joanne. "I met your husband yesterday, so I feel I'm getting to know more of my neighbours. Please come in."

I heard Joanne gasp as she looked around the hall and took in the magnificence of the décor.

"This place is amazing," she said.

"Allow me to give you the guided tour." Charles led her through into the living room. I stayed behind in the hallway and looked at the photographs again. I studied the photo of Ray's father, pondering about what the business-men had been discussing during their visit and whether I was right that the beautiful Li Na was showing more than a casual interest in Zhang Lei.

I joined Jack and Joanne on the tour. The place was even bigger than I'd appreciated. I'd only seen a small proportion the night before. There was a billiard room, indoor swimming pool, sauna and gym, as well as an area full of sporting equipment.

"The guns are shut away in that safe," said Charles. "We've also got a full range of fishing gear here. Hiking and climbing stuff, of course. We have a croquet lawn and a boules area out in the garden. All the equipment is kept here. You name it, we've got it. We try to provide a wide range of activities for our guests."

I reflected that this was the only room in the complex that actually looked like my preconceptions of a hunting lodge. Mercifully there were no heads mounted on the wall, but there were numerous framed photographs of guests holding up fish, or kneeling beside dead deer.

Charles shepherded us back to the living room where Mary had laid out a formal afternoon tea. At the end of a table spread with plates of sandwiches and cakes, she waited to pour tea.

"This is great, thank you," said Jack.

Mary smiled. "You are most welcome."

"Please help yourself to some light refreshments," Charles said. "Then make yourselves at home. You are welcome to try out the spa, sauna, gym. If you wish, you can explore the grounds. Consider yourselves our guests. Mary is here to assist you if there is anything you need. I leave you in her capable hands."

"What do you fancy doing?" I asked Jack.

"I wouldn't mind having a walk around the grounds. What about you?"

"Excellent idea," I nodded.

Joanne opted for the sauna and the spa, and after agreeing that we might join her later, Jack and I went outside.

CHAPTER TWELVE

"THERE'S A PICTURE OF LEE AND Ray's father in the hallway," I said. "With a group of other business people. Taken a year ago. Remember Lee said he was here last Labour Weekend? I asked Mary who the people in the photo were."

"It would be interesting to know if the police followed up with each of them once Zhang disappeared," Jack remarked. "It would also be relevant to know who went out on the muster with him. They were quarrelling all day, remember?"

We were walking along a gravelled path that meandered across the immaculate lawn. It was a cloudy afternoon but still pleasant enough to be outside, and the lack of bright sunshine had done nothing to detract from the beauty of the setting. I turned to look back at the lodge.

"They couldn't have positioned it better, could they?" I said, looking at the way the soft golden colour of the building was framed by the dark bush-covered hills beyond.

"Whoever designed it did a good job," agreed Jack, "and it won't have come cheap. A lot of money has been invested here. An enormous amount. Charles is still a young guy. It would be interesting to know where he got his funds from."

"Family funds?" I speculated.

"Maybe. He was introduced to us as the owner manager, but you have to ask yourself whether there are other investors involved as well. It's a big operation."

Money matters didn't interest me, so I listened with half an ear as we passed a little sign pointing to the croquet lawn.

What I really wanted to know was the identity of the body in the swamp. It seemed incredible that I'd only found it the day before yesterday. I half wanted it to be Ray and Lee's missing father, so they would know what had happened to him. At the same time, it would be less socially awkward if the corpse turned out to be someone unconnected with our host and the lodge.

The path led over a slight rise, past another discreet sign pointing to the boules court, then followed the contours of the land down towards the little stream I'd seen that morning.

A grassy area had been cleared on the bank, with a convenient seat from which to enjoy the pleasant view of a little waterfall tumbling over the boulders.

"Even this bears out what I was saying," said Jack as he sat down.

"What does?" I asked.

"This pleasant little scene."

"What's wrong with it?" I asked looking around. It looked fine to me.

"It's not a natural feature," said Jack dryly. "Look closely at the rocks and you'll see they aren't from around here. They're granite, and if you remember digging Lee out yesterday, you'll know what the local rock looks like – which isn't that. They've been brought in and carefully placed to create this nifty little waterfall and very nice staged area. The attention to detail is superb. And it will all have cost money."

"Well, they're in the business of entertaining celebs," I said, scrutinising the offending rocks and wondering if he was correct. "I can see their guests checking out deals on Trivago – not! They'll have serious money and won't mind paying for their pleasures."

"Hmm." Jack said nothing more, but a slight crease between

his eyebrows told me he was still considering Lodge's finances.

"Well, it's the only time I'm ever likely to stay in a place this posh. I'm determined to enjoy it, fake rocks or not. You wait until you have dinner; it was superb last night."

Jack grinned. "Frankly, I'd rather be on holiday with you and eating takeaways." His look was frankly lecherous. "Uncle Pat's guest bedroom has limited scope for activities."

"Well, I feel much the same, but if in Rome and all that . . . . I assume we can move on tomorrow?"

"We Are Out Of Here," said Jack, stressing each word. "I don't need earthquakes, bodies, family or any other nonsense to come between us and our time to relax together."

I sat down beside him and reached for his hand. "I totally agree."

Jack's larger hand wrapped around mine as he returned to his examination of our surroundings. "Let's see how far the cosmetic work on this stream has gone," he said eventually, as he stood and pulled me up with him.

At the far end of the clearing, the grassy area fused with a plantation of native trees and shrubs. A small, formed track led under the trees, and we followed it upstream.

We were no more than ten metres into the bush when the look of the stream changed completely and I could see what Jack was talking about. The rocks, smaller than those in the clearing, were soft golden brown and blended with the umber shade of the surrounding earth. Small pools between the rocks had wind-fallen leaves, and cobwebs clustered low on bushes that overhung the water. This was ungroomed and natural bush.

"I'm picking not many guests wander up this way," said Jack. "I think we've stumbled on the backstage area of this particular show."

Sure enough, after a few minutes, the track widened into a small clearing and as we turned a corner we reached an enormous shed set on a large gravelled area concealed, from the rest of the property by a large hedge.

"Garden and equipment shed? Definitely backstage," Jack said. I grinned at his smug complacency, even as I agreed with his assessment.

Tyre tracks in the gravel indicated heavy equipment. I approached the shed and stood on tiptoe to peer through the window.

"Only a tractor at the moment. It's enormous in there, but empty."

"It's well locked up," said Jack, indicating the heavy padlock on the sliding doors. "They're not taking any chances that a guest gets in and goes joy-riding."

"I don't think it's just the tractor they're safe-guarding. I'm betting this is where they store the helicopter. They'd land it on the trailer and tow it into the hangar to keep it safe overnight. Just like we do in Paraparaumu."

The track led on around the enclosing trees, and then divided. To the right I recognised the site of the helipad. Our route must have taken us in a large loop through the grounds. We were now much closer to the lodge than I'd realised. The design of the estate concealed how the various areas related to each other.

We turned in the other direction. In front of us was a long, low building.

"Servant's quarters," Jack said with some satisfaction. "See how they've managed to keep the roof profile low. I bet you can't even see it from the house. We're back to that clever designer again."

"You must be right. I'd wondered where the staff stayed."

"They'd all have to live in," said Jack. "There's no local village to commute from, and this place must take a few people to run it properly. There'll be a groundsman or two, Wu, Mary and probably cleaners as well."

"Not to mention the chef and Stephen the waiter."

"Plus the helicopter pilot," said Jack. "And there could well be more. Phil's probably the exception. I'd imagine there's a farm cottage somewhere for him."

"I'd forgotten Phil," I remarked. "Yeah, he didn't seem to have much to do with the main house, did he?"

Jack pointed. A golf cart was driving down the hill on our right. It pulled up by the door. Mary climbed out and went in. I watched the door swing shut behind her.

"Another woman used to work at the lodge," I said. "She was in the photo. Mary said she left."

"There's probably a high turnover. Not many staff would want to be stuck out here; it's very remote." Jack was looking around as we walked towards the building. "I'd say that's the main path to the lodge. It would be quite a hike in wet weather if they didn't use the carts."

The door opened again, and Charles stepped out. He paused for a moment then looked up, startled, as he registered our approach.

"Hi," he called.

"We've been exploring," I explained as we got closer.

"So I see. Well, you've reached the staff quarters. Not many of our guests make it down here." Charles looked amused. "Can I offer you a lift back to the main building? It looks as if it's going to start raining soon."

Jack looked at me and raised an eyebrow. "Shall we?"

"We'd better get back," I agreed. "If Joanne has been in the spa all this time, she'll be pickled."

I sat in the front beside Charles, and Jack squeezed into the seat behind.

The wide pathway took us up a slight rise to where we could see the main house in front of us.

"This is so beautiful," I said to Charles. "We were just saying how well everything, from the buildings to the landscaping, fits together so perfectly. Who designed it all?"

"It was designed by a Chinese architect currently living in Auckland. He'd done his early training in Shanghai and liked the opportunity of creating a blend of oriental and New Zealand themes. I think it works well."

"It's lovely. What about the grounds? Did he design those as well?"

"No. The grounds, as they are now, are fairly recent. The first design, which was here for several years, had a formal garden. Then a couple of years ago we decided to put in a swimming pool and tennis court, which meant we had to reorganise everything.

One of our guests offered to help create a new concept. She said we were ruining our best asset by the old, rigid geometric design, so she drew up a new landscape plan." Charles smiled. "She said she thought her function was like being a jeweller – taking a precious stone and enhancing it by creating a beautiful setting for the piece."

"Well, she did a lovely job of it."

"We think so too, although we were very nervous when the bulldozers came in and destroyed the first garden. But Li Na knew what she was doing. It's turned out well."

I gave a slight start.

"Is she the woman in the photograph you have in the hall? Mary mentioned her when we were discussing the group."

Charles threw me a surprised glance. "Mary discussed her with you?"

"I'd asked who the people were in the group. In most of the other pictures I could identify who the celebrity was, but I didn't recognise anyone in that particular photo. Did you say she originally came as a guest?"

"The first time she came here was with Wenjun."

That was interesting. Mary hadn't shared that nugget with me. I'd only gained the impression that she and Li Na were not on friendly terms.

"Who *is* Wenjun?" I asked. "I thought he was a guest, but he seems to be in every photo you have up on the wall. Is he part of the staff?"

Charles laughed. "He might as well be. He's here so often that he almost is part of the staff. No, Wenjun's a guest, but he does have a financial interest in the lodge as well. When I first built it, I was undercapitalised. As you can imagine, it's not cheap to run a facility such as this, and the early years were a struggle. Wenjun visited here, identified the problem and offered to put money into the business. He wanted a project to occupy him during his retirement. I needed an investor. At first he used to come at regular intervals, but he has been a permanent guest now for the last year or so. He tells me he's at the stage of his life where he appreciates solitude and tranquillity."

"And he brought Li Na to this beautiful place."

"At the time she was his ..." Charles paused, grasping for the word, "… companion. She loved this place, and of course later her designs and work were instrumental in shaping the lodge as it is today."

"So what happened to her? Mary said she'd left. Did she and Wenjun break up?"

"Ah." There was an awkward silence. "She became close to another guest," Charles said carefully, "and it caused trouble between her and Wenjun. They had a serious quarrel and without a word to the rest of us, she packed her bags and left. Wenjun drove her to Te Kuiti and dropped her off at the bus station. Apparently she intended to go back to China."

He sighed. "We haven't heard from her since, which is a great pity as she was well liked here and contributed so much. Mary was hurt that Li Na never said goodbye to her because they'd been friends. I don't know whether she's been in touch with Wenjun since, but he's never mentioned it."

We were still some distance from the lodge when the first heavy drops fell. Charles made an irritated noise, but stopped the cart, climbed out and rolled the plastic walls down around us. Jack and I helped zip them up and we continued the drive in a little plastic bubble. Within a minute the rain was pelting down.

"Just as well we accepted a ride," said Jack. "We'd have been thoroughly caught out otherwise."

"The forecast is for heavy rain this evening," said Charles.

"It's a holiday weekend," I said. "What else were you expecting? Of course it's going to rain."

As we reached the main building we heard the beat of helicopter blades. A minute later the Eurocopter flew over the lodge roof and hovered for a moment before settling on the landing pad.

"They've only just made it back in time," said Charles. "I'd been hoping they'd make it before the cloud was too low on the hills. I'll drop you two off and go and get Ray."

Inside, we found Joanne sitting in the lounge, sipping iced water.

"We thought you'd still be in the spa," said Jack.

"I had a lovely spa and then treated myself to the sauna. It was perfect luxury to just lie there and let the steam iron out my tensions," smiled Joanne.

"I thought you looked a little flushed," I said, taking a seat beside her.

"Mary's just given me some cold water to help me cool down. What did you two do?"

"Walked around the grounds. Fortunately Charles offered us a ride just before the rain started, otherwise we'd have got soaked."

"I noticed it was raining. It will have put paid to the shearing for the day," said Joanne. "Pat won't be pleased, but we'll see the men earlier than we expected."

"Let's hope it doesn't bring down any more slips," remarked Jack. "After yesterday's shake, some spots might be unstable."

Joanne shrugged. "The gangs have been out there clearing up today, so the worst of them should have been stabilised. This is an amazing place, isn't it," she said, changing the subject.

She looked round the lounge. "It's funny how little everyone in the area knows about this place. I mean, we know the lodge is here, but there isn't much interaction between it and the local community. I can't wait to tell my friends I've been here and used the facilities. They'll be most impressed."

"We're certainly mixing with high society," I said. "Or at least, we're where high society hangs out. Pity there aren't any celebs here at the moment for us to meet."

Jack shot me a look.

"Don't you want to meet the rich and famous?" I teased.

"Not particularly. This place is great, but I don't need to spend time with people who are only here to shore up how important and wealthy they are."

"What a cynical view you have of our visitors." Charles had entered the room unseen. "I assure you, wealthy and important as they are, most of our guests are charming."

I didn't often see Jack back-footed, so I was amused to see him look embarrassed.

"I'm sure many of them are delightful," he replied. "I just don't happen to subscribe to the cult of celebrity. I think your place is beautiful as it is, and I'm grateful I don't have to think of something to say to people I'm familiar with only from photos in the media and yet know nothing about. Of course, the women may think differently."

"I wouldn't say no to meeting George Clooney," Joanne said wistfully.

"He's already taken," I laughed.

"Just my luck," said Joanne.

"Pat will be here shortly," I assured her.

"Love Pat as I do, that's no consolation," she grumbled.

Charles smiled. "You ladies will just have to manage without George this evening and make do with us instead. In the meantime, may I pour anyone a drink?"

Jack settled for a beer, Joanne had a mint julep, "'because I've never had one,'" and I had a Chardonnay.

By the time Pat, Ian and Matt arrived we were on our second drinks and feeling very relaxed and cheerful.

Joanne looked up when Pat came in. "Hello, George," she shouted and then started to giggle at her own joke. I saw Pat's eyes widen, a response which immediately made me join in with Joanne.

The men watched tolerantly as Joanne and I leaned against each other and abandoned ourselves to laughter. The more Pat tried to intervene, or ask what the joke was, the more helplessly we convulsed.

"I wouldn't bother, mate," Jack said to Pat. "I'll explain it all later. In the meantime, have a drink and go with the flow."

It was Joanne who ended our laughing fit. "I need to pee," she announced. "I'll wet myself if I carry on like this."

By the time she returned from the bathroom, Jack and I had explained the joke to a still-confused Pat.

He shrugged. "I'll never understand women," he said as he accepted a beer. He sipped it appreciatively.

"Hell, we need this after driving through all that rain. It was a busy day in the yards until we had to stop because the sheep were getting wet. By the time we set off, the rain was coming down so hard we could barely see the road in front of us."

"How did the shearing go?" Jack asked.

It was a successful change of subject for a dyed-in-the wool farmer who could talk about his sheep for hours.

"The rain is a real pain," he said. "We'd have finished the job today if it hadn't come down that heavy. I just hope it dries out tomorrow, so we can get the rest of the mob shorn and back out onto the hills. It's not looking good, though."

"The forecast looks rough," said Ian. "Don't get your hopes up."

"We've had a very wet spring," said Charles. "I'd hoped we were over the worst of it, but winter doesn't seem to want to let go this year."

Discussion of the weather stopped with the arrival of Ray, Brett and Wenjun.

Charles made introductions all round. I watched as the men shook hands. Pat cocked his head sideways and looked at Wenjun sharply.

"We've met before, haven't we?" he asked. "Weren't you with us on the muster this time last year?"

There was a soft exclamation of surprise from Ray. "It was *you* with my father?"

I felt Jack stiffen beside me. It hadn't occurred to either of us that Zhang's companion on that ride had been Wenjun.

"Yes, I was indeed in that party," he said. His face gave nothing away. He was as casual as if he'd been discussing the weather.

"I heard Zhang spent the day quarrelling with you," said Jack. "What was that all about?"

"Quarrelling? No," replied Wenjun. "We had different politics, that's all. It was a discussion." He gave a slight smile. "In light of Zhang's disappearance, I can see it's natural you should ask me about it, but there was nothing sinister, I assure you."

There was a slight break in the conversation as everyone considered this.

"Can you update us on your brother's condition, Ray?" Charles changed the subject. He stepped into the awkward moment smoothly, as a good host should.

"Lee's OK. They operated and straightened the leg up, which is good at least. He's in traction and probably will be for several weeks. The leg is too swollen for it to be plastered so he has to stay in bed, harnessed to weights, until the bone starts to knit properly."

"Were you able to speak to him?" I asked.

Ray shook his head. "He was in theatre by the time I arrived and was only just starting to come around when we had to leave. I'll go and see him tomorrow. At some point we are going to have to make decisions about how we handle the situation. We're needed back in China for our business. But for now, Lee's safe and in the right place."

Mary arrived with the trolley of canapes and busied herself circulating amongst us, pouring and topping up drinks.

Charles, making an effort to get to know his neighbours, was talking to Joanne and Pat.

"You're quite right. We've been far too distant from the local community. Hopefully this will change."

Matt and Jack were sharing a joke, and Brett joined them. I got the impression he was trying to avoid me.

This left me with Ray and Wenjun. I realised that Wu was missing and I hadn't seen him all day. He was probably taking the day off to nurse his injured shoulder.

"I'm glad your brother looks as if he'll be all right," I said.

"We've still got to figure out what to do," said Ray. "With our father absent, we can't afford to be away from the business too long. I'm going to have to return to China soon, and I don't know whether Lee will be able to travel. I've emailed our mother. She might be able to come to New Zealand and be with him while he recovers, but she can't speak English and would be nervous travelling on her own." He looked stressed.

"It will work out," I assured him. "Things always do." I hate it when I find myself uttering platitudes, but I'm not very good at sympathetic small talk.

"Maybe there is someone from the Chinese community who could help her?" Wenjun suggested. "You could enquire if that was so."

I was eager to move the conversation into more cheerful territory. "You spoke to the police this morning?" I asked.

Ray also looked relieved at having moved away from the logistical problems he was facing.

"Yes. There was a detective inspector. A very tall man." Ray gave a slightly effeminate giggle. "I've never seen a man so tall and thin. It was like seeing a ghost or a demon."

I was inclined to agree. The resemblance between Alastair Taylor and Nick Cave was remarkable.

"Are they making any progress identifying the body?" I asked.

"Surely it would be too soon for information?" said Wenjun. "We shouldn't speculate," he added repressively.

I looked at him in surprise. I imagined we were all interested in finding out the details.

"This is so," said Ray, "but they already have some understanding."

Just then Charles clapped his hands.

"Ladies and gentlemen, I'm told that dinner is ready, if you would all like to follow me through to the dining room."

How frustrating! I thought Ray was about to tell us more on what the police had found.

I'd hoped to wangle a seat next to him at the table and carry on the conversation, instead of which I ended up sitting between Pat and Wenjun.

Predictably enough, the talk again drifted towards Pat's sheep.

"Did you manage to get them all down yesterday?" I asked. "The dogs must have had their work cut out after the quake to gather them all up again."

"Yeah. They're tuckered out today all right, but we got most of them down safely. If we missed a few, we'll pick them up in April. We were all grateful to reach the sheds last night."

"Jack said it was scary riding down the valley with that wall of slip behind you."

"It was that. There'll be a powerful amount of water caught up behind that dam now."

"What happens about it?" I asked. "Will the council come and clear it, or what?"

Pat shook his head. "We caught up with Vaughan Conroy when we drove here. He's the boss of the contracting outfit the council uses for maintenance. He wasn't very hopeful they could do much. Said he thought it was too dangerous for him to put a team in to clear it up. The whole slip is unstable, the slopes above have got huge boulders that could come down at any minute, and it would be a massive undertaking to get above them and clear them out."

"But what happens if the dam gives?" asked Wenjun, who had been quietly listening. "Surely that would put a wall of water down the valley which would be very dangerous."

"Civil defence will be looking at that, I imagine. It's going to be destructive, however that wall is breached. It might burst naturally – who knows? It's pissing down out there at the moment. Maybe the additional water will be enough to push through the debris and clear it. I'm just glad our place is high enough above the river not to have any issues when it does. I'm just sorry for the poor sods who live on flatter land downstream."

I gave a bit of a shiver as I thought of that massive pile of rubble and boulders being released down the riverbed and then thought of the damage that must already be occurring upriver of the dam. The spot where we forded the river yesterday morning would be metres underwater. The little stream we followed to the foot of the cliff was most probably drowned. However, or whenever, the blockage cleared, it would take years for the river to recover.

"It seems most unsatisfactory to leave clearing up the river to some random natural act," grumbled Wenjun. "Surely there must be a way to fix this problem?"

Pat stared at him. "I've been a countryman all my life, and I can say with some certainty you can't fix nature, particularly if, by that, you mean fix a river. If you try, you'll end up with more of a mess than when you started."

Wenjun subsided. I got the impression he thought this Kiwi laissez-faire attitude was very poor. Chinese engineers would have the whole issue done and dusted by now.

I smiled at him. Some cultural differences are impossible to bridge.

CHAPTER THIRTEEN

THE FOOD WAS DELICIOUS, THE WINE was poured generously, and Charles was an admirable host. If his intent was to build goodwill within the community, then treating Joanne and Pat to a slice of luxurious living was a good start. I'd no doubt Joanne would spread favourable reports of the lodge and its owner among her circle of friends and neighbours.

We'd reached the end of the last course before Brett, who'd been quiet throughout the meal, turned to Ray and asked the question that had been occupying my thoughts.

"How did you get on with the police this morning? Did you learn anything?"

The directness clearly startled Ray, who looked across to Charles, as if asking permission of his host to introduce the distasteful subject.

"I don't know whether a dinner party is the right place …?"

Charles shrugged. "Everyone here is going to be interested in what the police have to say. We can't pretend they don't exist. They've been camped out in our driveway for the last two days."

Ray nodded. "They didn't tell me a lot. The detective was more interested in asking why Lee and I were at the lodge and what we knew about our father's disappearance."

"Did they say they thought the body was your father?" Brett asked.

Ray shook his head slowly. "I got the impression they didn't think it was very likely." He looked around at us. "Of course, I wanted them to say they were certain they'd found him, but they didn't. They *did* say, if it was my father, they'd need me to look at items found with the body, but they didn't give me the impression that was going to happen."

There was silence as we each thought through the ramifications of this, then Joanne said what I'm certain we were all wondering. "So, if it wasn't your dad, who would it be?"

"It's beginning to be like the Bermuda Triangle," said Ian. "You come here, and people disappear." Perhaps realising too late from Charles's silence that the statement hadn't been very tactful, he hastily added, "Not that I'm saying that's what's been happening. But it still is very odd. It would make a good story."

"Let's hope it doesn't make a story," snapped Wenjun. "Not one that gets picked up by the newspapers or media anyway. That would be disastrous for business."

I was aware of a change in the general mood of the group. Wenjun looked annoyed. Charles seemed unhappy and was using his fork to draw circles on the tablecloth, and tension was radiating out from Brett. The rest of us were uneasy and embarrassed. Mary was the only one who looked composed.

"The police will sort it all out," she said calmly. "It's just coincidence the body was found here. There's probably no other connection with the lodge."

Jack looked across at Mary and smiled. "As you say, they'll sort it out. It's their job."

"Shall we go through for coffee?" Mary asked.

Charles rose abruptly. "Yes, let's go through to the living room."

I thought for a moment that Pat would decline and opt for leaving. He wasn't the sort of man who'd want to be caught up in the lodge's problems and he'd had a long working day, but Joanne followed Charles, so he tagged along.

Mary poured coffees and handed them out. The simple ritual

defused the tension that had been building up in the dining room. Rattled nerves were calmed, and anxieties smoothed over.

A gust of wind rattled the windows.

"The storm's getting up," remarked Matt. "It's not looking good for finishing the shearing tomorrow."

Pat gave a discontented grunt. "Bloody weather. We've just had the wettest October on record."

I looked up at the windows. It was too dark to see outside, but light reflected off the raindrops on the glass. It was obviously pouring with rain.

Pat stood up. "I think we should be going," he said. "It'll take us forty minutes to get home, and it's been a long day."

"Yeah, I agree," said Joanne. "Matt, will you come with us? Jack, can you drive my car? I've had a couple too many to drink. Thank you so much for your hospitality." She leaned towards Charles and gave him a light kiss on the cheek. "It's been lovely to be your guest and enjoy your wonderful facilities. You've a very beautiful place here."

"My pleasure," said Charles.

We said our goodbyes and shook hands with Wenjun and Mary. I noticed Brett had disappeared directly after dinner.

"Good luck," I said to Ray. "I hope your brother recovers well, and I hope the police can help you with your father."

Ray shrugged. "I hope so too. To think that we might never know what happened to him is a nightmare."

"Good luck then," Jack echoed.

"You are going home tomorrow?" Ray asked.

Jack nodded.

"The police here are concerned with the body in the swamp. To them, my father's disappearance is unimportant. If I can't get the case reopened here, may I call you when you return to work and see if there's anything you can do?"

"I don't know what difference I can make, but I will certainly ask a few questions on your behalf," said Jack.

The rain hadn't let up during the time we'd been at dinner, and there were deep puddles on the drive as we ran across to the vehicles. Pat and his family piled into one, Jack and I shared the other and Ian had his own ute. With the headlights on and windscreen wipers fighting the storm outside I felt warm, cosy and happy to be alone with Jack. His family were lovely, and the lodge had been quite an experience, but it was nice just to be the two of us.

We drove slowly. The visibility was atrocious even with the wipers working at full speed. We navigated the drive, guided by Pat's tail-lights and the small fluorescent markers which lined the sides of the road. Fortunately, like everything else here, the drive was in good condition and Jack didn't have to worry about unseen potholes.

We reached the main gate. The forensics team had left, and there was nothing now to mark the spot in the swamp where the body had been.

I couldn't repress a superstitious shiver.

"Are you OK?" Jack asked.

"Someone just walked over my grave," I said, eyeing the dark swamp where the body had lain. *Did ghosts haunt the spot where they died?*

Jack gave a chuckle. "Don't get morbid," he chided. "Do you want to drive?"

"Hell no," I muttered, my eyes on the faint blur of Pat's lights. "I like to see where I'm going. I may be an instrument-rated pilot, but cars don't have the right instruments."

"Soon, I imagine, self-driving cars will take over the world and they won't worry about such details," said Jack. "Hello, Pat's stopping."

We drew up behind his vehicle and watched as Pat got out. He was pointing a torch at the ground. Matt followed him.

"I'd better see what the problem is," said Jack.

He only had a light water-proof jacket on; he'd be soaked through in seconds. I decided to take refuge in my female status and stay in the warm, dry car. There are times when it pays to be a girl.

The headlights of Pat's car lit up the men as they walked forwards, and I saw Ian had joined them. They only went a few feet before they stopped, and I saw the beam of the torch swinging in a wide arc over the darkness in front of them.

After a few moments Pat and Ian moved a few metres to the left while Jack and Matt remained where they were, peering into the darkness. I tried to work out where we were. The rain and darkness hid any landmarks, but we hadn't come far from the lodge gates. I didn't think we'd crossed the bridge yet, and I hadn't noticed the war memorial either. The lack of visibility was so complete it was disorienting. Even with the headlights shining full on them, I could barely see the men.

Some lights were reflected in the mirror as another vehicle, warning lights flashing, slowly drove up behind us. It passed and pulled up in the middle of the road beside Pat's car.

It was a council truck, similar to the one we'd seen earlier in the day. The occupant climbed out and went forward to join the guys. Pat was pointing up river. I saw the newcomer gesturing with his arms.

Then, with no warning, the men were in full flight, running back towards us. There was something wrong with the way they were moving. Their legs seemed unnaturally slow. It was only as Jack reached the vehicle, opened the door and swung himself in that I realised they'd been running through water. In the seconds it took him to climb into the seat and slam the door the water had risen high enough to lap the door sill.

Jack had started the engine before his backside had even hit the seat.

"We're out of here," he said as he turned the wheel sharply, mirroring Pat's actions in front of us.

"What happened?" I said.

"The river's flowing again. It's already burst its banks. Fuck!"

Jack swore as the wheels spun uselessly for a second before gaining purchase with the road. "Don't let us down now," he grunted.

The roading truck had backed up a hundred metres, and I watched in the wing mirrors as it reversed and made a three-point turn.

Ahead of us, Pat's vehicle was now across the road. He appeared to be struggling to force it round in the turn, but slowly he began to make headway and completed the manoeuvre. As he passed us, making for higher ground, Jack started our own turn. Immediately I could feel the lack of response from our vehicle.

Disturbingly, it was easy to move forward into the rising flood of water, but any attempt to change direction met with resistance. I could feel the tyres slipping and skidding beneath us.

"The current's pulling it. Shit, I'm backing out of here," he said, looking over his shoulder as he put the car into reverse.

I was looking at the water ahead of us. In the last minute, the level had risen considerably and there was white foam on the surface, marking the speed of the flow. It was like watching the Huka Falls when the control gate opens. The flood was powerful, deadly and terrifying. If the door had still been open, the water would be pouring in by now. As it was, the sides of the car were absorbing the force of the water pressure.

There was a sudden loud bang and the car shuddered.

"What the fuck?"

"Some flotsam hit us," I explained. "Just keep driving, for God's sake!" In spite of an effort to sound calm, I could hear my voice come out in a suppressed shriek. Terror clawed at me as I watched the flood shove us sideways.

Beside me Jack kept up a steady stream of "Shit, shit, shit," as he wrestled with the controls. The car slipped, slid and shuddered beneath us as it struggled to gain traction.

Jesus! If Jack and I got swept away it would be such a futile way to die and the possibility was becoming increasingly real. I could feel the vehicle being buffeted by the water. We plunged and shook as the surging river pounded us. I'd have been sea-sick if I hadn't been so terrified. The water was high enough now that waves splashed up against the window beside me. Every passing second increased the amount of water around us, and the rain was still falling.

I watched Jack's white-knuckled hands on the steering wheel as he fought the current. The tyres skidded on the treacherous surface beneath the water, so we made no progress. It felt as if we were hovering in position, in spite of the sound of the engine revving.

I looked back over my shoulder. The other vehicles were several hundred metres away, up on the rise. They might as well have been on a different continent. There was no way they could help us. Anyone venturing into this maelstrom to connect a tow rope would be swept away instantly. Jack and I were on our own. I suppressed an involuntary moan and gripped my hands tightly together to steady myself. If I lost control now I'd never regain it and turning into a babbling idiot would solve nothing.

Abruptly the car lurched backwards over some unseen obstacle. I gasped as it lifted, then crashed down on the far side. Something must have been wedged behind, jamming us. With it gone, we began to move. Slowly, fighting the lateral pull of the waters all the way, Jack backed us up the road and out of the torrent.

Once clear of the flood he stopped and turned to me. We stared at each other for a long minute.

"You OK?" he asked eventually.

I nodded. I found I'd been holding my breath and let it out in a long exhale.

I gave Jack a shaky little grin. "Well done," I said softly, which drew a short choke of laughter from him.

He reached out, took my hand and clasped it firmly. "That was a bit too close for comfort," he remarked.

I curled my fingers into his. His jacket was wet at the wrist, and I realised his clothes were soaked.

"You're wet, you must be frozen."

"What? Oh, I didn't notice. I've been sweating too hard for the last few minutes for that to even register." He reached forward and turned the heating up. My hand felt empty without his covering it. After our close shave with disaster, the tangible reality of him felt good.

"We can chalk that one up as another adventure we've shared."

"Why are adventures always at night and usually involve being cold and wet?" I complained.

"Beats me," he replied. "I'm just glad we survived this one. There was a second or two when I didn't think we would." He gave me a wolfish grin. "I know it would be romantic to die together, but I'd rather put it off for a while."

"Talk about being swept away by passion," I murmured.

Jack turned the car, drove up the road and parked beside the other two vehicles.

Pat wound down his window.

"That was getting a bit close, eh?" I grinned at the understatement, wondering what it would take to shake Pat out of his permanently relaxed poise. Nothing ever seemed to rattle him.

"What happens now?" asked Jack.

"Kevin's just been on the RT. It seems the river's burst the dam upstream and is flooding. They're closing the road from the other side. Well, you saw the state of it. Nothing can get through there safely. We won't be able to get across tonight."

The council worker walked over. "Hi again," he said. "Great night, isn't it?"

At least his oilskins meant he was suitably dressed for the conditions. The rain was pelting down.

"What's the news?" asked Jack.

Kevin shook his head. "Not good. The road's closed. Nothing is going to get across that bridge until it, and the access to it, gets checked out by engineers – and that won't be until tomorrow morning at the earliest. The river will have to go down first, and if this rain keeps up, it could take a couple of days for the levels to drop. It's impossible to know how much damage is being done under all that water. For all we know, the bridge may not even still be there."

There was silence as we absorbed the information.

"But there's an alternative route, isn't there?" I asked.

Pat shook his head. "Nah. There's no way out of this valley apart from the bridge. The other end of this road runs into a big forestry block." He stared blankly out into the darkness. "We're stuck."

"This isn't looking good," said Matt.

"There's nothing we can do about it." Pat had reverted to laconic type.

"Can't we go back to the lodge? Surely they'd put us up –

even if we just doss down in their lounge for the night. At least we'd be warm, dry and safe." Joanne leaned across Pat to speak to us.

I didn't want to go back. The lodge was a lovely place and all that, but there were too many tensions surrounding the people there and I, at least, had outstayed my welcome. I'd rather snuggle down in the car, alone with Jack.

"I guess we'll have to," Jack said before I could say anything. "We're all soaked through. I could use a towel and a place to warm up."

I could hardly complain. I wasn't the one who was wet and cold. I stifled a sigh and sat back.

CHAPTER FOURTEEN

THERE WERE STILL LIGHTS ON INSIDE although it was several minutes before anyone responded to Pat's knocking and opened the door. We waited in the car and watched as he explained our plight. Charles looked across and beckoned us in.

"Looks like we're welcome," said Jack. We ran the short distance through the rain to the entrance.

"We're so sorry," apologised Joanne. "We don't mean to put you to any trouble."

Charles courteously implied the late-night arrival of half a dozen bedraggled visitors was no trouble at all.

"Of course you should have come back here to us. Where else would you go?" he said, smiling at Joanne. "We can easily put you up for the night."

He led us through to the living room where the mah-jong table had been in use. A game had evidently just ended.

"We have some visitors," Charles announced to Wenjun and Mary. "The bridge is out, and they can't get home." They were the only two in the room. Ray had presumably already gone to bed.

"Oh, you poor souls," exclaimed Mary as she jumped to her

feet. "You look frozen."

She rushed out of the room and came back a few minutes later with towels and blankets for the men. "Please, come by the fire," she urged them. "Let me take your jackets and I'll get them dried for you."

All four men looked cold. Matt was noticeably shivering as he pulled his jumper over his head, and Pat looked his age. Even Jack, normally robust, was unusually pale as he towelled his hair and face dry.

"Wrap these around you," Mary instructed, handing out the blankets.

"That feels better," said Matt as he snuggled the rug around himself. He glanced at his father and grinned. "We look like a pack of refugees."

Charles poured generous shots of whisky for us all.

"This will help," he said as he offered them round.

"Thanks," Pat replied and took his first sip.

"It was touch-and-go out there for a while," he said. "Jack had a bit of bother getting his car out of the flood. That water's bloody powerful."

Jack nodded. "It'll take a while for the river to settle and go back down after this," he said. "I hope people downstream got out of its way in time."

There was silence as we considered this.

"If the weather was better, I'd ask Brett to fly you back home," said Charles, "but he couldn't in these conditions. If the weather lifts tomorrow, maybe we can do it then. Your vehicles will be stuck here until they fix the bridge, of course."

"Are you sure there's no other way to cross the river?" I asked. "There's a swing bridge by your yards, isn't there, Pat?"

"Yes. But there's no way to get to it from here unless you bush-wacked your way over the ranges," said Pat.

"That's so," confirmed Charles. "The only transport out of here over the next few days is going to be by helicopter. The forestry block at the end of the road has a runway, and the owner visits occasionally on holiday weekends, but I've only ever seen his small aircraft fly in and out."

My ears pricked up, an automatic reaction to anything aviation related. If there was a plane and a runway, at least we had another way out of this valley. Not that it would do us much good. There was still the issue of getting the cars out.

"I'm afraid you're stuck here," Charles was saying.

He gave a rueful grin. "Who knows what's happened to my own car. It's probably part of the debris being washed down-river by now."

"It's probably what bumped into us," I said. "Something gave us a shove."

"If it's just a matter of cars, then it's not too important, is it?" said Joanne. "I know it's a nuisance, but there's always insurance. I just hope no people get hurt in all of this."

"Or stock," added Pat.

"It's just as well forensics finished their work down by the woolshed today," said Jack. "Trying to keep everything protected from the elements in these conditions would be almost impossible."

"I just want them to tell us whether or not it's Zhang," said Charles. "Ray seems convinced it is, although I can't see how a man we dropped off in Taupo could end up back here."

"Or how he came to be shot," added Joanne.

"What?" The question was explosive.

Mary, who'd been gathering up the wet jackets, straightened abruptly with a gasp and Wenjun was suddenly very still. I glanced at Jack as I realised the police hadn't shared that piece of information with the lodge.

"Shot?" The question shattered the stunned silence. "Are you saying the person had been shot? That it was murder?"

"So the detective said," said Jack, "although he didn't use the term murder, just that a bullet wound had been discovered."

"Why was he speaking to you?" Wenjun's voice was sharp. "What is your interest in this matter?"

"None, aside from being there when Claire discovered the remains," said Jack easily, not responding to the tension in Wenjun's tone. "I know D I Taylor as a colleague, that's all. When we drove past the police cordon this afternoon I said hello, and he mentioned the bullet wound. If they've discovered anything else he didn't say. The forensic team - from ESR- will have taken their samples for examination by now, and until the police get their results, there's unlikely to be much new in the way of evidence."

"This is terrible," said Charles. "Do they know yet how long the body has been there? It must date from before the time the lodge was built. Surely it can't involve us. The last thing we need is scandal and notoriety wrecking our reputation. It could ruin us."

There was no mistaking his frustration and distress.

Wenjun said something in Chinese I assumed was meant to be reassuring. Eventually Charles nodded his head. The rest of us sat in awkward silence.

"I'll go and organise the rooms. I'll get Stephen to help me," Mary said and left the room abruptly. The door swung with force and slammed shut behind her.

"I'm sure it's just a coincidence the remains were found on your land," offered Joanne in an effort to ease the tension. "The police will sort it all out. I wouldn't worry about it. You've got such a lovely place here."

"Thank you," said Charles. "I'm sure you're right." He gave a polite smile, although his voice didn't hold a great deal of conviction.

"Can I offer anyone another drink?" he asked, retreating to the bar. Ian accepted, but the rest of us declined. I noticed Charles poured himself a large glass of whisky as well. Poor guy. He looked really rattled.

I remembered he'd said Wenjun had a financial investment in the lodge and wondered how vulnerable each would be in the fall-out from a scandal.

"Are you feeling warmer now?" Wenjun asked Matt.

He grinned. "I feel like a survivor from the *Titanic*, all wrapped up in a blanket like this. But the warmth is beginning to penetrate, thank you. The whisky helps."

"I'm feeling good now as well," said Jack. "We owe you a great deal."

"Very hospitable," added Joanne. "Mary is wonderful, isn't she? Do you think she needs any help? I'd be happy to lend a hand."

I recognised the kind intent behind their comments. Jack's family were nice people and Charles's misery was automatically bringing out the best in them.

"No. She'll be happier left to organise things her own way," said Charles. He smiled slightly. "It would be a brave person who interfered with Mary and her domain."

"She's a cracker of a worker," said Pat.

The living room door opened again. I suppose we all expected it to be Mary returning, so it was a surprise when, instead, Ray stood in the doorway, his face blank with shock.

"Oh, hello. We thought you'd gone to bed," said Charles. "Would you like a drink?"

Ray looked at him oddly, as if he didn't understand the question and couldn't quite focus.

"The hospital has just called. Lee's dead."

CHAPTER FIFTEEN

THERE WAS A MOMENT'S SILENCE WHILE we all stared at him.

"Oh Ray, that's terrible. What happened? What went wrong?" I blurted.

"They think he had a heart attack, but it's too early to be certain. I must go to him," said Ray. "Oh God, I'll have to phone my mother. What can I tell her? She's still mourning for my father."

"Come and sit down, mate," said Matt, putting his arm around Ray's shoulders and drawing him towards the sofa. "Sit down there. Let Charles get you a drink."

"I can't believe all this is happening," said Ray. "First my father, now Lee. Why?"

Joanne sat beside him patting his hand.

"Tell us what the hospital said when they called you," asked Jack.

"They said they had bad news. That Lee had just passed away. He'd come around from the anaesthetic while I was with him. He was awake, just a bit groggy when I left, but there certainly didn't seem to be any problem at that point. I'd never have come back here otherwise." He shook his head in disbelief.

"Here, drink this." Charles handed him a generous shot of whisky.

Ray stared blankly at the glass in his hand. He made no move to drink from it.

"He was fine when I left. I'm sure he was, or I'd never have come back," he repeated. "And now he's dead." His voice broke on a sob. "What do I tell our mother?" he asked in despair.

"So, what actually happened?" Jack's quiet voice was professionally soothing.

"The nurse doing the rounds checked on him. He'd been drowsy after the operation, but that was quite normal, they said. At dinner time, he ate a small amount and went back to sleep afterwards. They gave him a morphine drip for pain, which he could self-administer, but he barely used it. Everything appeared normal, but next time the nurse looked at him, he was dead. They did CPR but it was too late. He'd already gone."

"That's the thing about heart attacks," Joanne said sympathetically. "They can come on so quickly."

"But there was nothing wrong with his heart," Ray insisted. "He was healthy, fit and young. Why would he have heart problems?"

"Yesterday was a pretty rugged day," Pat said. "A lot more happened to him than just a broken leg. He'd been buried under that slip, and if it hadn't been for Claire and the guy who dug him out, Lee would have suffocated. Maybe the stress of all that took a toll on his heart."

Shit. So much had gone on in the interim, I'd almost forgotten that part. The euphoria of getting Lee out of the slip and safely to hospital had erased the problems we'd faced earlier in the day. A vision of Wu and me frantically digging Lee out of the slip resurfaced. I gazed at my hands, still bruised and grazed.

A hideous possibility occurred to me.

"I gave him CPR," I reminded Ray. "Maybe I caused him some damage?"

"You revived him." Jack was firm. "He'd have died yesterday if you hadn't taken action then. But Pat may have a point. Perhaps that near-death experience put a strain on his system and made him vulnerable to the anaesthetic. You can't take responsibility for that, Claire."

Well, maybe not, and it was supportive of Jack to say so, but the possibility I might have contributed to Lee's death was horrifying.

Ray shook his head and gave me a small reassuring smile. "No, Claire, I'm sure nothing you did yesterday caused this." His gaze returned to the drink he held.

"I can't drink this," he said, and placed it on the table. "I've got to get to the hospital. Can I borrow a car?" he asked.

There was a moment's silence as the rest of us looked at each other.

"I'm sorry, Ray, the roads are closed," explained Charles. "The bridge has been washed out in the flood. There's no way we can leave the valley until the work crews have fixed it."

"What? But I have to go!" Complete disbelief coloured Ray's voice. "There must be a way out of here. I've *got* to get to the hospital."

Charles sighed. "I'll call Brett and see what he says. Flying out of here is the only option at the moment, but I'm fairly certain he won't be able to fly you out tonight. The cloud is right down on the deck."

Ray stared from one to the other of us.

"Surely you must see that I have to get there?" The desperation in his voice was heart wrenching.

Charles had turned away and was speaking into his phone.

"It may not be possible to get you out tonight," said Jack. "We tried to get home earlier ourselves and had to turn back. It's why we're all here. The bridge is the only way into and out of this valley."

"There must be a way," Ray said stubbornly. "This is the twenty-first century. I can't just be marooned in the middle of nowhere."

Charles shook his head as he hung up.

"Sorry, Ray, but Brett says he can't take the helicopter up in this weather. Conditions are way below the legal minima for flying. He can't do it. You'll have to wait until tomorrow."

Ray gave an anguished cry of frustration. "What the fuck am I supposed to do? My brother is dead at the hospital, my mother is in Shanghai and my father has disappeared. Now what do I do? I can't reach any of them."

"You can call your mother," said Joanne. "It won't be very pleasant, but at least you can do that. You'll have to let her know."

Ray took a deep breath and nodded. "I'm sorry if I seem unreasonable. This has all come as a shock."

He reached for his drink and sculled the whisky. "I need to make a few calls," he said as he stood up. "I'll say goodnight."

Joanne smiled and said goodnight, but the rest of us were quiet as Ray left the room.

"Poor guy," muttered Ian. "Things can't get much worse for him, can they?"

Pat gave a grunt.

When Mary and Stephen returned to tell us the rooms were ready, we were sitting in miserable silence. Charles had given up attempting to be a genial host, and no one else was prepared to make idle conversation. Too much had happened over the last two days. I was exhausted and leaning against Jack's shoulder.

"You're all very quiet," Mary remarked, looking round at us. "Is everyone all right?"

"Ray just let us know that his brother died tonight at the hospital," Charles told her. "It's shocked us all."

"A heart attack," Wenjun explained.

Mary looked shaken. "Poor Ray, that's terrible. He must be devastated. First his father, now this."

"Naturally he wants to go to the hospital," Charles said, "but we can't get him there. The weather is too bad to fly. We're all stuck here until the rain eases."

"Oh, that reminds me. Wu isn't in the annexe," Stephen told him. "I knocked on the door to see if he was OK, and when I didn't get a reply, I looked in to check if he needed something for his shoulder. He's not there. He must have gone out. I hope he isn't caught on the wrong side of the river."

"When did he leave?" asked Wenjun sharply. I saw Mary

glance at him with a frown.

"I don't know," Stephen said. "I haven't seen him all day. I assumed he was resting in his room after his accident."

"Mary, when did you see him last?" asked Charles.

"I took lunch in to him just after midday," Mary said. "I've been working since then, so I don't know where he's gone. I hope he's all right."

"Something else to worry about," said Charles gloomily. "I suppose he'll phone us if he gets into difficulty. Is a vehicle missing?"

"I didn't check. I wasn't going out in the rain to count cars."

Charles gave a snort of laughter. "No, I suppose not. The sooner we all get to bed and put this day behind us, the better."

"I've got two rooms ready," Mary said. "I think perhaps Mr and Mrs Crombie in one and Claire and her partner in the other?" She gave me a questioning look. "Is that all right?" I nodded approval.

"I'm sorry," she said to Ian and Matt, "but would you mind if I put you up in the staff annex? We have no more rooms open in the lodge itself, but Stephen's made up a couple of spare beds over there if you're prepared to share a room."

"That's fine," Ian said. "I'm just grateful to be out of the weather and have a bed for the night. You don't snore, do you, Matt?"

"I'll drive you over there now," said Charles.

I gave a sigh of relief when Jack shut our bedroom door and the two of us were alone.

"Tired?" he asked.

"Knackered. But mainly overwhelmed by everything and everybody. I can't believe Lee's dead. That's just awful. Poor Ray."

Jack looked at me closely. "I meant what I said earlier. You did everything you could to save him and his death is not your fault. Don't start beating yourself up over it. You're not responsible for everything, even though you like to think you are."

I gave a twisted smile. "Are you telling me I like to micromanage things?"

"No, you're just bossy," he smiled, then laughed when I stuck my tongue out at him.

"That's better. Now I know you're OK."

We busied ourselves getting ready for bed. It was my second night of being without my own toothbrush. At least I kept my own hairbrush in my bag. Yes, the lodge supplied these items, but who doesn't prefer to use their own stuff? "Maybe I need to start carrying emergency supplies," I muttered as I brushed out my hair. "Deodorant, toothpaste, knickers. This is starting to become a habit."

"Hm," muttered Jack.

"What, you think it's a good idea?"

"No," he said as he got into bed. I snuggled up beside him and he put his arm around me.

"I was just curious where Wu went today and how long he's been gone."

CHAPTER
SIXTEEN

IN SPITE OF THE PREVIOUS NIGHT'S drama we were all up very early.

As so often seems to happen after a disaster, the storm had cleared and the sky was a fresh clear blue. The change from wild weather bomb to warm spring morning was almost too much to absorb. Only the large puddles on the drive showed how much rain had fallen.

Phil arrived while we were having breakfast.

"G'day," he said when Charles showed him into the dining room. "I came up to let everyone know the bridge got washed out last night. I didn't realise you lot were still here."

"We got stranded," said Pat. "Fortunately Charles let us stay. Now we've got to figure out how to get home."

"Well you won't get home via the bridge," Phil said flatly. "My guess is it will be out for weeks. I went down and looked at it first thing and it's a right mess. The river flooded the road, and there are boulders and debris everywhere."

"Have a seat," Charles said, "and help yourself to coffee. Is our land all right?"

"Yes, fortunately all lodge land and the farm is well above the flood line, so we're fine," replied Phil, "but other places won't have been that lucky. Your place should be OK, shouldn't it, Pat?"

"Should be. The sooner I can get back though, and see for myself, the better," grunted Pat.

"What are our options?" asked Jack.

"Well, you could try the old flying fox across the river from the Styles's place if you fancy a thrill. It's about a kilometre down the road," said Phil with a grin on his face, "but I wouldn't recommend it. It was pretty dodgy back when I was a kid."

"No, it would be most unsafe to use that zip-line. I've seen it. Getting Brett to fly you home is the only realistic option," said Charles. "I'll speak to him and see when he can take you."

"Is there absolutely no other way we can get out?" asked Joanne. "It's going to be a right pain if all our vehicles are stuck here. We need them at home."

Charles shook his head. "The road is the only way in."

"What about tracks?" Jack asked Phil. "Didn't you say yesterday there are logging tracks all through these hills and that Pat's place is really only over the ridge as the crow flies? Are they a possibility? Could we give them a try?"

"No way. I was talking about thirty years ago," said Phil with a short laugh. "Me and my mates used to ride them when we were young. They'll be overgrown now. There could be trees across the tracks. And when I said Pat's place was just over the ridge, I was exaggerating slightly – it's wild, rugged country up there. Probably a day's ride on a horse. Quicker obviously in a motor vehicle – but equally, you could get stuck and it would be a sod of a job to get you out."

"We've got some fairly grunty four-wheel drives," Pat reminded him. "Isn't it worth a try? The bridge could take weeks to fix, and I've got a mob of sheep waiting in the yards. We can't run a farm without vehicles."

"Why don't we at least go and see?" asked Matt.

"I'm up for it," said Ian with a grin. "You've got a quad bike, haven't you, Phil? We could use that. You must have one here as well?" he asked Charles.

Charles hesitated and shrugged. "It doesn't sound very safe, but I suppose you could give it a go if you're that desperate to get the vehicles out. We've got a couple of bikes. You're welcome to borrow them if you think it's worthwhile."

We all eventually agreed that Matt, Ian, Pat and Phil would take the quad bikes and investigate the state of the track and whether getting the farm vehicles over them was a viable option. The rest of us would leave by helicopter later in the day after Brett had dropped Ray at the hospital.

"Thank you," said Ray. The initial shock hearing of Lee's death had worn off and he looked less wild-eyed and distraught this morning. Overnight his face had settled into sad, haggard lines of grief. It must have been a rugged night for him, coping with his own misery and then having to tell his mother that her son was dead.

"I don't know how long I'll need to be in Hamilton," he said. "I suppose I'll have to make arrangements with the hospital. My mother wants Lee's body to go home to China and it could take some time for me to organise this and find out what formalities are involved."

Charles was adamant. "Brett will stay with you until you're finished. When you've done everything you need to, he'll bring you back here. Don't worry about that."

"But I might hold Claire and her friend up."

"We have plenty of time," I said. Joanne murmured her agreement. "First we've got to find out whether the men can get through the tracks anyway. Then, if they're successful, we may all be able to drive out. Don't worry about us."

The men left to get ready. I half-thought Jack would want to go with them, but he shook his head.

"These guys know their way around the country and the bush. They handle quad bikes every day over all sorts of terrain. I'd just get in the way." He gave me a wry grin. "I wouldn't be much use to them."

"Townie," I teased.

We waited in the living room. Ray was wandering around in the hallway talking into his mobile. We left him in peace. Mary offered us coffee, then departed, promising to return when the chef had finished making a batch of biscuits.

We were a quiet group, content to sit in silence.

When his phone rang, Charles answered the call and walked away from us into his office across the hall.

Mary returned with freshly baked cookies and handed them around. It was far too close to breakfast for anyone to be remotely hungry, but we nibbled on them politely.

Charles had been gone some time, but when he returned he looked troubled.

"That was the police," he said. "They wanted to tell us the remains in the swamp cannot possibly be Ray's father. It's a woman. They plan to be here later today to question lodge staff. They want to see whether anyone can identify things they found on the body."

There was a horrified gasp from Mary and I turned in time to see the biscuits slide dangerously across the plate. I took it from her, but I'm not sure she noticed as she launched into a furious tirade in Chinese directed at Charles.

The rest of us sat watching in horrified fascination as she screamed at him. I thought I caught the name Li Na.

Ray was now standing in the doorway listening to the tirade.

Charles kept shaking his head and expostulating. I gathered he was defending himself against whatever she was accusing him of.

Finally, Mary gave a great sob and fled the room, leaving Charles standing very still and pale. He turned and realised we were watching.

"I'm sorry you had to see that," he said to us eventually. "She was upset." And on that complete understatement he retreated to his office, leaving us staring at each other.

"What was she saying?" Jack asked Ray.

"She accused Charles of murdering a woman called Li Na," said Ray. He was visibly shaken. "I hoped – no, I thought – the remains would be those of my father. But they're not. Why would Mary suggest Charles had anything to do with it?"

"She told me Li Na had left here," I said.

"Mary said Li Na never said goodbye. Just left. Disappeared

without warning. And it was Charles who told her that Li Na had gone back to China after a quarrel with Wenjun. Now she questions that. It's why she was shouting at Charles."

"Jesus," said Joanne. "This place is toxic. The sooner we're out of here the better. Let's hope the guys find a way through the hill tracks. Ian was right. It *is* like the Bermuda Triangle, with missing people and unexplained disappearances."

"Stall turns," I said.

"What?"

"It's an aerobatic manoeuvre. You fly in one direction, climb the plane until it's vertical then cartwheel sideways down again. Now you're going in the opposite direction to the way you started. It's what's happening here. Just as soon as you think you've got a fix on the situation, it all goes topsy-turvy."

The men were organised for the recce into the bush by nine. I watched for a while as they loaded up the bikes with chainsaws, crow-bars, chains and spades. Jack helped them tie the gear on.

"That should do it." Phil gave an approving nod as the last straps were tightened.

"You look as if you're going on a major expedition," I remarked.

Pat smiled at me. "You better believe it, girlie. We don't know what the tracks are going to be like. Better be prepared for the worst. Yesterday's earthquake may have shaken things up as well."

I wondered just how bad conditions might be up in the hills. At the very least, the tracks would be wet and slippery.

"Take care," Joanne said, giving Pat a casual peck on the cheek as he left.

"You seem remarkably calm," I said.

"Sweetie, I couldn't stop them if I tried. Matt and Ian are gagging for an adventure, and Pat isn't going to want to be left behind. Phil's only protesting because he's not certain they can get through. Frankly, I'm surprised Jack hasn't insisted on going."

"He thought he might hold them up. As he said, they know the country and conditions. He claimed to be a townie."

Joanne snorted. "A pretty competent townie, if you ask me."

She looked at me narrowly. "Is it serious between you two?"

I felt a flush of colour rise in my cheeks.

"Sort of," I said hesitantly. "It's still early days for us both. This holiday has been the longest time we've spent together, so a lot of it is in the 'trial-and-error' phase. I like him a lot, but I don't know how he feels about me."

Despite my efforts to be casual, I could hear the resentment in my voice. Was it too much to expect him to reciprocate my impetuous statement and say he loved me? Tit for tat seemed fair. Instead I felt I was dangling in no-man's (make that no-woman's) land.

Joanne looked at me. "You don't know?" Her tone was incredulous. "What's the matter with you, woman? Every time he looks at you he lights up. He can hardly keep a smile off his face when you walk into the room."

Her words surprised me. Jack always seemed so damned cool and relaxed. I certainly hadn't noticed any overt display of affection.

"He hasn't said anything to me." Again I registered my sulky tone and winced. How infantile could I be?

"He's a bloke, Claire. He's a Kiwi male. What are you expecting? Hearts and flowers? However much he claims to be a townie, I doubt he's going to write you a sonnet to tell you how he feels."

I gave a reluctant smile. "Maybe not."

"If he's anything like his Uncle Pat he'll *show* you how he feels, not tell you. You just have to read the signs. If he looks like he loves you and acts like he loves you, then what have you got?"

"A duck," I said and laughed at her look of incomprehension.

We were interrupted by the bikes revving up and paused to wave to the men as they headed off down the drive.

Joanne shrugged. "If we're going to be stuck here, I'm taking advantage of the situation and getting back to that sauna," Joanne said. "I might as well pamper myself while I've got the chance. Do you want to join me?"

I shook my head. "Nah. I'll see what Jack's doing first, or maybe go for a walk. I feel a bit cooped up at the moment and the grounds *are* lovely."

Jack, it turned out, had offered to help Charles clear a fallen tree that was partly blocking the drive. Wu, who would normally have managed the project, was still missing, presumed stranded on the far side of the river.

"I won't be long," he assured me. "Stay with Joanne and don't get into trouble."

I snorted.

Deprived of Jack's company, but in no mind to help him haul timber out of the way, I took myself off for a solitary stroll.

Joanne's words had both encouraged and depressed me. I wanted to believe she had picked up clues about Jack's feelings for me. At the same time, I found myself irritated and unconvinced that a man as urbane and charming as Jack would be inarticulate when it mattered.

A Kiwi male he might be, but Jack wasn't his uncle or his cousin. If Joanne had been describing Matt, I'd have agreed with her, but I had good reason to be aware that Jack was a very good communicator.

He'd told me once he wanted a less exciting girlfriend, but since we'd known each other we had lurched from crisis to crisis together, usually over something I was involved in. Even Roger, my boss, described me as a magnet for trouble. And here we were, once again in a situation associated with a dead body. Two, I suppose, if you included Lee's unexpected death.

I stomped along the garden path feeling thoroughly miserable. If the weather gods had been kind, Jack and I would have been long gone from this valley, not coping with earthquake, floods and washed-out bridges. What next, I asked myself gloomily – fire? It was all too apocalyptic for one woman to cope with. The sooner I was back at work dealing with the simple laws of physics pertaining to aviation, the better.

When I looked up, I discovered that without conscious intent I was following the path Jack and I had taken the previous day.

CHAPTER SEVENTEEN

EVEN UNDER OVERCAST CONDITIONS YESTERDAY THE garden had been pretty. Today, in the fresh morning sunlight, it glowed like a jewel. There were some silver puddles on the gravel tracks, the lawns gleamed emerald green and the small drops of water on ferns and shrubs that lined the path refracted the light and sparkled like diamonds.

When I reached the clearing I took a seat on the bench and watched the flowing water. This morning the water level was much higher and the little stream was turbulent, rushing around and over the artfully arranged rocks and cascading in waterfalls between larger boulders. As the water tumbled its way through the glade, the effect was wilder and more dramatic than yesterday, but still no less charming.

My imagination churned in time with the water. I thought of the woman who had designed this lovely place. Was Mary right, and was it Li Na's body I'd stumbled upon in the swamp? The woman in the photograph was beautiful in her own right. Li Na, Zhang and Wenjun – I tried to make sense of them and their connection.

Zhang and Wenjun had ridden on last year's muster. They'd been heard to argue, and Zhang had subsequently disappeared.

Charles had told me that Li Na and Wenjun had been an item before they too quarrelled. Assuming the body was Li Na's, had the argument been severe enough to have led to her death? It seemed reasonable to assume the woman in the swamp had been murdered. Alastair Taylor said the skull had a bullet hole in it. Could it have been suicide? In which case, they must have found a gun close by.

The three names intertwined. Li Na, Zhang and Wenjun. Two of the three had disappeared.

Mary claimed Charles had lied and told her Li Na had gone back to China.

Which then raised the question, did Charles know what had happened to Zhang and Li Na? Was he responsible for their disappearance?

I shuddered. Joanne was right. The lodge *was* toxic. No wonder I felt on edge.

I felt a sudden acute wish not to be alone. I stood up and went in search of Jack.

I reasoned the fastest way to find him would be to carry on along the track we'd followed the day before. It led, via the staff quarters, back to the drive where Jack would be working and was a quicker option than retracing my steps to the lodge.

I walked upstream along the bush trail. The storm had dumped twigs and branches on the track which I had to step around. In a couple of places puddles and muddy edges made the going hazardous. I picked my way with care.

For most of the way, the sound of rushing water from the stream beside me drowned out other noises, but as I turned the final corner I heard the motorised sound of heavy hangar doors being moved.

I stopped at the edge of the clearing.

The doors were already half-way open and slowly sliding further apart. Brett sat on the idling tractor in the space between them, clearly waiting for them to open completely. As they got wider, I saw the tractor was hitched up to the helicopter trailer. I'd been right when I told Jack that the chopper was kept locked away safely when not in use.

Brett didn't notice me as he focused on the task in hand. I was amused to note I'd no more desire to speak to him than he did to me. I stayed where I was, partially concealed by bushes, as he carefully towed the trailer out. The hangar was large, but so was the aircraft, and Brett was taking due care not to damage his precious Eurocopter.

Once he was well clear of the doorway, Brett stopped and jumped down, leaving the tractor idling as he went back to the building. The noise of the tractor's engine meant I couldn't hear, but it was obvious Brett was talking to someone I couldn't see.

Eventually Brett returned and drove away up the track. He must have been getting ready for Ray's trip to Hamilton.

Once he was out of the way I strolled down to take a look at the hangar. It was about the same size as the one we had at work, but Kapiti Aviation had several aircraft to park up, as well as our Hughes 300. A hangar this size simply for one helicopter seemed excessive, even if the Eurocopter was a substantial aircraft. I was curious about what other machinery was stored in it.

I had almost reached the doors when a man stepped out. He gave a slight start as he registered my presence.

"Wu!" I exclaimed in surprise. "I thought you were stranded on the wrong side of the river. Have you been here all the time?"

His eyes flickered and I wondered again how much English he actually understood. His silence conveyed clearly enough that he wasn't pleased to see me.

I gave a slight shrug. "Oh well. Good to see you're here. How's the shoulder?"

Again no reply. I gave him a polite nod, then stepped past him smartly to look inside the hangar.

My move took him by surprise. He'd obviously expected me to turn and leave; consequently, I was well inside before he managed to catch up with me.

He subjected me to a torrent of indignant Chinese as he tried to hustle me out. He could have been raising Health and Safety concerns, but who knows? It was time for some reciprocal incomprehension. I gave him a blank look and carried on with my inspection of the hangar.

It was at least the size of the one we had at work. This was a steel sided construction designed to hold large machinery. A digger and a bulldozer were parked on the left. On the right was a service pit with steps down into it. Above this hung chains and winches. I realised this was as much a working garage as it was a hangar.

Against the wall was a work bench with professional-grade tools neatly hung above it on a board. Health and Safety notices were pinned up alongside whiteboards with various cryptic comments relating to the work they did here. Beside the bench I recognised an air compressor and welding gear. *They must do all the lodge's mechanical maintenance here on site. I suppose it makes sense. – they're a long way from a local garage.*

Towards the rear of the building two steel trap-doors were set in the floor, presumably concealing some other storage or service facility beneath. Along the back wall windows allowed the office behind them to look into the main hangar. It was a very impressive set-up, and I made a point of telling Wu so with approving smiles and gestures.

Wu was making it very clear I wasn't welcome. He hadn't actually laid hands on me, but I felt I'd pushed his tolerance as far as it would go. With one arm still in a sling, his physical options were limited, but he was making the most of his verbal weapons. The tirade had stopped, but he was speaking to me now in short, sharp, angry sentences, each interspersed with a jab of his index finger. I thought it time to leave.

"Thank you so much for showing me around," I said. "It's a great facility."

I could feel his eyes burning a hole between my shoulder blades as I walked away. I'd been discourteously pushy, but his unpleasantness seemed disproportionate. I was, however tenuously, a guest at the lodge. He must surely be used to other nosy visitors.

Jack was hard at work clearing the tree. I took a moment to admire his unexpected skill with a chainsaw. I like competent men, and our relationship was still fresh enough to discover new and unexpected insights into each other's experience and abilities.

Stephen worked with him, stacking the cut logs onto a trailer. The debris was obvious here, with twigs and leaves scattering the drive. Most of the work had been done, and the log Jack laboured over was a stubborn bit of stump. As I watched, the blade bisected the wood and Jack straightened, turning off the saw.

"Hey, you," I said, then realised he couldn't hear me through the protective helmet and earmuffs. I moved nearer. He caught sight of me, smiled and removed the helmet.

"Hey, you," I said again.

"Hey yourself," he said. "What have you been up to?"

"I went for a walk past the glade we were in yesterday and ended up at the hangar. Guess who was there? Wu! So he *wasn't* caught the other side of the river last night. I had a good look round the hangar while I was there as well."

"Wu showed you around his hangar?" Stephen's tone was incredulous. "How did you achieve that? He never lets anyone in there. It's his private little kingdom."

"He didn't really show me around," I confessed. "I just walked in. He was trying to say something to me, but I couldn't understand him. I ignored him and had a nosy around. It's an incredible set-up in there. Part hangar, part engineering shop. It's got hoists and pulleys, pits and all sorts. My boss would be jealous if he ever saw it."

Stephen looked impressed. "Good on you. You've been further in than I've ever managed."

"Brett was there getting the helicopter out," I said. "Maybe it's just you he doesn't like, Stephen."

Stephen laughed. "Well, Wu and Brett are good mates, so I suppose it's different."

"Hang on," I said. "If they're mates, does Brett speak Chinese? I didn't realise that."

"No." Stephen sounded surprised. "They speak English. I wouldn't think Brett knows Chinese."

"But I didn't think Wu spoke English? He made it quite clear to me that he doesn't."

Stephen snorted. "He's probably just being difficult, pretending not to understand. I don't think Wu likes most people."

He nodded to Jack. "I'll drive the trailer up. Do you guys want a lift?"

"We'll walk," Jack said abruptly, and waited until Stephen had driven away.

"What the hell were you thinking of?"

"What do you mean?" I asked, surprised.

"I told you to stay with Joanne."

"So?" I didn't like his tone, let alone that he was frowning at me. "I wanted to go out, that's all. Joanne wanted another sauna. What's your problem?"

"Didn't you hear Mary this morning?" Jack said in exasperation. "Those remains belonged to a woman, and Mary was throwing some nasty accusations at Charles. We don't know whether the lodge is involved or not, but at least use some common sense and don't go wandering around on your own."

"I hardly think I'm in danger," I retorted. "No-one's got any reason to attack me."

"Wu has, by the sound of it, if you forced your way into his hangar."

"I might have annoyed him, but that doesn't mean he's going to harm me. He just thinks I'm nosy."

"You've no idea what he thinks. You've already said you weren't certain about him on the day of the muster. Why put yourself at risk?"

"Well, I don't consider I was at risk."

"You've no way of being certain of that. A man is missing, a woman has been murdered and it looks very likely the lodge is implicated in some way. Use your head and don't go off on your own, particularly if you're going to annoy the staff."

"You're over-reacting," I said shortly. "I'm quite capable of looking after myself."

"I'm not bloody over-reacting. All I'm saying is keep yourself safe. We don't understand what's going on here."

We weren't quite quarrelling, but it was the nearest we'd come to it yet and we walked back to the lodge in uncomfortable silence.

We were both off kilter. Too much had happened. Jack and I'd had a lovely holiday and rounded it up with a bit of adventure. But now it was too much. I was losing my sense of proportion. We needed a return to normality. I needed to go home.

I decided I missed my home, my cat and my job. I kicked moodily at the leaves and twigs scattered on the drive. Until the trail blazers on the quads came back to tell us it was safe to drive the tracks, we couldn't even resolve our situation by leaving.

I glanced at Jack. He walked, hands jammed into his jacket pockets, his head down. I decided it was time to offer an olive branch.

"Why would Wu pretend he doesn't understand English? After all, *we* don't care whether he does or doesn't. It makes no difference. It's just been a pain trying to communicate with him in sign language."

Jack glanced up. "I've been thinking about that one. I don't think his pretence has been directed at us. We're just collateral. It was Ray and Lee he wanted to deceive."

"Why?"

"Because if they thought he couldn't understand them, they might say something in English that he wanted to overhear?"

"Lee thought Wu knew who they were and why they'd come to the lodge," I said. "In which case . . ."

"In which case he wanted to hear what they said about Zhang."

We walked for a while, both considering the implications.

"I agree this sounds like Wu is somehow involved in Zhang's disappearance, but does it mean Wu knows what happened, or did he want to find out if Lee and Ray knew anything about it?"

Jack gave a short grunt of affirmation. "I would say it's obvious the brothers didn't know what happened to their father. Otherwise they wouldn't have visited the lodge and they certainly wouldn't have tried to stay here incognito."

"Which means Zhang's disappearance involved Wu, and he wanted to make sure Lee and Ray didn't suspect him – or at least he wanted to know if they *did*."

"And that," said Jack, "is a good argument in favour of

keeping out of his way and not going off on your own."

CHAPTER EIGHTEEN

RAY JOINED US AT LUNCH AND took the seat beside me at the table. His trip to Hamilton hadn't eventuated. "The hospital says there has to be a post-mortem before Lee's body can be released," he explained. "There wasn't any point going to the hospital if I couldn't see Lee, so I've spent the morning phoning funeral directors, airlines and going through the legal process which will allow me to take him home."

"It must be awful," I sympathised. "How's your mother?"

"Hysterical," Ray said. "I've phoned her a couple of times, but she can't stop crying. Her sister is with her, but I need to get back home as soon as possible."

I nodded. "Dealing with all the red tape can't be easy."

"It's a nightmare," he said. "My English is fine for most purposes but dealing with bureaucracy is difficult in any language, and now I have to cope with the paperwork involved in transporting a body. Apparently Lee will have to be embalmed before he can be taken on the plane. There's a lot to deal with."

He gave me a rueful look. "I feel incredibly alien here."

Lunch was a quiet affair. None of us felt like being chatty. Charles and Wenjun asked a few questions about how we'd all spent our morning, but although Joanne and Jack both replied, the conversation languished. It was obvious we were all simply going through the motions. Charles looked strained and unhappy, and we ended up eating in silence. It was an uncomfortable meal and I was glad when it ended.

Mary served coffee and disappeared as soon as lunch was over.

I curled up in a seat by the window and read while Jack and Joanne played Scrabble.

It was after lunch before Pat and the others returned.

"We're back," Pat announced.

Charles emerged from his office to greet them.

"Did you make it? Can we get home?" Joanne asked excitedly.

Pat frowned. "It's a bit gnarly in places, but I reckon we'll get the vehicles through safely enough with a bit more bush-bashing."

"Woo-hoo! Let's go then," said Joanne. "I can't wait to get home." She registered Charles's presence. "I'm sorry. I didn't mean to suggest that you haven't been the most generous and hospitable of hosts," she rushed to assure him, "but we've trespassed on your hospitality long enough, and I'm worried about our own place and our animals. I want to check it out and make sure everything is OK before I relax."

Charles gave a slight smile and waved away her apology.

"I understand completely, and I would feel the same if our positions were reversed."

Joanne smiled. "Then what's keeping us? Let's load up and go."

Pat gave a quiet cough. "Well, that's the thing," he said. "I'd much prefer it if you and Claire didn't come with us on this trip. As I said, it's still a bit gnarly, and the track's muddy and churned up in places. It's not going to be a joy ride. I'm fairly confident we can get through, but I'd feel much better if I didn't have to worry about you two."

He turned to Charles. "Would it be possible for Claire and Joanne to stay here this afternoon until we're through the bush track and safely back on the road the other side of the ridge? It would take a weight off my mind. Then perhaps you'd be prepared to get them helicoptered home? We'd pay for it, of course."

"No, no." Charles shook his head. "There's no need to talk about payment. We're neighbours and help each other out. Right?"

He smiled at me and Joanne. "Of course you are welcome to stay – although," he added after a glance at Joanne's face, "I understand how hard it is for you to be patient."

I thought I heard Joanne grind her teeth in frustration. Her face was a study as she managed to combine glaring at her husband, with smiling politely at Charles.

"Thank you, Charles. But darling, I'd much rather come with you. I promise we won't be in the way."

Pat shook his head. "Not possible, Jo. I don't want the men distracted looking after you two. I want their hands on the wheel and their minds on the track. If something goes wrong, they'll need all their concentration to correct it. You wouldn't mean to be in the way, but you'd skew their focus at the wrong moment."

I shared Joanne's frustration. I'd much rather be bounced around in the seat of a car struggling along muddy tracks, than stay here any longer. I glanced at Pat's face. It wore the same steely resolve he'd shown yesterday when he'd hustled me off my horse and into the helicopter with Charles. Clearly his modus operandi in any action was to clear camp followers out of the line of fire as quickly and efficiently as possible.

Joanne tried a few pleas, but if anything, Pat grew more intractable. There was a certain mulish tightening around his mouth that suggested he wasn't having any argument.

I looked across at Jack, who raised his eyebrows at me and gave a slight shrug. As clearly as if he'd spoken, he told me this wasn't our fight. We'd do as we were told.

I sighed and saw Jack grin. I scowled back. It was fine for him to be cheerful. I'd have laid good money down that he'd be included in the adventure while Joanne and I would be left there twiddling our thumbs.

"Matt, you'll come with me," ordered Pat. "Jack, you can come second. Ian, bring up the rear if you would. Your old Land

Rover is probably the toughest vehicle we've got. I want us to stay in visual contact so we can help each other out if we hit a snag. Equally, don't drive up the arse of the car in front. Keep enough space to accelerate and manoeuvre as needed. Any questions?"

Jack and Ian shook their heads.

Pat turned to Joanne and me. "It should take us about three hours, but we've got plenty of light. If Charles can get you dropped back to the farm by five o'clock, we'll see you there."

"Not a problem," said Charles.

Pat gave Joanne a smile as he turned away.

"OK. Let's get going."

He led the way through the door and Charles went out with them to wave goodbye.

"See you later. Don't get into any trouble," Jack said, giving my shoulder a brief squeeze as he followed Ian and Matt out.

"Bastards," I heard Joanne mutter as they left.

"I know what you mean," I murmured.

We looked at each other, sharing a moment of frustration and female solidarity, before she grinned.

"Bloody men," she said at last. "Always think they know what's best."

She gave a resigned sigh. "What are you like at Scrabble?"

CHAPTER NINETEEN

JOANNE AND I PLAYED TWO ROUNDS of Scrabble. At least the game kept us occupied, although neither of us showed much enthusiasm. My thoughts were with the men making their way up through the bush and wishing I was with them. I didn't underestimate how difficult the drive might be – I'd had a taste of the countryside on the muster. However much horsepower the cars had, it would be manoeuvrability and driver skill which would count in the end.

Sometime later I glanced up through the windows and saw Ray standing outside. It looked as if he was going for a stroll, and I realised neither Jack nor I had told him our suspicions about Wu. It probably wasn't a good idea for him to be wandering around by himself.

"I'm going out," I told Joanne.

"Now?"

"With Ray," I explained. "He's outside. I won't be on my own. I just think he could do with some company."

She hesitated. "Are you sure I can't tempt you to a rematch? I'm two up on you."

"I was just lulling you into a false sense of security, but I was going to win in the long run," I teased.

"Oi, I don't think so. I'm way ahead of you at the moment."

I smiled. "Let's wait and see how it pans out if we have a rematch, when I'm concentrating on the game. Do you want to come with us?" I asked.

"Nah, I'll stay here and read. Ray's grief probably needs one-on-one time and you know him better than me. Enjoy your walk," she said.

I caught up with Ray by the croquet lawn where he'd stopped.

"Mind if I join you?" I asked.

"What? No, of course not." Ray gestured towards the lawn. "Lee and I played a game here the first day we arrived. It seems incredible that he's gone. I can't get my head around it."

"I felt like that when my mum died. I'd see her at the shops, or out on the street, and wave before I'd realise it was someone else. It took me ages to get used to her not being at the other end of the phone."

"I can't believe it was a heart attack. He was too young, too fit," Ray said fretfully.

"I assume they'll call you after the post-mortem and let you know what happened?" I asked.

He nodded.

"Whatever the cause, he's still gone." Ray gave a bitter laugh. "I'm going to miss him. Our whole business is going to miss him. Lee was very like our father, and when Father disappeared, Lee was the one who held the company together. I'm just a glorified accountant really, only useful for the money side of things. He built networks of people. He remembered contacts he made – their names, families, interests. He had a phenomenal memory for faces and names. He even recognised Wenjun when they were introduced."

"They'd met before?" I asked, surprised.

"So Lee said. When Lee was at a trade conference with our father. Wenjun was there to talk about China's gold purchasing policy. Lee said he was certain he went by a different name then. He wasn't sure he was right of course, but he did say he wondered why a prominent man would have changed his name. It was what Lee was researching on the computer the night before the muster. I think it was why he was so concerned when he thought someone had been snooping."

I remembered Lee having mentioned something along these lines on the muster.

"He didn't tell you what the original name was?"

Ray shook his head. "If he did, I don't recall it." He gave me a sheepish look. "We were going under assumed names ourselves and I was more concerned with our father's disappearance. If Wenjun also had a secret, it didn't seem very important."

We walked together for a while, both deep in our own thoughts. I wondered how Jack and the others were getting on.

"I discovered something odd today," I said eventually. "I thought Wu didn't speak English."

Ray glanced at me. "He doesn't."

"But he does. Stephen told Jack and me. He said Brett and Wu were friends. I was surprised and asked if Brett spoke Chinese. Stephen said, no, Wu speaks English."

Ray frowned. "Are you sure? He didn't seem to understand anything Lee or I said in English."

"But that's the point," I explained. "Jack thinks Wu wanted to eavesdrop on what you and Lee were talking about. As you thought he couldn't understand, you might say something about your father without realising he was listening. Remember how you thought everyone knew who you and Lee were before you told Charles your real name? I bet it was Wu who told them."

"They must have been suspicious from when we first arrived, though," said Ray thoughtfully, "because the deception was there from the very beginning."

"Maybe they were just being wary. After all, Zhang disappears – a year later two young men of an age to be his sons turn up. It's not difficult to research people on Wikipedia, and your father was a prominent man, wasn't he? There's likely an article about him online. They'd probably expected someone from the family to turn up. It wouldn't be hard to put two and two together."

We'd reached the place where the path divided.

"Where would you like to go?" asked Ray.

"Not that way," I said, indicating the path I'd taken earlier.

"It's a bit muddy. Let's try going left. I don't know where it goes, but it'll probably be better underfoot."

The gravel path wound across swathes of lawn, gradually turning towards the front of the lodge. I hadn't seen it outside from this angle before. The stone was a warm honey colour in the afternoon sunlight. The lawns came almost to the edge of the building. With delight I saw a peacock strutting across the green.

"This is such a heavenly looking place," I sighed to Ray. "It's hard to believe anything could go wrong here, it's so peaceful."

Ray's grunt was non-committal.

"Maybe there's nothing wrong here. It might all be coincidence. Maybe Wu was just curious about you. Maybe the woman was a suicide. Just a sad, personal story that doesn't involve anyone else."

Ray shook his head. "There are too many unexplained incidents. You forget, Wu tried to attack Lee on the morning of the muster. He pushed him deliberately into the tangle of creeper. I'm certain it wasn't an accident, whatever Lee said. If Pat hadn't come back to get us, Lee could easily have been killed. Wu chose where the track was at its steepest. If the horse had panicked and Lee had fallen down that cliff it was unlikely he would have survived."

"But why?" I objected. "What possible reason could Wu have?"

"I've no idea," said Ray. "I can only report what I saw. We were in a risky situation and Wu tried to profit from it. Likewise, if you hadn't been there with Wu when Lee was found after the earthquake, I don't believe Lee would have lived then."

"When I first saw Wu I wondered what he was trying to hammer with the stone," I said. "But when I got there Wu helped me dig Lee out, so I gave him the benefit of the doubt. It's possible he was trying to break up some of the bigger rubble. He only had one workable arm, so it kind of makes sense."

"We'll never know," Ray said bleakly. "Lee's dead anyway and nothing will change that now." He turned away. "I only hope they release his body quickly so I can take him back to China." I heard his anguish and my eyes teared up automatically in response. We walked on in silence until we heard the beat of rotor blades. I looked up as a red and white helicopter flew up the valley and over the lodge.

"It must have landed on the helipad," I said as the noise faded out a few minutes later. "At least we've still got some contact with the outside world, even if we can't cross the bridge."

The path we were on forked again.

"Which way this time?" I asked.

Ray shrugged. "Right. The other looks as if it goes back to the lodge and I'd prefer to be away from there for a while."

"Fair enough." The new track bent to the right and disappeared behind a small shrubbery.

"Ray!" We turned as Stephen came jogging up behind us. "I've been sent to find you. It was just good luck I saw you two out of the window. The police are here and want to speak to you."

"To me?" asked Ray.

"Yeah. I'll take you back to them," said Stephen.

Ray looked at me and raised an eyebrow.

"You go," I said. "I'll make my own way back. I'll just see where this track goes to. I'm too keyed up worrying whether the guys are OK and how soon Joanne and I can leave. I'm not ready to go and settle down to a good book indoors. I'll see you shortly."

I followed the path through some bushes and heard a startled squawk and a flapping of wings as I disturbed a tui feeding on the early flowers of the kowhai trees. A few metres further on, the path stopped. I sat on the conveniently placed bench and looked past the fence at the farm-land beyond. Half a dozen cattle stared back at me curiously from the adjoining paddock. I had reached the end of the gardens. Even on the lodge side of the fence the grass was longer and the garden rather less well manicured than the rest of the grounds. I suspected this was an area of the estate where few visitors came.

It was lovely to be alone for a few minutes. I felt for Ray, but his grief had tugged at my own emotions. With him gone, a weight lifted, and I experienced a guilty sense of relief.

Somewhere in the hills behind me, Jack and the others would be struggling to get the vehicles through the rough tracks. With any luck they'd be successful, and within the next hour or so Joanne and I would be flown back to the farm, leaving this place and all its unanswered mysteries behind.

I sat back, closed my eyes and let the peace of the countryside soothe out the crinkles and tensions of the last few days.

CHAPTER TWENTY

I HAD A FEW MOMENTS ENJOYING the peace before a troubled voice in my sub-conscious began nagging at me. I was doing, it told me, precisely what Jack had warned against – being alone.

I mentally shrugged my shoulders. I didn't take Jack's concerns seriously. I wasn't a risk to anyone at the lodge, so it was unlikely I was in danger, regardless of the mysterious disappearances of Zhang and Li Na. Even so, to my irritation, I couldn't repress a childish feeling of guilt as if I was doing something naughty.

I checked my watch – 4. It was time for me to return to Joanne anyway. With any luck by the time I made it back I'd find Brett ready to fly us home.

I'd reached the croquet lawn when I heard my name being called and turned to see Mary coming towards me.

"I've been looking for you," she said.

"You've found me," I smiled. I waited to hear what she wanted, but instead she fell into step beside me.

"You seemed upset earlier," I prompted after a few moments' silence.

She nodded. "I …" she started then abruptly cut herself off.

She caught my glance and bit her lip. "I don't know where to start," she said. "I need your advice."

I looked at her in surprise. Her uncertainty was uncharacteristic. Mary was always poised and collected.

"I don't know that I can advise you about anything," I said, "but I'm happy to listen."

"There's no one else I can talk to. Everyone works for the lodge and I don't know who to trust. I'm too frightened to talk to anyone here. You're a stranger, and a woman."

I took a breath. "I'm all that," I agreed. Her words made me pause for a moment.

If she was afraid, or at least thought she had reason to be so, then it reinforced Jack's warnings. On the other hand, if she was going to tell me what had been going on here and throw some light on what had happened to Zhang and Li Na, then it was too good an opportunity to turn down.

"So, what is it you want to tell me?"

She hesitated. "It would be best perhaps if I showed you, then you can give me your advice. Follow me please."

"Where are we going?"

"Quickly now." She looked back at the building behind us. "We mustn't be seen."

"This is a bit cryptic," I observed. But I let her lead me back along the path I'd followed that morning, through the glade and along the bush track towards the hangar.

She stopped by the door which, as usual, was locked.

I was just about to point this out to her when she floored me by rummaging around in her pocket and producing a key.

"You have a key to the hangar?" I asked in surprise. "I assumed only Wu would hold the key."

"Both he and Brett have keys," she said. "This is Wu's. I took it from his room."

Was it possible she didn't know he'd been there this morning? I wondered whether I should tell her I'd seen him.

She opened the door and stepped inside.

"Come in," she said. "I'll shut the door so no one knows we're in here."

I was beginning to wonder what exactly we were up to.

"Should we be here?" I asked.

Mary gave a short sniff. "Wu is so secretive about this place that I got curious. Now I understand why."

She led the way to the rear of the hangar and stopped by the big metal trap doors in the floor and gave one a tug.

"Help me lift them," she asked. "I'll grab a wrench to give us leverage."

I moved up beside her. Together we levered and lifted the doors up and laid them flat on the ground. I stared down into the pit that we'd exposed.

There were steps at the far end leading down into a kind of bunker. Otherwise the space was completely empty.

"There's nothing here."

"Wait," said Mary. "We have to climb down."

I watched her make her way down the steps.

"Why?" I asked.

"Come on," she urged, "and I'll show you."

I descended onto the third step down and waited She was still holding the wrench and fumbled a little as she used her free hand to pull the keys out of her pocket again. She pressed a small device attached to the ring and I realised it was a remote control. She pointed it at the blank wall in front of her.

"I discovered this by chance," she said. "I pressed this button and heard a door move. It took me a while to find out where the noise was coming from. Then I investigated down here."

The control mechanism squeaked and rattled as the whole side of the bunker slowly slid sideways.

"Look," Mary commanded, pointing into the cavity.

I stepped down beside her.

"My God, what the hell is that smell?" I asked. The opening door had released the most revolting stench. Involuntarily I put my hand over my mouth and nose.

"Look," said Mary again. "Tell me what you think I should do."

I bent forward unwillingly to peer into the opening. I wasn't at all keen on getting close to the source of the smell. I already knew I wouldn't like what I was going to find.

"What is it?" I asked. "There's got to be something dead in there to cause this sort of stink." The light from the opening didn't penetrate far enough into the cavity to provide much illumination. I made out a lumpish shape in the gloom but could see no details.

"I'll need a torch if you want me to see what that is."

I was completely unprepared for the blow that fell across the back of my neck and knocked me out.

CHAPTER TWENTY ONE

I OPENED MY EYES TO A blackness so intense that I put my hands to my face to check my eyelids had in fact lifted. When that failed to give me vision I decided I was dreaming. The back of my head ached, and I was lying uncomfortably. I shifted my position and closed my eyes again, but instead of sinking further into the dream, small details nagged for my attention.

I was lying on a rock-hard surface with no comfortable bedding to snuggle into.

I was sore. I put a hand to the back of my head and gave a soft gasp as I pressed the skin. I must have a massive bruise there, because it hurt like hell.

I was still fully dressed.

Worst of all, I was then sufficiently awake to register the smell. The stench impregnated the air so thoroughly it must have been clinging to every molecule of oxygen. I could almost feel the miasma spreading itself over my skin.

Mary. I remembered. She'd wanted to show me something.

This wasn't a dream. I opened my eyes again and registered the utter absence of light. Tentatively, I reached my arm up into it. I could feel nothing above me. I reached to the right and encountered a hard surface. I traced my hand down it and let my fingers explore the right angle of floor and wall.

It wasn't much, but that small amount of physical orientation served to anchor me. I pushed myself up into a sitting position and leaned back against the wall.

What the hell had happened? Mary must have hit me, but why?

I shifted uncomfortably on the floor, felt something hard pressing into my hip and pulled my phone out of my pocket. I fumbled with the buttons, discovering in the process that my hands were shaking. The absolute darkness held no visual clues and I hadn't realised just how unsteady I was.

The light was too bright. I had to turn my head away as my eyes adjusted. The torch lit up a rectangular chamber three metres long, a metre and a half deep and about a metre in height. The ceiling was only just above my head.

The shape I'd seen and the source of the smell, occupied most of the floor space. My foot was touching it. I snatched my leg away.

I suppose courage comes in many forms, and I don't claim to have a great amount of it. All I know is it took all my reserves of nerve to turn the beam on that shape and force myself to investigate what it was.

He lay on his side, his back to me. I ran the light along, from the shoes that my own feet had been touching, over the fine wool suit and up to his head of short black hair. It didn't take a genius to work out who this body had belonged to.

"Mr Zhang, I presume," I murmured. This feeble attempt at flippancy was my only defence against the rising realisation of the horror of my situation. If I yielded to that tide, I'd scream until my throat was raw, then curl up in a foetal ball until I died.

Had Zhang already been dead when he'd been entombed here, or had he died a slow, lingering death alone in the dark? Was that going to be my fate?

I've always been mildly claustrophobic, and the walls of this bunker were definitely beginning to close in on me. The combination of terror, stench and confinement was making my stomach churn. I put a hand over my mouth as a surge of nausea hit me.

I sat back and turned the light away. It seemed an unwarranted intrusion into his privacy. For a man who'd been dead a year, he was still in remarkably good nick. The cool, dry conditions must have hindered decay.

"I'm sorry you died," I said at last. "Your sons were looking for you. They missed you very much."

I wondered if his spirit lingered here. What a hideous place to spend eternity. I swallowed to suppress the fear and nausea that thought entailed and tried to think.

I checked the phone. It was down to 35% battery life and there was no signal. I tried repeatedly to phone out – Jack, my sister, 111. The mobile obstinately declined to connect to a service.

"Fuck," I swore. It seemed I had a highly technical, over-engineered torch and nothing more.

The battery wouldn't last forever. If I was to have any chance of getting out of here, I had to find it now.

I swung the beam around the space. With the exception of Zhang and me, there was nothing to be seen, just blank sheets of concrete on three sides. I raked the walls and corners, top and bottom. Nothing.

Eventually I wriggled round enough to examine the wall I'd been leaning on. Bingo. Above my head was the track for the sliding door. I followed its length with the light and at the far end found the box with the housing mechanism.

To reach it I had to crawl the length of Zhang's body, something I accomplished with a superstitious mixture of fear, revulsion and apology. Despite my best efforts, I couldn't avoid touching him.

"I'm really sorry," I apologised, "but I owe it to both of us to get us out of here if I can."

It was even worse when I reached the box and had to shift my position to squat beside it. My hip jammed against Zhang's head, and I felt the body move as I eased my legs out along the wall. I gave an audible gulp of horror that sounded like a sob as I tried to wedge myself into the smallest possible space.

This small movement had caused a marked increase in the stench. My stomach knotted and dry heaved as I breathed in the rotten vapour.

"Gross, gross, gross," I muttered.

I turned my attention to the box. As I'd suspected, the track ran through it.

Another wave of dry-retching overwhelmed me before I was able to reach and examine the chain that ran along the tracking. Surely there had to be some way to manually override this thing, some way of pulling the chain along the housing and forcing the door to slide open?

I couldn't see clearly enough in the gloom and glanced at the phone. The battery level was now 25% and falling fast.

I returned to the track. I couldn't get a purchase on the chain, although I picked and scrabbled at it until my fingers, already damaged from digging in the slip the day before, were bloody and sore. Nor could I force the cover off the box. In desperation I swung my body around, ignoring poor Zhang and the indignity my contortions were causing his corpse. I needed to be able to kick at that housing.

I booted the mechanism repeatedly with all my strength, but I was in a cramped position and couldn't get a great deal of force into my kick.

Panic was beginning to set in. My kicks became more frantic and even less effective. The level of light dropped again, and the phone screen helpfully advised my battery was now at 15% and I needed to recharge it.

I screamed in rage. Even when my burning throat forced me to shut up, the echo of that cry travelled around the walls of my tomb.

Had Zhang shared this despair in his final hours? I'd never felt so utterly helpless, or needed such a desperate release from the fear, anger and panic that clenched in me.

I still needed to feel effective but that little box defeated me. I crawled back to reach it with my fingers. I shook, twisted and hit it. All in vain. Whoever had designed the system had probably never imagined a need to open it from this side of the wall.

Long minutes later I was still trying to force the box to cooperate when the phone abruptly switched off.

The transition to darkness was so complete it came as a physical shock. There were still stars playing, bright motes of colour that danced uselessly inside my eyelids while the blackness pressed against my skin with an almost tangible weight.

I gave a choking sob of horror, pulled my knees up towards my chin and wrapped my arms around them. My forehead fell forward to rest on my knees in the classic foetal position.

In the darkness the air seemed denser. I'd become partially accustomed to the foul smell, but in the absence of light, the atmosphere thickened, and it became harder to breathe.

It occurred to me that the preserved state of Zhang's body might owe a lot to an absence of oxygen in this tomb, in which case I might not be in for a long, lingering death in the dark. Mortality might come much quicker from asphyxiation.

I closed my eyes and clung to my legs. Against my will, tears began to trickle as I thought of Jack. He'd be so angry with me. He'd warned me about not going off alone.

But then, I'd never get to hear what he thought of my stupidity. I wouldn't be seeing him again.

Self-pitying tears ran down my face. I rubbed my cheeks against my knees to dry them.

When he heard I was missing, Jack would tear the place apart looking for me. I knew that. But people had searched for Zhang and never found him. If Mary denied seeing me this afternoon, the last sighting would be where Ray and Stephen had left me.

I wouldn't see my sister again either. Nor my nieces. Nor my boss, Roger. I wouldn't fly again.

The list of farewells I'd never get to say grew longer, and I grew increasingly maudlin as I snivelled in the dark.

At last I must have exhausted myself with emotion because, for an indeterminate period, I remember nothing. I don't think it was resignation, just a bone-deep weariness that made me close my eyes. I may have dozed off.

I snapped back into wakefulness all too soon and then panic really had free rein. There was no plan or reason as I hammered at the wall, shouted, scratched at the tracks and chain of the opening mechanism. My throat hurt from all my shouting, my nails ripped, and my fists were bruised from beating the door. It made no difference.

Eventually I ran out of energy, gave up and leaned back against the wall. I had no idea of the time, but I wondered whether the men had successfully made it through to Pat's place. Had anyone noticed I was missing yet? There was no way of knowing how long I'd been entombed. It felt like hours. It might even be night time.

The wall was hard against my back. I shifted uncomfortably, then jolted forward in shock as light shone suddenly from the control box. With a grinding clank, the chain above my head began to move and the panel slowly slid sideways.

Daylight blinded me, but there were voices and hands urgent on my shoulders.

"Claire, thank god we found you."

"Fucking hell. Here, Claire. Hold my hand. Can you stand?"

I heard someone retching. "God help us, it stinks in there."

"Let's get her out, quickly."

My light-sensitive eyes were flooded with tears. Gentle hands helped me crawl from the cavity and supported me as I got to my feet.

I blinked hard.

"Are you all right?" Joanne asked.

I nodded.

"Come on, up the stairs." Brett had his arm around me. "Can you walk OK?"

I wasn't sure I could. I staggered when I tried to take a step and felt Brett's arm tighten in support.

"I can carry you."

That woke me up. I don't like being helpless.

"No, I can manage." My eyes were beginning to focus and, with that, my sense of balance began to return.

"If you give me a hand, I can get up the stairs."

Brett led me, and Joanne followed as back-up. I felt her hand steady against my spine, but I managed.

I still couldn't understand what had happened. "Fuck, Mary shut me in there deliberately!"

Joanne gave a gasp. "Mary? Jesus, she was helping me search for you. No wonder I couldn't find you."

"Are the police still here with Ray? We must tell them about Zhang!" I said.

"The police left ages ago," said Joanne. "I heard them leave when I was trying to find you."

"How *did* you find me?" I asked.

"It was pure chance. Brett came into the lodge and said he was ready to fly us home, so I went to look for you, but I couldn't find you anywhere. I must have searched for an hour or more, and I started getting worried. In the end I saw Mary and asked her to help me, but of course she steered me well clear of the hangar. Then we found Brett. I told him you'd disappeared. He led me here and had keys to the hangar."

Brett interrupted her. "We've got to get you two out of here. If you can make it as far as the door, you can get on the quad."

"But Zhang…" I protested.

"Isn't going anywhere." Brett's tone was curt as he bustled me out of the hangar towards the quad bike.

"You'll have to keep her steady," he told Joanne as I took my place on the carrier.

"I'll be fine," I said, taking a firm grip on the rail. "I don't understand why Mary wanted to kill me. Because I *would* have died if you hadn't found me."

"You'd been asking too many questions," said Brett. "I warned you to keep your nose out of lodge business."

"I didn't," I protested. "I might have annoyed Wu this morning when I had pushed my way into the hangar, but I haven't done anything to upset Mary."

Brett gave a snort.

"She's Wu's wife," he said. "Whatever happens, they stick together."

"Wife? Oh shit," I said, as the implications sank in. "No one mentioned that."

"But why?" asked Joanne. "What's going on here?"

"I don't ask. I just keep my head down and do my job," said Brett.

"But you knew where Claire was as soon as I told you she was missing," accused Joanne. "I'm sure you did. I saw you and Mary staring at each other and wondered what it was all about. I didn't understand then, but you must have realised what had happened, because you led me straight to the hangar while Mary made excuses and left very speedily."

Brett ignored her as he put the quad into gear. The bike leapt forward, and I was glad I was hanging on tightly as Brett drove aggressively up the track to the helipad.

"Stay there while I do a quick pre-flight," he ordered.

I sat on the quad bike and watched as he busied himself around the helicopter. I still felt a bit wobbly. Joanne slid off the luggage rack and stood leaning against the handle bars.

"How long was I in there?" I asked.

"A couple of hours or so, I'd guess. Long enough for me to be really worried about you. I don't understand any of this," Joanne said.

"Neither do I. I just want to get out of here," I said. "We can report everything to the police when Brett gets us back to your place. Until then, I just want to stay safe."

"Brett knew there was a body hidden in that hangar. You should have seen his face when I told him you'd disappeared. He went chalk white. And when we got to the hangar, he knew just where you were and how to open the door of that cubby-hole."

We both stared at Brett who was slowly working his way around the machine.

"He warned me off asking questions two days ago," I said. "He may not be responsible for whatever happened to Zhang, but he knew about it. And now we're going to go up in a helicopter with him."

Joanne looked at me. "Do you think we should go?"

"I don't think we've got a choice," I answered. "We've got to get away from here and the chopper is the only practicable means available. And he did just rescue me."

Brett finished his checks. "OK. We're good to go. Come and

take your seats," he shouted.

Joanne was on her feet and reaching her hand out to support me when we heard a shout and saw Wu running across the grass towards us.

"No, stop!" he shouted to Brett. "What are you doing?"

"I'm getting them out of here," Brett called back. "Let it go, Wu. It's all over, mate."

"They can't go," Wu shouted. "They know too much. You can't do this."

He'd reached Brett, and we could see they were having a furious argument. They'd dropped their voices, and were just too far away for us to be able to hear exactly what was being said, but the substance was clear.

Brett stood his ground. We heard him say, "No. No!" loudly in reply to some statement of Wu's.

Wu was getting more and more wound up. The hand on his good arm was waving around as he made his points and his voice got louder.

His fists clenched, and I thought he was going to hit Brett. Brett evidently thought so as well, because he took a couple of steps back.

The men stood staring at each other.

"They go with me." Brett's shouted words were forceful and final. "No more, Wu. It's over. This is it."

He turned away.

"Get over here," he called to Joanne and me.

He'd turned his back on Wu and wouldn't have seen Wu whip the handgun from his jacket. But Joanne and I did.

"Fuck!" Joanne gasped. She jumped astride the quad, turned the key and had us moving before I'd even properly registered what was going on.

"Hold on!" she yelled.

I was lucky I wasn't spun off as she swung the bike around and accelerated down the drive.

We were already sweeping around the corner, out of sight of the pair, when we heard the sound of the shot.

"Jesus!"

We'd left the groomed gardens of the lodge and were now flying down the main drive heading to the entrance of the property.

I had to hand it to Joanne. She drove that bike like a pro. I clung on like grim death as we tore down the race. I chanced a glance behind to see if we were being followed but could see nothing.

We reached the gateway and Joanne slowed down.

"Which way?" she yelled over her shoulder.

Left would take us down towards the broken bridge and closed road. If Wu was pursuing us, we'd be trapped there.

"Right," I said.

I'd barely got the word out before Joanne had swung us hard into a right-hand turn and was burning along the valley road.

"We need to get help," Joanne shouted back to me. She was driving like a maniac.

"Do you think Wu killed Brett?" I had to lean forward to hear her.

"I hope not. I feel gutless running away and not trying to help him. Brett was trying to get us out of there." I was breathless enough with shock and reaction. A shouted conversation with Joanne was taking it out of me.

The bike slowed as we went around a corner. "For what it's worth, I feel bad too, but we couldn't have done anything," she yelled over her shoulder. "Wu had already pointed that gun. We had to look after ourselves. Whatever's been going on, Brett is mixed up in it, remember. He's hardly an innocent party."

I sighed. Joanne was right, of course, even if I couldn't quite square our actions with my conscience. I could only be impressed by her pragmatism.

Joanne slowed the quad down a little as we scanned each side of the road for a suitable sanctuary. Open grassland had given way to forestry soon after we'd left the lodge's farmland. Radiata pines grew straight and tall on either side of us, and the fence line ran along the edge of the road with no break to indicate a homestead or worksite we could seek help from.

I kept glancing over my shoulder to check for pursuit. If Wu was chasing us, it wouldn't take him long to get down the road to the washed-out bridge, find we weren't there and follow us up the valley instead. He'd also be aware of any potential bolt holes available to us.

"Still no sign of him?" Joanne asked.

"Nah," I replied. "But he can't be far behind us." An uneasy possibility suggested itself. "Unless of course he knows it's a dead end and we've nowhere to run. In which case he can take his time and pick us up at his leisure."

I'd barely finished speaking when we rounded a bend in the road and found ourselves in a large cul-de-sac.

CHAPTER TWENTY TWO

THE LARGE, CIRCULAR TURNING AREA WAS fringed with tall pines that grew so thick it was hard to see through into the dark undergrowth of ferns and lupins. A wide, gravelled road led through the forest and curved out of sight a hundred metres ahead. Unfortunately, solid three-metre high gates, with no obvious means of opening them, blocked any access.

"They're electric," I said after a brief look. To the right of the gates stood a post with a swipe mechanism and key-pad. Without a passcode we were stuck.

Joanne groaned. "That's it for us and the quad then," she said as she turned the machine off.

"'Fraid so," I said, studying the barrier. "Do you want to give the other one a try?"

Set to one side, and guarding the drive, a smaller gate was cut into the fencing. It was too narrow for the farm-bike, but wide enough to walk through if you were prepared to duck beneath the barbed wire running just above head height.

"We'll be on foot," said Joanne dubiously. "We could walk into that forest for ages and not come across another human being to help us. Didn't Charles say it was a massive plantation?"

"He also said the owner had a pad up here which he visited sometimes," I reminded her. "It's a holiday weekend – maybe he came up here for a break."

"If so, he'll be as stranded as we are," remarked Joanne. She stared at the gate for a few minutes, chewing her bottom lip. "I don't know…" she said at last.

She heard it before I did. "Shit!" she exclaimed. "We're out of here."

I turned my head and caught the far-off low engine rumble of a vehicle coming up the road behind us. We abandoned the quad, and I followed Joanne through the gate, running up the road as fast as we could.

I'm no sprinter, and the track ran uphill, but I cleared the distance like an Olympic athlete. Once we reached the curve and were safely out of the line of sight we stopped. She leaned against a tree, while I bent over, hands and weight resting on my knees as I tried to catch my breath.

Eventually my heart rate slowed and steadied. I looked at Joanne who was barely puffing.

"Shit, you're fit," I muttered.

"Marathons," she explained briefly. "It's the Auckland one next weekend. I'm supposed to be in training."

I nodded my understanding.

We heard a car door slam.

"Off the track," urged Joanne.

On each side of the road the ground between the trees was cluttered with branches from various prunings. Tangling these together, a rich mix of weeds had taken up residence in the litter. It wasn't easy to forge a path, but desperation drove us, and we pushed our way through, clambering and scrabbling over logs, twigs and pine cones. I recognised young foxgloves, ink weed, re-colonising native plants and, unfortunately, the occasional blackberry that grabbed and scratched us as we passed.

It was hideous, ankle-turning stuff and pitifully slow to scramble through, but it provided brilliant cover from pursuit. Even if we'd left footprints in the soft earth as we left the road, they'd be impossible to follow very far, and we were now some sixty metres away from the track.

"Claire!" he called. "Claire! Joanne! Please come out."

We ducked lower into the shelter of the fallen branch we'd hidden behind.

"That's not Wu," Joanne mouthed at me.

"Charles," I whispered.

"Ladies, please! Let me help you. You'll be safe with me. I've spoken to Brett and he told me everything. Please. You must trust me to look after you and get you safely home. Wu can't hurt you anymore."

Joanne and I looked at each other.

"What do you think?" she mouthed.

I shook my head. "We can't chance it. If we get it wrong and he's not kosher we'll both end up dead. It's too much of a risk. We'd be two more bodies in hidden graves."

I didn't add I was reasonably certain that, if I disappeared, Jack would get a crew of digging machines to excavate the entire valley to find me. Although I acknowledged sadly his primary motivation would be the urge to throttle me for my folly.

Joanne nodded. She looked about as glum as I felt.

To add to the misery, the ground we knelt on was sodden and the damp had penetrated right through my jeans. The spring evening was getting chilly and the water was cold.

I shifted uncomfortably. A nubbin of wood was digging into my knee – a small discomfort that was rapidly becoming intolerable. Try as I might, I couldn't divert my attention from it, and even the tension of listening to Charles calling us wasn't enough to help me ignore it. The effort of resisting its irritation was beginning to put my whole leg into spasm. I began to understand how victims voluntarily surrendered to their attackers rather than endure the continued strain of concealment. I could feel sweat beading down my back from the tension.

Eventually we were aware of Charles's calls moving away as he searched further up the road. I sat back, carefully eased my poor leg straight, and rubbed my knee.

"What do we do now?" asked Joanne.

I shrugged. "Wait until he comes back to his car. Then we go up this track as far as we can and hopefully find a house."

I reached automatically for my phone and gave a tsk of impatience when I remembered it had no power.

"Have you got your phone with you?" I asked. "Mine's flat."

Joanne stared at me as if I had three heads, before her face cleared.

"Oh my god, I completely forgot," she said. "How dumb is that?" She groped in her jacket pocket and dragged it out.

"Text Pat or Jack," I suggested. "They can get the police in."

Joanne bent over her phone. "No reception!" she complained. She eased herself up onto her knees, held the phone above her head and twisted around to face different directions.

"There," she said excitedly. "I've got some bars."

"Use them before you lose them."

She busied herself with the phone, her fingers flashing across the keys. "I've asked Pat to text back when he gets this and then I'll call him. It's got to be quicker to let him know what's happening if I can speak to him and explain it all."

I suppressed a surge of irritation. Naturally she'd turn to her husband, but I wished she'd texted Jack who had the experience and the contacts to get us support quickly.

"Mind you," Joanne said, "Pat will turn it all straight over to Jack. This is more his territory, isn't it?"

I made a non-committal noise. Who the fuck knew whose territory we were in? Armed offenders squad for one, I supposed.

Joanne kept an eye on her screen. "Shit. It's lost signal again. The text hasn't gone."

"If it's sitting there, it will go as soon as we get reception again, won't it?" I asked.

"Dunno. I suppose so. Or maybe I'll have to press resend. Either way, the message hasn't gone."

I felt my shoulders sag. If only we knew whether we could trust Charles or not. But with no certainty, we had to ignore him. Our best chance was to find a friendly person at the house up the road. Or at least find somewhere to hide until the police could rescue us.

We'd kept our speech at a whisper, and Joanne settled back

below the shelter of the log. I was sitting up taller so I could watch the road. It had been a while since we'd last heard Charles call, and I wanted to know when he returned from his search. With any luck we'd see him pass us on his way back to the car.

In spite of my vigilance, I almost missed him. The light was starting to soften, the undergrowth between us and the road was thick, and Charles's jacket was a non-descript colour which faded into the natural hues of the forest.

If he hadn't moved a hand to wave something from his face, I wouldn't have seen him. I caught the movement of the pale skin, but it took me longer to make out the rest. He was moving purposefully down the road towards the car.

I shrank back down behind the log.

"He's out there," I whispered.

Joanne laid her phone on the earth between us. Huddled together in silence we watched as the minutes rolled by.

In the end, we allowed fifteen minutes to elapse before we thought it safe to sit up and take stock. There was no sign of Charles, but we were losing visibility fast as the early spring evening darkened. Clouds had rolled back in during the afternoon and contributed to the gloom. We were fortunate the clocks had already gone forward for summer time, otherwise we'd be in complete darkness by now.

"Move out?" Joanne whispered.

I nodded.

It was a sod of a job extricating ourselves from the branches and creeper that snagged our ankles as we clambered our way back to the track. What had been a tricky passage earlier, in daylight, was fraught with difficulty in dusk's shadows. Joanne swore as she rolled an ankle on a pinecone hidden beneath the rubbish.

"Are you OK?" I hissed.

"Fine," she muttered. "Let's just get out of here." She was hobbling by the time we made it to the road, but I said nothing. Truth was, it didn't matter what condition either of us was in, we still had to find shelter and help.

CHAPTER TWENTY THREE

IT TOOK QUARTER OF AN HOUR to reach the fork in the road, and by then the rain had started in earnest. This, combined with a cold wind, soon had us chilled.

"We made it!" I said.

"Thank fuck for that," replied Joanne. She caught my glance. "I'll be glad to put this foot up."

"Do you need to lean on me?"

She shook her head. "Nah, it's just a bit sore. We'll be right."

The logging track continued straight ahead but curving from it, a sealed drive led down the hill towards a house.

"Someone's home! There are lights on and cars parked in the drive."

"Let's hope they're prepared to help," Joanne said. "Or at least give us shelter until Pat or the police arrive."

"Let's hope so," I agreed. We were both still wearing the clothes we'd worn for the evening at the lodge. They'd been smart when I first put mine on, but subsequently, they'd been crumpled, I'd rolled around inside a tomb and both of us had clambered over sticky, resinous pine logs and through the mud. The steady drizzle was beginning to soak us, adding to our dubious charms. Our gear was now well and truly travel-stained.

"We looked like disreputable tramps," I remarked. "Let's pray they can see beyond appearances."

Joanne sniffed. "We look disgusting," she agreed.

Clear of the pine trees there was still enough light to follow the path down the hill to the pleasant bungalow – a modern structure – designed in the style of an older colonial home. A wide verandah ran around the outside and gave us welcome shelter from the rain. Five metres from the house our presence evidently triggered an external security light which guided us around the corner to the front door.

I searched for a door bell, failed to find one and knocked.

I looked up and saw a security camera directed at us from the corner. Further inspection revealed another one, at the far end of the verandah, and yet another at the opposite end. We'd probably been under surveillance since we entered the property. Whoever owned this place took security seriously.

"Lights, cameras, action…." I muttered.

"What?" Joanne looked confused.

"I'll explain later," I said as I turned to face the door. I was trying to organise my thoughts. I needed to present our story in the best light, but for the life of me I couldn't sort out how to tell a complete stranger I'd been buried alive, we'd been threatened with a hand gun and we feared for our safety.

"Hello." The man who opened the door was short and stocky. "Can I help you?"

He was Asian. I looked at Joanne and saw her face reflect my concern. Rural neighbours are close-knit and tend to know a lot about each other's business. Proximity alone would make it likely that this man knew the people at the lodge. Did their shared ethnicity represent a closer relationship?

"Um, sorry to disturb you, but we need your help," I mumbled.

I saw him take in the bedraggled state of our clothing and raise an eyebrow. He looked beyond us at the falling rain and smiled.

"It's too cold to hang around out here. Please, step inside and tell me what you need."

He opened the door wider and we crossed the threshold in

silence.

We stood in the hall. The relief of being out of the weather was immediate.

"Now, what can I do to help?" he asked.

Mercifully Joanne took control and stepped forward with her hand extended.

"Hi, I'm Joanne Crombie, we farm the block on the far side of the ridge."

"A neighbour then!" he said as he shook her hand. "And you need my help? Of course, I'll do what I can. Why don't you come through to the living room where it's warm. My name is Paul by the way." He gestured to Joanne to precede him.

"No, no," she protested. "Please, after you."

I had a terrible sinking feeling as we followed him down the hallway into the warm living room.

"Make yourselves comfortable, then you can tell me what brings you here." He indicated the sofa.

"I'll stand by the fire if you don't mind," I said. "It was getting cold out there."

"And wet."

We stood with our backs to the fire. I hadn't realised how chilled we were. Neither of us had warm clothing. Joanne only had a light jacket which was now soaked, and my long-sleeved shirt wasn't enough to keep out the spring chill.

"So, please tell me. What happened to you?" asked Paul.

"We were staying at the lodge," I began. He gave an encouraging smile.

"And…" he prompted.

"We were in danger, so we left," interrupted Joanne. "We need to contact our family, so they can come and get us, and we need somewhere safe to stay in the meantime."

I nodded in agreement.

"You were in danger at Retakure Lodge?" said Paul. "I've heard it's a very pleasant place to stay."

"It is," I said. "But there's something's bad going on as well. There's a dead body on the property and some of the staff are involved. Joanne and I were threatened, and I was almost killed."

Paul looked startled. "Then certainly you must stay here where you are safe. I want to hear your story. After that, we can decide what best to do. You both look very cold. Can I pour you a drink to warm you up?"

"Please."

He poured generous measures of whisky. "Would you like ice?" he asked.

"Ice for me please," said Joanne.

"Give me a second, I'll get some from the kitchen," said Paul.

Joanne waited until he'd left the room. "I think it's going to be OK."

I nodded agreement.

Paul came back with the ice and fixed Joanne's drink. He raised his eyebrows in question at me.

"Straight for me, thanks."

I gulped rather than sipped the fiery liquid and coughed as its warmth poured down my throat.

"Careful," murmured Joanne. "You don't want to choke."

"God, that's good," I said. I smiled at Paul. "Thanks. That's cut through the cold in my bones." I felt an immediate lift in my spirits and took another, more careful sip of the potent spirit. Euphoria surged through me. We were warm, safe and alive, and somewhere out there, Jack was waiting for me.

Paul smiled at me and walked towards us, his own drink in his hand, then sat down.

"Perhaps you should tell me your story?"

"It started with me finding some human remains in the swamp," I began.

"I heard about it," Paul said. "It's been the talk of the valley."

The warmth and whisky had relaxed me, and I found myself enjoying telling Paul about the last few days.

I was warm enough now to sit down on one of the sofas. Joanne joined me.

I detailed finding the remains and then the muster.

Joanne, also mellowing under the influence of the alcohol, chipped in with any bits I missed and between us, we detailed everything that had happened.

"Do you realise what's really odd about all this?" I asked. "It was only four days ago that Jack and I stumbled over those remains. It feels like we've been here for weeks."

It occurred to me that Joanne might feel offended by this reflection on her hospitality.

"It's been lovely staying with Pat and Joanne of course," I added, "but it's been a very hectic few days."

"It's not the usual entertainment we provide our guests," agreed Joanne dryly.

Paul had been very quiet, evidently studying his feet, while we told our tale. It was a moment before he moved and looked at us.

"Why?" he asked.

"Why what?" I replied.

"You say this woman, Mary, deliberately shut you in that room. Why would she do that?"

"I wondered that. I think it was because I'd been asking questions about Zhang and Li Na. Mind you, I hadn't found out anything."

"On top of that you'd been poking around that hangar in the morning, hadn't you?" said Joanne. "Maybe Mary – or perhaps Wu – thought you were getting too close to the body."

"Or maybe everyone is just twitchy," I replied. "Brett told me not to ask questions. He's the helicopter pilot," I explained to Paul. "They're all on edge."

"But by her action, Mary would seem to have confirmed any suspicions you already had. A little counter-productive, wouldn't you think?"

Actually, I was finding it difficult to think about anything. The whisky, gulped down far too quickly, was making my head woozy and my eyes heavy. I blinked to clear them.

"I bet she was set up by Wu," I said. "He's always struck me as psycha…,psycho…, you know, mad." For the life of me I couldn't get the word out. I licked my lips. I must be tired; even my voice sounded slurry.

"Your boyfriend is a detective, isn't he?" Paul asked.

I saw Joanne frown. "Where did you hear that? We haven't

mentioned it."

"It was part of the gossip when I heard you'd found a body," Paul shrugged. "You know how everyone knows everybody's business in the country."

Joanne gave a wry smile. "That's true enough." She took a long pull on her whisky and sighed with pleasure.

"This drink's a life saver. I hadn't realised how cold I was." She stretched her legs out. "It's even dulling the pain in my ankle," she said. "Perhaps it will come right in time for me to run in Auckland after all."

"Marathon," I explained to Paul. I noticed he was watching Joanne closely. I turned my head to look at her as well, but my eyes were tired. I felt them droop. It seemed too much effort to open them, so I kept them shut. Nothing seemed to need my attention so I let myself drift. It had been one hell of a day.

I was floating somewhere between being awake and asleep. I was aware of the lounge door opening and shutting but couldn't be bothered stirring myself to check it out.

"They're out to it?" I felt myself frown. I recognised the voice but couldn't place it.

"They're well gone." Paul's voice, amused. "You'll have to help me get them out of here."

"Are you sure we shouldn't just bury them?" I realised it was Wenjun talking. How had he got here? Was I dreaming? I let the thought go.

"What, and make it obvious that there have been two more murders?" Paul snapped.

"Don't be stupid. We wouldn't be in this mess if that psychopath you keep as a servant hadn't run amok this weekend. I've told you before you've lost control of him. He needed to be terminated months ago."

"Just asking." Wenjun sounded annoyed. "Wu's useful. Getting rid of him would cause more problems than it would solve."

"What he's done has caused us a whole *heap* of problems we're going to have to sort out. What the fuck was he doing trying to get rid of this girl? How did he think he was going to explain away her disappearance?"

"He thought she knew something incriminating."

"He didn't think at all."

"Well, I didn't ask him to dispose of her. What are you going to do with these two?"

"It's a cold night. They'll die of hypothermia fast enough if we leave them outside. They're not going anywhere in the state they're in now. They'll sleep their way to death. All we have to do is dump them somewhere they won't be found for a couple of days and the result will be death by natural causes. The drug will be out of their system in a few hours, and no one will be any the wiser."

"They'll find the bike by the gate."

"So what? The women wandered onto a forestry block of their own volition and have only themselves to blame if they die out in the open on a cold night, dressed inappropriately. They should have come and asked me for help. We don't even have to edit the CCTV footage. I stopped recording when Charles came up here looking for them." Even half asleep I could hear the laughter undercutting his sarcasm.

Drugged. The idea floated in my brain, a vagrant thread among many. I tried to concentrate. Somewhere, a faint alarm bell rang. Had the whisky been spiked? A mere second later the thought had passed. I suppressed a smile. It felt *soooo* good. I slipped back into the warm current of my dreams and let myself float. Jack's face came and went. He was smiling, the warm man I'd come to love.

Later he was angry with me, like he'd been this morning. I moaned in distress. I couldn't hear the words, but I knew he was telling me I was in danger. His face swam away. I couldn't see him although I looked around.

Hard hands gripped my arms and pulled me upright. I muttered in discomfort as I was manhandled.

"Careful. Don't damage her." Paul's voice again. "Not in any way that can't be explained by her running around in the forest."

There was ragged breathing close to my ear. My arms hurt from being dragged but the discomfort was brief. I was lifted, then there was a hard surface beneath me where I settled back to sleep. I don't recall when they dumped us on the ground, but the fading noise of the tractor's engine merged with the thunder as my dreams turned ugly and I ran from a faceless pursuer. Later, I was aware of cold water beneath me, saturating my clothes, but there was warmth beside me so I rolled over to snuggle against it.

The relief was temporary. I was beginning to wake up.

CHAPTER TWENTY FOUR

MY TONGUE WAS THICK AND DRY, and my mouth tasted foul. I had a colossal headache and worst of all, I was chilled to the bone. I'd never realised how apt the phrase was. I ached with the cold.

I was lying pressed against Joanne's back which had kept my front half slightly protected from the driving rain, but my back was soaked. I moved to separate us. Deep chills ran through me. My shoulders and hips seemed to have frozen, and when I tried to push myself up, I couldn't coordinate my legs and arms.

My brain also seemed to have frozen – thoughts moved with painful sluggishness as I struggled up. Snatches of conversation I'd heard in that dreamlike fugue surfaced sufficiently for me to understand we were here to die.

I wasn't sure I cared. Shutting my eyes again and letting the world take care of itself for a while was incredibly tempting. I was exhausted.

The nausea was the only thing pushing me on. I needed to be sick. My stomach hurt. I had to vomit. For that, I had to at least be on hands and knees – even better if I was standing up.

I scrambled on all fours and let the spasms empty my stomach. I was groaning with misery by the time I'd finished, but the contractions had at least woken me up and freed me from my torpor.

It was pitch black here under the trees. I reached out to Joanne and ran my hands over her.

She still lay unmoving, but two thoughts were now clear in my head. We would die if we didn't make the effort to move, and it was my job to get Joanne to cover.

I wasn't gentle. When yelling her name didn't work, I tried shaking her and in the end resorted to slapping her hard.

"Joanne, come on. You have to wake up." I shook her again.

"Joanne, you must make an effort." I didn't think I could lift her. For all her slenderness, Joanne had a lot of muscle mass. She'd be heavy.

In despair I slapped her again. "Joanne, wake up!" This time I felt her flinch.

"Go away," she muttered.

I was so relieved I could have hugged her.

"Don't go back to sleep. You've got to listen to me. Wake *up* Joanne. Or we'll die!"

It took several minutes, but gradually she came around.

"Shit." She put her hand to her face. "You've hit me!" Her voice was as plaintive and confused as a child's. "What's going on?"

"I'll explain later. Right now, we have to move and find shelter. We'll die of hypothermia if we can't get under cover soon and start warming up."

She was painfully slow, and I had to bully and manhandle her a bit, but together we got both of us upright.

"Crap," she exclaimed as her bad ankle hit the ground. "That hurts."

"Lean on me," I said. "Put your arm around my shoulder. I'll support you if you can hop on your good leg."

She obeyed. The area between our bodies was marginally warmer than the rest of us. I did my best to help her through, but half the time I dragged her, struggling, through the undergrowth. I doubt you could find a more miserable situation.

"I don't suppose you've still got your phone?" I asked. I'd

already checked my pocket and found it empty.

Joanne patted herself. "No. I must have dropped it."

I shook my head. "Nah. They'll have taken them and dumped them somewhere. We'll have to manage without a torch."

It was impossible, of course. We had no visibility, I didn't know which direction to go in and Joanne was still dazed and wobbly.

We had to get out of the forest and find a road. Climbing around the branches and weeds had been challenging enough when we had clear sight of what we were struggling over. Now it was a nightmare, and Joanne was already lame.

I was beyond rational thought. I just knew we had to move, so that was what we did. My brain had shut itself away in some deep part of my system and left my legs and arms on auto-pilot. Step by step, we trudged on, tripping on the debris underfoot and feeling our way around obstacles. I'm not even certain we went in a straight line.

I tripped on a rock and had to scramble back to my feet to get over it. Each time I fell I seemed to have less energy to straighten up again. We stumbled on a few more painful paces before I gradually became aware that the going was easier.

"Stop," I said. "Just stand still a second." When she was balanced safely I bent over and ran my hands over the ground.

"We're on a road. We've reached a road. We're on clear ground!"

"What should we do?"

With some relief I heard strength returning to Joanne's voice. We weren't out of the woods – pun intended – yet, but life was going to be easier if we had two brains working on the problems.

"Up or down," I wondered. "If we go down, we should eventually get to the front gate and back out to the road, but it takes us past the house, and if a car drives up, we'll be possums in the headlights. Our main need is to find shelter, just to get us through the night. Maybe there'll be a shed or something if we go uphill?"

I was finding it incredibly hard work to make my brain focus. Sharing the load would be a godsend.

"We didn't pass any machinery sheds when we came in this afternoon. Maybe they're up ahead."

"Maybe." I was dubious. We had no way of knowing how far into the forest Paul and Wenjun had brought us. I tried to remember what Paul had said. Something about putting us where no one would find us. Unfortunately, I remembered nothing more specific.

"It's just as likely any sheds are located behind us, further down the hill."

"We go up," said Joanne.

I hesitated.

"It's a wild guess either way, isn't it?" she asked. "So, let's go up. I've got a good feeling about it. and it's stopped raining as well." Without waiting, she removed her arm from my shoulder and started limping her way up the road.

I had to smile as I followed her. The small encouragement of finding a road had put new courage into both of us, and that had been pure good luck. Perhaps we were finally on a winning streak.

The going was easier now, the gravel smooth and even, but we couldn't see what we were walking on. Even away from the cover of the trees, the night was still incredibly dark. We navigated primarily by looking up at the sky where the route was marked by a lighter line running between the lines of trees. As a tactic, it served us well enough, as long as we remembered to look upwards.

The surge of energy we'd experienced when we found the road faded quickly. It might have stopped raining, but the clearing sky meant the night was getting colder.

I soon sank back into that mindless state where my brain went to sleep, leaving my legs plodding onwards. Even that was becoming increasingly difficult. I was breathing through my mouth and heard myself making strange, involuntary groaning noises.

Joanne was no better. She stumbled against me a few times, evidently having trouble keeping a straight line. Even looking upwards to check the line of the road was getting impossibly hard.

It was only at the last second that some primitive sensory awareness made me look up before I hit a solid object. Instinctively I put my hands up to protect myself and felt the unmistakable shape of corrugated iron beneath my fingers. I ran my hands out across the surface and established we'd found something substantial.

Joanne had stopped right behind me.

"We've found something," I whispered. "A building."

She didn't reply.

"Joanne?" I reached for her and got no response when I touched her shoulder. She just stood there like a shaky zombie.

"Shit. Don't give up now" I gave her a little shake. "Come on. We've got to find out how to get inside."

I grabbed her by the arm and pulled her with me as I walked along-side the building. The wall appeared featureless and seemed to go forever – in fact I'd begun to worry that it was only a wall – before I reached a corner and followed the road around it.

It was lighter on this side of the building and easier to make out some details. We were free of the trees and in a large open clearing. This side of the building was shorter. I used my hands, patting the walls anywhere I thought I could discern some unevenness that might indicate a door or window.

Before long, I found a small ledge. Further investigation discovered the glass window above the sill. It was shut, of course, but if I couldn't find any other way in, I'd break it.

Joanne had revived to the point of whimpering softly, which I thought was a positive sign. I tugged her along with me again. I didn't dare let go in case she collapsed, and I couldn't stop to look after her here. The priority was to get into some shelter.

A few metres further on I found a door. My fingers traced its height, identified the hinges on the right and then explored the other side for a handle. I assumed it would be locked, but when I gripped the handle and turned it, the door opened.

I stared at the blank doorway in shock for an appreciable moment before recollecting myself.

"Come," I said tugging Joanne across the threshold with me and shutting the door quickly.

We stood together in the dark while I tried to get a sense of where we were, or, more importantly, whether we were alone.

We were surrounded by silence. After a few moments, I turned to explore the wall behind us in search of a light switch.

It took me a while, partly because the lights were controlled by heavy industrial-type switches that had to be turned, rather than the domestic up-and-down fitting I expected. I'd just figured this out – we had similar switches in the hangar at Paraparaumu – and was about to rotate the switch when caution stopped me.

I'd already realised the building stood clear of the surrounding trees. It was also true we had climbed uphill once we reached the road. So, we were in a clear area, high on a hillside? Some latent part of my brain must have been working. Who knew how visible we'd be if I turned the light on? The window just beside me was testament to how easy a vagrant light would broadcast our presence to any watcher.

With regret I let my hand drop and leaned back against the door.

"Joanne?" I'd felt her slump to the floor as I shut the door.

"Joanne? Are you OK?"

There was no answer.

"Holy crap," I muttered. I hoped she was simply asleep and hadn't passed out.

I had a purely selfish moment of despair and shut my eyes. I didn't have the strength to keep myself going, let alone any spare energy to support Joanne.

Later, this moment of weakness would shame me deeply.

Joanne had literally saved my life when she found me in that tomb, and again when she'd ridden the quad away from Wu, yet in a moment of weariness I couldn't help her? I aspire to higher standards and it was humiliating to realise how completely I'd failed. A saying of my father's surfaced:

"'Tiredness won't kill you.'"

My head touched soft material. I turned and rubbed my cheek against it, nuzzling the cosy surface in a rapture of comfort. It took a second or so before an imperative penetrated my fog addled brain.

"Investigate this," it clamoured.

Slowly I lifted my head from the fabric, turned, and gave the door I was leaning against a pat-down. It didn't take much to establish I'd discovered a garment hanging from a hook on the back of the door. Even better, when I tried to lift it off, it turned out there was another hook, and both held warm garments.

"Joanne!" I sank down on the ground.

There was no reply, so I searched for her on the floor. I found her sitting, slumped against the wall next to the door. I tapped but got no response.

"Joanne, you have to help me get you into a jacket." She didn't respond.

A sob surfaced. I couldn't deal with this shit…. I gulped and forced myself to concentrate. Yes, I could cope, and all Joanne needed was warmth. I wouldn't extrapolate on other possibilities.

"Joanne, wake up. You've got to get out of your wet jacket and into something dry. Put this on."

It was easy enough to tug the wet one off, but trying to sort out the shape of the new garment was a nightmare. I fancied it was a jacket, but trying to find the sleeves, collar and buttonholes in the dark with a seriously befuddled brain was a challenge.

Finally I managed to organise it into something usable and forced Joanne into it. She wasn't actually comatose, but she was seriously uncooperative. At one point, she complained of being too hot and hit my hands away before slumping back, unresponsive.

Once I had her sufficiently covered, I pulled the other jacket over myself. Holy crap, it was good. For the first time, in what seemed like hours, I could feel warmth gradually seeping back into my body – as it happened, not the most comfortable of sensations, even while I welcomed the good it represented. I dragged the jacket around me and immediately I was too hot, then too cold. My fingers itched and burned as blood circulated and feeling returned. It hurt. I believe I moaned and Joanne, probably experiencing the same things, was making the same noises. I settled myself against her and pulled her into the circle of my arm.

Some survival programme I'd once watched had explained that living creatures had enough warmth, if shared, to resuscitate a victim of hypothermia. I settled down to snuggle up to Joanne and ensure we both stayed alive.

When I stretched my legs out, I discovered I'd inadvertently pulled a third item from the pegs, which was currently tangling my feet. It was rougher, long and made me sneeze. It was long enough, I found as I dragged it up, to cover our legs and keep us warm between feet and shoulders. I pulled it over us and tucked it under our legs. If the sky outside was any guide, we were still a couple of hours short of the dawn, hopefully long enough for us to warm up and make some sensible decisions once we were in a better condition.

Despite intending to keep watch, I was asleep within minutes.

"How're you feeling?" Joanne's voice, clear and un-slurred, came as a relief. If she was speaking, she must be feeling better.

I opened my eyes. Pale grey light shone beyond the window. I must have been asleep for at least a couple of hours. I turned to look at Joanne.

How did I feel? *Like shit*. My mouth still tasted foul, my head hurt and I ached all over. I assumed she felt the same. She certainly looked awful, but then I wasn't feeling too flash myself, so I moderated my reply.

"Tingly, itchy and tired, but OK. I hope you don't mind me cuddling up to you, but I thought we'd better share our warmth."

"It's fine, no worries." Joanne sounded lazily amused. "When Jack said he was bringing you to meet us, he didn't tell us we were going to get this close so soon."

I gave a small laugh. "I think it's called developing closer ties."

There was a long silence.

"I wasn't sure we'd get through the night," Joanne said softly.

"Me neither. Last night I felt my whole brain go numb with the cold. At least now I can think."

"Hot food and drink would be good too." Joanne was quiet for a bit. I shifted closer beside her. We still needed all the warmth we could generate.

"What do you really think's been going on at the lodge?" she asked after a while.

I hesitated, trying to put the pieces together.

"I think it's to do with Wenjun," I said. "Ray said Lee recognised him from earlier in China, although his name was different then. Ray was too wrapped up in their own concerns trying to find their father to be very interested, but it makes you wonder who Wenjun actually is, why he changed his name and what he's doing in a remote part of New Zealand. Jack said he was sure the police would have investigated political links when Zhang disappeared, but of course, they wouldn't have known Wenjun isn't who he says he is."

Joanne considered this. "There must be something Wenjun's covering up, which is why he tried to get rid of us tonight, and it looks like Wu is Wenjun's fixer. He must have thought you'd discovered something in the hangar because you pushed past him to have a look around. It would be why he got Mary to attack you. By extension, that led to the attack on both of us. Perhaps Wenjun thought he had to protect his position when Zhang and Lee recognised him, and we're just collateral damage."

We were both quiet for a while as we thought things through.

"Brett already knew about Zhang," Joanne said with certainty. "It's how he knew where to find you. Even if he wasn't actually involved in Zhang's death, he was aware of it and helped cover it up."

"Lee said his father's friend, the premier, had been cutting back on corruption," I added. "Maybe Wenjun's been a bad boy, fiddled the books and got caught? But how does that explain Paul? He's obviously involved somehow too."

"Didn't you say Wenjun was one of the investors in the lodge? That would be a lot of money," said Joanne. "Maybe it's a way of Paul and Wenjun laundering cash."

"It's all conjecture," I sighed. "We need the police. Now they have a new body to deal with. If the remains in the swamp are Li Na, how did she fit in to all this, and why was she killed? When

I first saw the photo on the wall, I thought she was looking at Zhang. Maybe they had a thing going? Charles said she got close to a guest – maybe he was talking about Zhang. Maybe Wenjun was jealous? At least with the discovery of Zhang's body, the police will have to go right back to scratch and reopen the case into his disappearance as well. Maybe they can sort it out."

"Maybe," Joanne yawned.

I smiled at her.

"Dawn's nearly breaking. Are you OK if I get up and see what I can find around the place? There's almost enough light now for me to have a look around without walking into something."

"See if you can find a magic carpet so I can get back home to Pat."

"If only," I said. I'd be pretty happy as well if I could find such a thing. I was sure I wanted to see Jack just as much as she wanted to see Pat.

I levered myself up onto my feet. I was stiff and bruised, but there was no serious damage. I was careful to stand to the side of the window when I looked out. It seemed unlikely anyone would be waiting outside, but it didn't hurt to be careful.

The sky outside had the soft muted monochrome shades that pre-empt dawn. The sun would rise on the opposite side of the building but already the upper leaves on the trees I could see had a lighter tinge to them. There was sufficient visibility in the building for me to make out some details.

It turned out that Joanne and I had settled down in an area divided from the rest of the building by a series of metal storage cabinets that effectively formed a small ante-room. I went around them and found the area beyond was still quite dark. My eyes were gradually adjusting and I crept forward into the gloom.

I'd thought at first that I could follow the line of the wall around the space but had to reconsider that plan when I kept stumbling into items stored on the floor at the base of the wall. Going out further seemed risky, but in fact the floor there was largely clear of debris.

I'd gone some way into the space before I thought to turn and check behind me.

Against the light it was easy to see the large shape I'd been walking around and missed before. I'd come within inches of banging into it.

I gave a little crow of pleasure. "Hey, Joanne, I think I've found your magic carpet."

What I'd actually found was a good deal better. Even as a child, I'd never been completely convinced about the aerodynamic properties of magic carpets and largely rejected their presence in the *Arabian Nights* in favour of winged horses.

Now, silhouetted against the light I could see the sturdy Cessna 182 that filled the space. We'd stumbled on a hangar.

I tried to remember what Charles had said…. something about the owner keeping an aircraft here so he could fly in and out of his property. Well, if he kept the keys near-by as well, I'd be happy to borrow his plane and take Joanne and myself home. I assumed the owner was Paul, and we didn't owe him any favours.

CHAPTER TWENTY FIVE

"WHAT DO YOU MEAN?" JOANNE CAME forward into the hangar. "I can't see anything."

"Come towards me slowly and you'll see it," I said. "Just be careful you don't bang your head." It was brightening, but it was still dim inside.

"Oh, it's a plane! Can you fly it?"

"I sure as hell intend to," I said. I opened the pilot's door, reached in and groped along the dashboard. Nothing.

"What are you doing?" asked Joanne.

"Hoping Paul leaves his keys in the aircraft," I said. "If we're lucky, he does"

I ran my hands over the panel instruments on the console. In the poor light it was hard to see what they were. If I remembered the layout of a 182 correctly, the slot for keyed ignition should be down on the left-hand side of the column.

"Bingo. Found them."

"Jeez, are we on a roll?"

"I guess, but this is his plane, parked securely in his own hangar. He probably never bothers to remove them."

I paced around the aircraft for a cursory pre-flight inspection. "If we can get airborne and across that river, we'll be safe. Even if the paddock by your house isn't long enough to land on, in the worst-case scenario, I can put down on a farm track. The main thing is to get out of this valley."

"Let's see how the hangar doors open, but I don't want to actually open them until the last minute, so we don't alert anyone to our presence. You try at this end and I'll look at the far end. They must slide or fold somehow."

"Of course, if they're padlocked we've got a problem," Joanne said gloomily as she bent to feel around the floor.

"Maybe," I said, "but the door wasn't locked so maybe Paul's casual about security all the way up here." The door I was examining abutted the wall smoothly with no obvious locking device at ground level. I stood and ran my hands up the edge of the frame.

"Ah," I said as my hand encountered a chain. I fiddled with it for a few minutes but couldn't work out how it was fixed.

"Damn. I wish I had a torch. There isn't enough light to see how this works, and my hands are so sore after the last couple of days. My fingers feel like sausages."

"There's a bolt down here," Joanne reported. "I can wiggle it." There was a pause before I heard her give a soft, satisfied grunt. "Got it. I've pulled it out. I think if you can unlatch your end, we should be able to slide the doors."

"I'm working on it," I muttered as I carried on fumbling with the chain. I could feel it caught on something but couldn't work out how to free it.

"Crap!" I swore in frustration, pulling as hard as I could.

"Got it!" and with a final lift and tug hook was free of the locking contraption on the frame.

"We've done it," crowed Joanne. "Do you think we should just try and slide it a little bit to see if it works?"

I weighed the options. At some point we were going to have to open the doors, even if there was the nightmare risk that Wenjun and Paul were waiting outside. My plan was to get the aircraft ready and only open them once we were ready to fly. On the other hand, I still had some checks to do, and in the murk of the hangar it was going to be difficult to see the fuel level on a dipstick.

"In a second," I replied. "I just want to see where Paul stores his fuel. He must have a tank or even jerry cans somewhere around."

I could see more clearly now as I searched, but even so, I only found where the oil was stored when I backed into a shelf I hadn't noticed. At the rear, a large tank was standing on a trailer.

"Bingo again," I said. "I guarantee that's fuel. It's even got a pump mechanism on top of the tank. I hope there's enough in the plane already, but if we need more, at least there's some here if we need it."

I walked back to the doors and took a breath. "I guess it's now or never. Let's do it!"

Once we'd got them moving, the heavy metal doors were surprisingly easy to. I winced at every squeak they made. As soon I'd created a big enough gap I stuck my head through and looked around. The coast appeared to be clear. We had to hope that Paul and Wenjun were so certain we were dead or dying out in the forest that they hadn't bothered to check.

"All clear?" asked Joanne as I pulled my head back in and continued pushing the doors.

"So far, so good," I said. "Let's hope those murdering bastards are having a nice lie-in this morning and assume we're dead."

When both doors were open I returned to the aircraft. With the hangar now filled with soft morning light, it was easy for me to complete the checks.

"Hop in," I said, "and get your safety belt on. Once I get this machine moving I'm not stopping for anything. We'll do a rolling take-off and get out of here."

I strapped myself in and turned to Joanne to check she'd done the same.

"Shit, I left my jacket in the other room. I'll just get it."

I exploded. "For fuck's sake! Really?" Her face looked so shocked I immediately felt guilty.

"Sorry, Joanne. Get it. Quickly. I'm starting the engine up, so don't go around the front of the plane. Come around the back of the tail."

"OK. I'll hurry, I promise."

I ran through my mental check list as I primed the engine, switched on master and magnetos and turned the key. The aircraft might not have been used in a while, but after I tried a second time the engine took and roared into life.

I throttled back and let it idle. It wouldn't hurt the engine to have a bit of a warm-up.

I opened my door and looked back for Joanne. She was standing at the entrance to the ante-chamber where we'd been sleeping, her jacket in her hand.

"Come on!" I yelled. "Go around the back of the aircraft and get in. Don't go forward of the wing struts."

She shook her head but didn't move.

From the darkness behind her, Wenjun stepped up beside her. His hand gripped her arm.

"Get out of the plane!" he shouted. I could barely hear him over the noise of the engine, but his meaning was clear.

I stared at them both and felt my stomach drop. We'd been so bloody close to being safe I'd almost begun to believe in a happy ending. Now we were back to square one. I was so tired I could have cried. I turned and looked forward at the airstrip past the hangar doors. The desperate need to go, to get away from this place, was almost overwhelming. I craved the freedom of being in the air, in a world I understood and controlled.

"Claire, go! Go, get help!" Joanne yelled at the top of her voice.

I turned back to look at them.

Wenjun shook her.

"Go!" Joanne begged me.

Slowly, watching me all the time, a big smile on his face, Wenjun pulled a handgun and put it to her head.

He said nothing, just kept looking at me as he gave a slight shrug. "'Your choice'," it said.

There *was* no choice. Joanne had grabbed me and abandoned Brett to his fate yesterday, but Brett was a compromised character. Joanne, by any definition, was innocent. If I hadn't been nosy, if I'd obeyed Jack and refrained from meddling in Wu's business, she wouldn't be in danger today.

I considered my options and left the aircraft idling while I released my safety belt and stepped down from the plane.

"I'm so sorry," she said as I drew closer. "I'm so very sorry."

"Not your fault," I said shortly. I was angry and frustrated with her, with me, and most of all with the situation.

Wenjun had lowered his weapon as he saw me approach.

"I told Paul to kill you," he said bluntly. "Direct ways are always the most effective."

"But not the most intelligent." Paul had entered the hangar behind Wenjun. "You two are a problem," he said pleasantly, as he walked around his partner. "I thought we'd fixed that problem last night, but no, here you are, alive and well and trying to steal my plane. We can't let you go, and getting rid of you is proving difficult. It's a bit of a dilemma."

He sauntered past me and switched off the ignition. He was frowning when he turned back.

"Just as well we came up here to fly ourselves out to Auckland this morning, otherwise we might have missed you. Horse thieves used to be hanged. I imagine the same could apply to aircraft thieves."

"Why are you doing this?" I asked. "How are you connected to the lodge and Wenjun?"

Keep him talking, my inner voice advised. If he's talking, he's not killing you.

He gave a low chuckle. "Well now, that would take far too long to explain. You know, I really should just let you take that plane on your own. The crash when you discovered you couldn't control it would solve all our problems and I'd get to claim the insurance as a bonus."

I said nothing but tried to look suitably terrified.

"She's a pilot," Wenjun said impatiently. "Of course she can fly the bloody thing."

"Are you now?" Paul looked at me as if he were seeing me for the first time. "What a clever girl. I had no idea."

Again, ridiculous given the situation, I felt that familiar forging of camaraderie. Not that I thought it would help us. Even as I watched, I saw his eyes narrow in calculation.

"You've given me an idea," he said. "Keep an eye on them," he ordered Wenjun. "I won't be a second."

His voice sounded artificially loud in the sudden quiet of the hangar. He picked up a couple of tools from the bench against the wall. I watched suspiciously as he lifted the engine cowling and fossicked around inside. Most light aircraft have simple engines that anyone with a small amount of mechanical knowledge can fathom. By extension, it's equally simple for anyone armed with that knowledge and a screwdriver to disable or at least inhibit the engine's performance.

If Paul thought I was piloting an aircraft into the air when he'd been mucking around under the cowling, he was going to have to think again.

"Just a slight modification." He smiled at me as he screwed the cowling on.

"There you go, ladies. All ready to step aboard." He gestured at the aircraft.

"You don't seriously think I'm flying a plane you've tampered with, do you?"

There's good reason that all pilots pre-flight check their aircraft. It's preferable to find a problem before you take off than have to deal with the issue once in the sky. After all, you can't pull over and park on a convenient cloud while you fix your plane. To get behind the controls of a compromised aircraft knowingly went against all my training.

There was no way I was going to get into that aircraft willingly. On the other hand, the degree to which he'd compromised the plane depended on what exactly he had done to it, which in turn depended on how extensive his aviation experience and knowledge was.

As far as I was able to tell from watching him, Paul hadn't damaged the ailerons, rudder and elevators, collectively known as 'flight controls' which enable aircraft to be manoeuvred and steered. His tinkering had most likely involved the oil or fuel system. The question was, how badly?

Few people outside the aviation industry realise that aircraft don't plummet from the sky simply because an engine stops working. In twin-engine aircraft, the one remaining engine will, in most cases, be able to keep the plane airborne until it can make a safe landing.

In a single-engine aircraft such as Paul's Cessna, a failed engine simply converts the plane into a rather heavy glider, descending at 500 feet or so a minute. Assuming the plane reached sufficient altitude before the engine failed, it's possible to cover a considerable distance before touchdown. More than sufficient time to cross the river. If we were lucky.

And there lay the problem. I knew we were already high up, probably towards the top of the hill. If we had the opportunity to get safely airborne above the trees and ridge line, the chances were we could glide a fair way out of the valley. But this still depended on what Paul had done. If the aircraft couldn't get sufficient height, we'd crash into the trees which was unlikely to have a happy ending.

Death by bullet, or death by aircraft. Which was it to be? I didn't fancy either.

I glanced at Joanne who was staring blankly back at me and realised I would have to make the decision unaided. Joanne was gutsy, but she knew nothing about aviation. The gamble, and the responsibility, would be mine.

"Get on the plane." Wenjun shoved Joanne. She stumbled forward and he pointed his gun at the back of her head.

The gesture spawned a moment of clarity. I suddenly understood.

"It was you! You shot Li Na!" I accused. "The body in the swamp, that was your doing!"

Wenjun swung the gun towards me. "Shut up and get in the plane," he snarled.

"She had fallen for Zhang, so you shot her," I stated with growing confidence. "Or maybe she knew you'd killed Zhang and would have betrayed you, so you had to get rid of her. It's all becoming clear." I paused. "You didn't tell Mary, though, did you? She didn't know her friend was dead, although she knew about Zhang."

I'd hoped asking him questions would buy us time. I'd read somewhere that murderers liked to discuss their crimes.

"Your name isn't Wenjun either, is it?" I said. "Zhang knew who you were, just like his son Lee knew. Is it associated with crimes back in China? Are you hiding out in the lodge? Was that why you killed them both? They knew your real name?"

He paled, and my certainty grew. Wenjun was the nexus of the evil at the lodge, and Wu, if I'd heard the conversation right last night, was his lackey.

"What did you do? Ray seemed to think you were something to do with buying gold for China. Did you defraud the government?"

Unfortunately, Wenjun wasn't the talkative type.

His eyes narrowed into a glare of undiluted viciousness, and the gun in his hand wavered erratically. I abruptly shut up and took a step back. Jack once told me most people couldn't hit a barn door with a handgun unless they stood closer than two metres in front of it. This may have been true, but I didn't want to test the hypothesis.

"I think you should get into the aircraft now." Paul's voice was quiet behind me. "You're pushing your luck. I won't be able to control Wenjun if you rile him too much, and I don't want more bodies with bullet holes to dispose of. Much better if you die doing what you love, don't you think?"

I allowed him to pull me around by the arm and lead me to the plane. Behind, I heard Joanne protesting as Wenjun chivvied her to the other side of the aircraft.

Paul opened the door for me. "Have a safe flight."

I glared at him. "What have you done to the plane?"

"Ah, that would be telling," he smiled. "Much more fun for you to find out for yourself."

"You fucking bastard!" I was shivering with nerves.

"Don't forget your safety belt, will you?" he reminded me with an evil smile as he shut the door.

Wenjun shoved Joanne in beside me. We shared a glance, her eyes were frightened.

Paul and Wenjun had retreated to safety behind the aircraft.

Unfortunately, I wouldn't be able to attack them with the propeller once I'd started the plane

"What's going to happen?" Joanne asked.

"We're going to taxi up the strip. That will put some distance between us and these two. I will also put the heater on, so we'll be warm. Once we're rolling, I'll have a chance to check oil and fuel pressure gauges. If I knew what Paul did to the engine, it would help. He's probably disconnected a fuel hose, but I can't be certain. I didn't see any fuel dripping under the plane, which I would have expected."

"Can we even take off?" Her voice wavered. Pity engulfed me. Her hands were clenched tightly in her lap. At least I had something to do – she had to be passive and hope I made the right call.

"Honestly? I don't know if we can, or if we should. But if we stay here we'll have a bullet in us for certain. At least this gives us another option. I'm sorry, I can't think what else to do."

I turned the switches on and listened closely to the engine's beat. As far as I could tell, it sounded fine. I slipped the brake and we rolled forward. I wanted to put as much distance between Paul, Wenjun and us as I could.

A windsock was positioned on the opposite side of the runway. I turned the aircraft downwind and taxied towards the far end of the airstrip.

"The way I see it, we have two choices," I said. "I take us up to the end of the runway and the two of us jump out of the plane and hightail it into the trees. We'd have a head start on Paul and Wenjun, so maybe we could try and hide ourselves again in the forest."

"Oh, shit no!" Joanne sounded horrified. She gave me a sheepish look. "I'm absolutely knackered. I don't think we could survive another few hours out there, even if they didn't catch us and I couldn't run away if they did." She bit her lip. "Sorry, I'm being feeble."

"I'm much the same," I said. "I'm running on empty. No, I don't think either of us are in a state for more orienteering, which leaves the second choice. We hope the damage Paul has done isn't too serious and that we can get enough altitude to glide to safety if the engine conks out. Neither of them are very attractive options."

Joanne gave me a slight smile. "It's OK, I trust you."

I wanted to say I wasn't entitled to her trust. Instead I nodded, and gave her a wry smile.

Apart from peripheral glances outside the aircraft to check we were tracking straight up the runway, most of my attention was focused on the control panel inside the little plane as I tried to assess what, if any, damage there was. The flight controls were all operating freely and fully, and the gauges showed a proper degree of pressure. It was most perplexing.

We reached the end of the runway and I swung the Cessna around to face the wind. We'd come some 500 metres uphill from the hangar.

Paul and Wenjun stood watching. Blood-thirsty ghouls at a public execution.

"Fucking bastards," swore Joanne.

"Morituri te salutant," I muttered grimly.

"What?"

"Sorry, I'm nervous and it was a bit of bad taste. It means *'We who are about to die salute you'.*"

"Oh, like gladiators?"

"Just like gladiators."

"Well, some gladiators lived," said Joanne staunchly. "I watched the TV series."

"Too bloody right," I said, thrusting the throttle through to full. "Today is not our day to die."

The Cessna accelerated down the airstrip. It was nearly flying as we passed the watching men and the hangar. I held it on the ground for as long as I could before letting her lift.

I'd loved flying since my first lesson, and I'd had my share of scary moments over the years, but the terror I felt at that moment was unprecedented and crippling in its intensity. I held on to the yoke with a white-knuckled grip as if I could coerce the plane into the air by sheer force and will-power. If the engine failed now and we crashed into the trees ahead, we'd be dead.

My entire focus was on the aircraft and our need to achieve as much altitude as possible. We'd never survive an emergency without sufficient height. I listened to the engine, studying the gauges and instruments with a fierce concentration.

We'd lifted high enough already to clear the trees surrounding the airstrip, and I kept in as steep a climb as I could.

Joanne was silent beside me. She must have been terrified. I didn't even know if she'd been in a light aircraft before.

To my relief we were soon high enough to be able to see over the trees and down into the valley beyond. Not too far in front of us was rolling farmland, and I could see the road we'd travelled on the quad.

I'd considered flying over the ridge which Phil had said separated this valley from Pat's. It was tempting – and by far the most direct route to safety on the far side of the river. The drawback was the thick bush that covered the hillsides. If something went wrong, there'd be nowhere to put down safely.

With regret I flagged the notion and carried on following the road down the valley.

Retakure Lodge was in sight on our left when I decided we were probably high enough.

I heaved a sigh of relief and looked across at Joanne.

"So far so good," I said as I lowered the nose of the aircraft into the attitude for level flight.

She gave a tremulous smile. "Well done."

I pulled the throttle back to cruise mode. Nothing happened. I pulled again, but the throttle wouldn't shift. I tugged harder.

"What the fuck?"

"What's the matter?" Joanne sounded terrified.

"The throttle's jammed on full power. I can't shift it."

"What do you mean?"

"I mean I can't slow us down. We're on full power."

"Does that mean we can only go fast?"

I was wrenching at the throttle so hard it was a wonder it didn't break off in my hand.

"No. Well, not entirely. It means we can't descend and prepare for a landing in the usual way. I'll have to turn the engine off otherwise we won't get out of the air."

"Is this what Paul did?"

"I suppose so, although I'm fucked if I know how."

I glanced across at her. "It's not as bad as it sounds. We train for this. For landing a plane without power, I mean. We just need to get across the river, pick somewhere to land and go through the drills."

All of which sounded confident, and as I'd hoped, Joanne relaxed a little. There is, of course, a massive difference between practising drills and coping with a real emergency, and my nerves were at full stretch. At least I knew I had the skills necessary to complete the task. My immediate concern was the way the gauge showed the engine temperature rising.

I looked outside. We'd passed the lodge and were approaching the washed-out bridge. From the air we could see the extent of the damage and how completely the river had destroyed the structure. Boulders and debris spread across the bank on the lodge side and littered the road. Only one piling from the bridge had survived, standing forlornly in the middle of the mess. The far side was high enough not to have been affected.

We were right over the water when the engine suddenly gave a cough. A nano-second later it caught again for a moment or two, which meant we'd crossed the river before it missed again, stuttered, then failed completely.

I stared through the window as the turning propeller slowed and stopped.

"It never rains but it pours. This is the real thing," I said. "A text book forced landing with no power."

I trimmed the plane up for a glide and looked about for a suitable landing site. When our problems consisted purely of a stuck throttle, I'd envisaged flying overhead Pat and Joanne's farm, picking a likely paddock and landing there. That was no longer an option. We were going to have to land within the next few minutes.

It was perhaps inevitable that the perfect spot to put the aircraft down was on the lodge side of the river. I had sufficient altitude to retreat to the paddocks on the far side, but we'd taken such risks to escape I wasn't prepared to give up and go back there.

On our side, the road ran beside a scrub-covered cliff several metres above level of the water. I didn't know what lay beyond the cliff and didn't have the altitude or the time to explore it on the off chance there was a good site up there.

I circled to see if there were any other options before making my decision. I pointed to the road beneath us.

"That's our landing strip."

At least there was a long, straight stretch to land on, so I wouldn't have to worry about traffic.

"Keep an eye out for wires," I instructed Joanne. There was no street lighting this deep in the rural heartland, but electricity and phone lines strung across the road would kill us if I didn't notice them in time.

I thought there was a slightly different feel to the aircraft with the propeller stationary than during simulated drills, and with no headset I couldn't make the necessary radio calls. Otherwise my training kicked in as I positioned us for our final turn onto the road.

I ran through the final checks, lowered the flaps then reached forward and flicked off the switches and ignition.

"We're committed now. No point in risking the engine firing up again."

It was impossibly hard to judge from altitude whether the width of the road would be adequate. I worried about clipping a wing on a power pole or an overhanging branch. Either could prove disastrous, with a massive drop to the river on one side and a rock wall on the other.

"Please keep an eye out and tell me if you see any power lines in the way," I reminded Joanne.

If I'd missed spotting any, we were done for. There were no second chances on this approach.

The road proved wide enough although I had to duck and dive around hazards on the final approach. The ground seemed to come up to meet us incredibly fast. It wasn't the smoothest landing I've ever done, but we touched down with space to spare on each wing tip and rolled forward.

I let go of the yoke, leaned back and shut my eyes. We'd made it.

The relief was so great that without Joanne I think I'd have stayed there, unmoving, and gone to sleep.

"Hey, up there!" Joanne's shout made me open my eyes and look out the window.

"Hallelujah!" I exclaimed as a helicopter came into sight over the edge of the cliff to our right. "The cavalry's arrived. It's the police chopper."

"Jump out, wave to them," I instructed.

She scrambled away from the plane as I checked I'd shut down the engine correctly and released the seat belt.

CHAPTER TWENTY SIX

B Y THE TIME I GOT OUT, the helicopter had landed 50 metres down the road. I leaned against the Cessna's empennage and watched the occupants climb out.

DI Alastair Taylor was recognisable by his height and leanness. A policewoman clambered out after him, followed by another man. I let my breath out in a long sigh of relief when the last one emerged and I saw it was Jack.

I couldn't have moved if I'd wanted to. The relief that flooded through me had sapped the last strength from my legs, and I stood there shaking, completely vulnerable, as reaction set in. God alone knew what I looked like. I watched as Jack scanned my face then hurried towards me.

Behind him Joanne was talking to Alastair and gesturing towards the remains of the bridge. I shut my eyes in exhaustion.

"Claire?" I felt Jack's arms around me as I was pulled into his embrace.

"Sweet Jesus, are you OK?"

I rested against him, my face buried into his shoulder. I couldn't stop shivering. I felt his arms tighten.

"Oh, baby, are you all right?"

I managed a slight nod.

I felt his warm breath on my forehead. "It's OK. You're safe now. I've got you. The police are here and it's all over." His comfort and sympathy undid me, and I felt my eyes welling with tears. I shivered and shook against him.

His lips lightly brushed my hair. "Thank God we found you. Pat and I have been frantic."

I snuggled deeper into his shoulder as sobs continued to wrack me. Who knew heaven could be standing safe and loved in a man's warm embrace? The notion sat awkwardly with me. I generally avoid romantic fiction, but I fancied this was one of its tropes.

"Oh, sweetheart." The sympathy in his voice simply made the tears flow more freely.

I despise easy tears, and I'm not keen on women who resort to them at the first opportunity. It was disturbing to realise how shaken up I was. It took a while, but I gradually managed to regain control.

Jack must have felt the change in me because he loosened his arms.

"I'm sorry," I said. "I didn't mean to break down."

Aside from anything else, I was professionally embarrassed. I didn't want him to think the forced landing had caused my outburst. That came with my job.

It was everything else Joanne and I had been through, and I simply lacked the words and energy to begin to explain the last twenty-four hours.

He smiled. "Think nothing of it. It's been another adventure, right?"

I smiled back wryly. "Sort of."

He opened the Cessna's door and helped me back into my seat before climbing in beside me. He reached over for my hand. His fingers curled around mine and I gave a little smile.

"What happened to the plane? Why did you land here?"

"Engine failure," I said.

"Fucking hell. But you're OK?"

I nodded.

"Shit happens, I suppose," he said. "Just as well you're a

capable pilot."

"It wasn't that," I said. "The plane was tampered with." My anger at the deliberate mutilation of the aircraft reignited, and the surge of rage I had felt at Paul's actions fuelled my energy. Suddenly words poured from me as I explained what he'd done.

Jack looked puzzled. "Who's Paul, and why did he want to kill you? Why did you go to the forestry block in the first place? I thought Brett was going to fly you and Joanne back to the farm? What went wrong?"

I belatedly realised I'd launched into a tirade about Paul without any other introduction. No wonder Jack looked confused.

"I haven't explained this very well, have I?" I said sheepishly. "I need to go back to the beginning, from when you guys left us."

Jack was gazing out of the window.

"Save it till later. You'll have to tell the police anyway. I can hear it then."

I looked up the road to where Joanne was now talking to the policewoman. Alastair was heading towards us.

Jack climbed down to greet him. I followed. I was over the immediate emotional reaction, but that didn't mean I wasn't tired, hunger, and sore. I needed a hot bath to ease away the aches and pains, and some hot food.

Alastair shook my hand. "OK?" he asked. "Joanne's already told us the gist of what happened to you. Sarah's phoning Joanne's husband so he can come and pick you all up. We're going to the lodge. You know there was trouble there last night? Now Joanne's information changes things. It may be the case has now cracked wide open. We'll take your statements later"

I nodded. All I wanted was to get back home with Jack and be in my own place, but in the meantime the farm, dinner and a hot soak sounded like a fine interim destination.

"What about you, Jack?" asked Alastair. "Do you want to come with us or go back with the others?"

Jack didn't hesitate. "I'll go back with Claire," he said, "unless you need me."

Alastair shook his head. "We've got reinforcements coming

in. Given everything that's going on, there'll be at least one new crime scene to set up – maybe more. You stay, and I'll catch up with you later."

He studied the Cessna and then spoke to me. "Is there some way of clearing this plane to the side of the road? It's a quiet spot, but it could pose a hazard at night if it's still here."

"I'll push it as clear as I can," I said. "It's not going anywhere else until an engineer has checked it. It's well and truly stuffed at the moment."

"I'll warn the council so the road crew can put some warning lights on it," Alastair nodded. "OK. I'll see you all later when we've finished across the river."

He headed back to the helicopter and Jack helped me shove the aircraft off the road. There was a clear area by the war memorial, opposite the bridge, and we pushed it there. He helped me secure the poor plane safely, clear of the road. I took the logbook and manuals with me. I'd give them to Alastair when I saw him again. I wondered what would happen to the Cessna. I supposed it would eventually have to be dismantled and trucked out.

CHAPTER TWENTY SEVEN

PAT MUST HAVE BROKEN THE SPEED record. I remember the drive from the lodge to the farm taking forty minutes. He achieved it in just under twenty. The tyres actually squealed as he applied the brakes when he drew up beside us.

We'd been sitting in the Cessna to keep out of the cold. The temperature was in fact fairly warm, but Joanne and I seemed to share a heightened sensitivity after our night in the forest. We'd been too busy coping with the plane to notice, but now the adrenalin was leaving our systems we were chilled and shivering. Jack had given me his jacket and passed his jumper to Joanne, but they couldn't stop the deep shudders that ran through both of us.

Jack climbed out and turned to help Joanne out of the back seat. I clambered out on my own.

Jack stayed beside me as I slowly locked up the doors and luggage hatch. Pat and Joanne needed a couple of moments alone.

After we'd given them a tactful moment or two, we went over to Pat's vehicle to find Joanne sobbing in Pat's arms.

I saw Jack's wry smile as we eased our way into the back seat.

Neither of us said anything, but my brain churned.

Joanne was no snowflake. She'd kept her poise and been composed and helpful to the police since we'd landed. She'd proved herself gutsy, capable, loyal and determined, and yet now she was sobbing in Pat's arms like a child.

It pretty much mirrored what I'd done with Jack. Even as I processed Joanne's tears, I already knew the answer. Pat was her husband, had been for years. Her tears represented trust that she could be vulnerable with him and not lose her dignity. He was her safe place.

I glanced at Jack and found him looking at me. He quirked an eyebrow and I found myself smiling in response.

It seemed I'd already decided he was *my* safe place. I carefully steered away from any thoughts of a future together. What would be, would be.

Joanne and Pat finally took their seats in the vehicle. I was behind Pat, so couldn't see Joanne. What gave me pause was seeing Pat's red-rimmed eyes reflected in the rear-vision mirror. Jack had said Pat was beside himself the night before. I could only guess at the intensity of emotion that had pushed such a controlled and laconic man to tears.

Pat drove back to the farm at a fraction of the speed he'd come over at. I was half asleep against Jack's shoulder when we turned into the farm drive.

"Food or bath?" Pat was asking as we walked into the kitchen.

"Food," said Joanne. I agreed. We hadn't eaten since lunch-time yesterday and since then we'd been drugged, been close to hypothermia, slept rough and gone through a forced landing. I was starving.

"I can do baked beans on toast?" said Pat awkwardly. I guessed Joanne always did the cooking, but she sat slumped on a kitchen stool looking as shagged as I felt and clearly wasn't going to be cooking anything.

"If you like, I'll poach some eggs to go with that," offered Jack.

I already knew Jack could cook, but it was obvious Pat was out of his element in a kitchen. Still, between them, they cobbled up a meal within twenty minutes. Baked beans on toast with poached eggs. It was the sort of meal Mum used to make when my sister and I were school kids.

While they'd been cooking, Joanne and I filled them in on everything that had happened since the men left us yesterday. She did most of the talking while I added details and filled in the story of Mary's perfidy. I flinched a little when I had to describe how I'd stupidly followed her into the hangar, imagining Jack's unspoken criticism.

It was too late to worry about it, and besides, I was too tired to care.

"Last night was a nightmare," Pat said, as soon as we finished.

"When we couldn't reach your mobiles, Jack called the lodge. Charles answered and told us you'd disappeared; that the quad bike had been found at the end of the road but there was no sign of you. He said Ray, Stephen and some others were out searching for you. Another body had been found on the property, two of his staff had been in a fight and one was hurt, so he was waiting for emergency services."

"It was more than a nightmare," said Jack. "I don't think either of us got any sleep."

His hands rested on my shoulders as if he couldn't bear *not* to touch me.

I scoffed a full double portion of food, appreciating its warmth as much as its quantity. Joanne wasn't far behind me in the trencherman stakes. I wondered how this affected her carbohydrate loading, or whatever it was marathon runners did before a big race.

I washed it down with scalding tea. Jack helped me up the stairs and scrubbed my back in the bath.

The food and the warmth of the hot water briefly revived me.

I was already in bed when I finally plucked up courage.

"I feel I owe you an apology," I said.

"What? Why's that?"

"Because I didn't take your advice about not being alone and followed Mary into the hangar. I thought you'd be angry."

Jack stared at me for a long moment before sitting beside me.

"Claire, I'm not angry with you. Yes, I warned you, but how could I be angry? You don't have to take my advice. I just wanted to keep you safe, and I worry about you. You're so brave and bold that sometimes you don't see the danger."

"Oh," I said. I tried to see myself as that brave, bold, woman, and failed. I'd spent an appreciable part of the last few days in an almost constant state of terror. I was nervous of everything, and I knew I tended to over-think things.

Jack reached out and took my hand.

"Baby, I love you to pieces, you must know that. I went through hell last night worrying about you. I love you for everything you are and wouldn't have you any other way. It's just as well you're so bloody competent, because you're fucking hard to keep up with, let alone protect. Last night must have taken years off my life span."

"You've never said that before," I said.

"What?"

"That you love me."

"Of course I have."

I shook my head. "No. You've never said the words." I gave a little laugh. "It's been bugging me, because I told you I loved you. I felt a bit of a dork."

"Shit. I thought I had – or that you knew anyway." Jack tugged me across the bed so he could get his arm around me and cuddle me tight against his body.

"I'm *so* sorry," he said ruefully. "Will you forgive me? I'm such an idiot. I hadn't realised."

Damn it, I felt tears starting to well again. I must stop this emotional response to every little thing.

I dropped my head to hide my face.

"Yes," I said, sounding a little unsteady.

"Joanne said it was because you were a Kiwi male."

"You discussed this with Joanne?" Jack sounded horrified. "Now I'm the one who looks like a dork. My family will never let me live it down."

"I don't think Joanne will talk. She told me it was obvious to everyone you loved me."

"I do."

The kiss that followed was long and satisfactory.

"I don't deserve you," Jack said at last.

"I probably don't deserve you either, so it's just as well we've got each other."

He kissed me again.

"Go to sleep," he said, "and never, for one second, doubt that I love you."

It was evening when he woke me.

"Alastair's downstairs and wants to talk to you. I'd have put him off so as not to wake you, but if we want to be out of here tomorrow, I thought it best to get it over with."

I nodded, still groggy with sleep. "Good thinking," I said as I forced myself to sit up. I fumbled about trying to find clean clothes.

Those I'd worn yesterday were irretrievably ruined – sticky and stained with pine resin, ripped on brambles and twigs as we'd forged through the forest and dirty beyond belief. I hoped it was only my imagination, but I thought I could still detect the nauseating stench of Zhang's dead body on them. I didn't intend to even try and save them so they were consigned to the rubbish.

But I was down to my last pair of jeans and sweatshirt. If we didn't go home the next day, my wardrobe would be in trouble.

The others were assembled in the kitchen by the time I made it down the stairs.

Joanne was pouring tea at the bench. She studied me as I walked in.

"You look better," she said.

"So do you. Did you get a nap?"

"I assume I did. I can't remember anything that happened after lunch until Pat woke me. I must have been dead to the world, but I feel all the better for it."

I accepted a cup of tea and sat down beside Jack. Alastair introduced the woman beside him as Sergeant Sarah Adams.

"Hi," she said.

Joanne came and sat on the other side of me.

"OK," said Alastair. We need to take statements from both of

you. Claire, I gather from Jack that you'll be leaving tomorrow?"
I nodded.

"Fine, we should have all the paperwork in place."

Alastair took a sip of his tea. "Before going into that I thought you'd like an update."

Joanne and I nodded.

"You've heard the body in the swamp was a woman? We've had provisional identification she was a previous employee at the lodge – Li Na. Apparently she disappeared, and it was assumed she'd returned to China after a quarrel with her partner. This is now a homicide case, and our enquiries are continuing.

"The body in the bunker will be a different investigation. Again, the assumption is this is the missing man Zhang. Forensics are already on-site collecting evidence, and their findings will determine proceedings going forward."

"Wenjun killed Li Na," I said. "I'm absolutely certain of it. I accused him of it when we were in the hangar."

"Did he say anything?" Alastair asked.

I shook my head. "No, but I'd got to him. I could tell. His body language screamed his guilt. He started waving his gun around, and Paul basically told me to shut up because he couldn't control Wenjun. I'm sure he killed Zhang as well. If not, you can guarantee Wu did it for him."

"Hmm," Alastair grunted. "You should be aware that both Paul and Wenjun claim they never saw you last night or this morning. They agree Charles had told them you were on the forestry block and they say they went out to see if they could find you but were unsuccessful."

"That's a crock of shit," grumbled Joanne.

"They also accuse you of stealing the Cessna from the hangar."

"The filthy lying bastards," Joanne exploded. "They drugged us, left us out in the cold to die and then damaged the plane trying to kill us."

Alastair looked at me. "As to the damage on the aircraft, have you any idea how it was interfered with?"

I shook my head. "I assumed he'd cut a fuel line or damaged the oil flow. In the end, we had a stuck throttle, which was something I hadn't expected. Then the engine failed, which makes it two completely different incidents. They could be associated, but I wouldn't know. You'd need an aircraft engineer to tell you. Maybe the engine overheated and seized due to being run at high speed for so long, although I wouldn't have thought so."

Alastair grunted. "I'm having the plane trucked to Hamilton. The engineers say they can take the wings off for easy transportation. They'll look at it and tell us what happened. If it shows signs of tampering, then obviously Paul and Wenjun's credibility will be in question."

"That's pretty much where things stand at the moment," he said. "Crime scenes have been set up and it's a work in progress. If the remains in the bunker are those of the missing man, you may have helped us unravel this case."

"When we fled yesterday, Wu was pointing a gun at Brett. Then we heard a shot. What happened?" I asked.

"Brett's the pilot?"

"Yes,"

"He sustained a gunshot wound to the chest and was airlifted out this morning. I understand his condition isn't critical. The owner of the lodge called emergency services yesterday evening, but they couldn't get in. In the interim, he subdued Wu and shut him in a storage room overnight. We arrested Wu this morning."

"Brett led me to Claire when she was in the bunker," said Joanne. "He tried to save us."

Alastair shrugged and looked at Jack. "In Ray's statement he claimed Wenjun is operating under a false name. We've contacted our colleagues in China to confirm this. It might be he's used the lodge to hide from justice in his own country."

"He also financed the lodge," said Jack. "That wouldn't have been cheap."

Alastair shook his head. "Money laundering? Gambling? Theft? Who knows? At least we're now looking in the right direction."

"Any questions? OK, let's get the statements taken."

Joanne and I recorded our stories, and Sarah typed them into her laptop.

"We're all done here," she told Alastair.

"OK. Then we're good to go." Alastair stood up.

"I've got one question before you leave," I said. "What happened to Ray's brother, Lee? Was his death natural?"

Alistair shrugged. "I haven't heard otherwise. If a post-mortem finds something suspicious, it will be investigated."

"Wu was away from the lodge the night Lee died," I said. "If it wasn't a natural death, maybe Wu killed him."

"How did he get back to the lodge again yesterday?" asked Alastair. "The road was out, remember?"

I didn't know. I liked my theory, in spite of its flaws.

"He could have got across if he was determined," Pat said unexpectedly. "He'd have been mad to try it, but there's a flying fox across the river at the back of the Styles's place. It's dodgy as, but it's got a pulley system, so you can cross both ways. I never let my kids play on it, but if you were desperate, and knew it was there, you might give it a go."

We all considered the weather and the state of the river the night of the storm. I gave a little shudder at the thought of it.

Alastair smiled. "OK, it's a hypothesis. We need to work with actual evidence, but I'll bear it in mind if Lee's death does come back as suspicious."

"Do you really think Lee was murdered?" Joanne asked me after Alastair had left.

"Maybe. It's just one more coincidental death. I'm starting to see murder everywhere."

Jack grinned. "As long as you don't think it when you look at me, that's fine."

"Don't tempt me," I replied.

It was hard to process the enormity of events at the lodge, and even harder to accept the bizarre series of coincidences that had inserted us, as innocent bystanders, into the story. We were all subdued, and it was a quiet evening.

Joanne perked up enough to reclaim her kitchen. She served hot soup and toast for supper, after which we said our good nights and headed for bed.

My head rested comfortably against Jack's shoulder. He'd been particularly warm and attentive and had so frequently assured me he loved me, I had to smile.

I thought I'd better deflect things before the conversation veered off into even more dangerously sentimental territory.

"Tomorrow we go home?"

"Home," Jack confirmed.

I allowed myself to luxuriate in the word. *Home*. Warmth, safety, Nelson my cat, my job and, of course, Jack.

"Home is where the heart is," I said lazily.

Jack's arm tightened around me as he gave a low chuckle. "I guess we both know where my home is then."

ACKNOWLEDGEMENTS

Being a writer can be an odd, solitary occupation. For weeks an author covers pages with words dredged from their own imagination and experience. In time, with some coaxing, polishing and revision, a novel is born and the days of solitude are over. It only takes one person to write a manuscript, but it takes a team to 'make' a book and I have been particularly fortunate in those who help put *Stall Turns* together.

Firstly I owe an inestimable debt to Kelly Pettitt for her frank but constructive criticism during the various revisions of the original draft and for her meticulously detailed notes. She is also responsible for the cover artwork, the photograph of me inside the back cover, the design and format of the layout.

Ruth Holman, Eden Smith, Sara-Lee Smith, and Belinda Hughes, all from my office, were pressed into service as beta readers and provided comment and input.

Sue Reidy, who has worked with me on all my books provided her usual helpful advice, guidance and encouragement during the revision process. Likewise Tina Shaw.

I also owe thanks to Debbie Watson for early proofreading. Finally, my deepest thanks to Adrienne Morris who edited and proofread the final manuscript.

My gratitude as ever to my husband Cavan who sustains me, helps in a thousand ways and never fails to encourage me.

Finally, my thanks to Reilly for spending the long hours with me and wagging encouragement; Pascal who lay on my lap as I typed on the keyboard; and Bandit, on whose broad back I cantered away from the frustrations inherent in the creative process.

ABOUT THE AUTHOR

Penelope came to New Zealand as an eleven-year-old after a childhood spent in India and Pakistan. As an only child, reading was her hobby – she read everything that came her way, a habit which has continued throughout her life.

On leaving school she trained as a nurse, without fully considering that a brisk default attitude of 'pull yourself together and stop whining' might not be an ideal prerequisite for the industry. Conceding, at last, that nurturing was not her dominant characteristic, she changed career path and after graduating with a BA (Hons) in English Literature, moved into management consultancy, which better suited her personality type.

After some years of family life she worked as a commercial pilot and flight instructor, spending her days ferrying clients into strips in the Marlborough Sounds and discouraging students from killing her as she taught them to fly.

Penelope lives with her husband, dog, cat and horse in Otaki, New Zealand.

The *Claire Hardcastle* series is set at three-monthly intervals roughly following the seasons.

Death on D'Urville (Autumn)

Straight and Level (Winter)

Stall Turns (Spring)

Her previous novels are *The Lost One* and *Helen Had a Sister.*

All novels are available in various formats from Amazon. com.

Paperback editions can be purchased within New Zealand from Paper Plus, Unity Books and other reputable book stores and suppliers. Alternatively, they can be ordered from Penelope's website - www.penelopehaines.com, and you can visit Penelope on Facebook @penelopehainesbooks.